FALLEN HERO

DISCOVER OTHER TITLES BY RILEY EDWARDS

Downrange

Fixed Asset

Hollow Point

Playing with Lies

Playing with Danger

Playing with Love

Playing with Forever

Takeback

Dangerous Love

Dangerous Rescue

Dangerous Games

Dangerous Encounter

Dangerous Mind

Dangerous Hearts

Dangerous Affair

Gemini Group

Nixon's Promise

Jameson's Salvation

Weston's Treasure

Alec's Dream

Chasin's Surrender

Holden's Resurrection

Jonny's Redemption

Red Team: Susan Stoker's Universe

Nightstalker

Protecting Olivia

Redeeming Violet

Recovering Ivy

Rescuing Erin

Gold Team: Susan Stoker's Universe

Brooks

Thaddeus

Kyle

Maximus

Declan

Blue Team: Susan Stoker's Universe

Owen

Gabe

Myles

Kevin

Cooper

Garrett

Silver Team

Theo

Easton

Smith

Jonas

Cash

The 707 Freedom Series

Free

Freeing Jasper

Finally Free

Freedom

The Next Generation (707 Spinoff)

Saving Meadow

Chasing Honor

Finding Mercy

Claiming Tuesday

Adoring Delaney

Keeping Quinn

Taking Liberty

Triple Canopy

Damaged

Flawed

Imperfect

Tarnished

Tainted

Conquered

Shattered

Fractured

The Collective

Unbroken

Trust

Stand-Alone Titles

Romancing Rayne

Falling for the Deltas (cowritten with Susan Stoker)

FALLEN HERO

RILEY EDWARDS

This is a work of fiction. Names, characters, organizations, places, events, and incidents are either products of the author's imagination or are used fictitiously. Otherwise, any resemblance to actual persons, living or dead, is purely coincidental.

Published by Montlake, Seattle

www.apub.com

EU product safety contact:
Amazon Media EU S. à r.l.
38, avenue John F. Kennedy, L-1855 Luxembourg
amazonpublishing-gpsr@amazon.com

ISBN-13: 9781662532726 (paperback)
ISBN-13: 9781662532719 (digital)

Cover design by Hang Le
Cover image: © Wander Aguiar Photography

Printed in the United States of America

To my family—my team—my tribe.
This is for you.

Prologue

Calista Ventura
Abu Dhabi, United Arab Emirates

"It's time for you to call Saint and his team."

Even though Tom couldn't see me, since he was three thousand miles away and we were speaking on the phone, I still rolled my eyes at his use of Pete's real name. For some reason—and I hadn't asked—Tom didn't like calling Pete 'Pete.'

"I already told you, Mason Hughes is going to be a problem. I don't want him involved."

That was the lie I'd told Tom on the plane out of Mexico, when I'd adamantly turned down his suggestion to ask Mason and his team to help me. The lie *wasn't* that Mason was going to be a problem because he was going to dig through my past, my present, and he'd find out who I really was and who I really worked for.

The true problem was I found him attractive—in the I-wanted-to-jump-his-bones kind of way. And the more he irritated me, the more I wanted to bang him. Which in my estimation was the definition of insanity. Or maybe it was unhealthy. Though I wasn't sure I even knew what healthy was. After Liliya was taken, my life spiraled into a tangled mess of dysfunction and grief.

"There's nothing for him to find."

"Be that as it may, Tom, I don't want—"

"I'm not asking, Calli," Tom interrupted me. "Your choices are call Saint or I'm pulling you."

The asshole would pull me out of some foolish sense of obligation to my father.

"I think you've paid your debt to my father tenfold. You don't need to keep riding in to the rescue every time you think danger's close." I'd shocked the man into silence. I took a second to savor the moment. "And just as a reminder, I didn't need help back in Mexico. I'd gotten myself out of that situation just fine and got us the authorization to go after Ahmad Sindi."

Still nothing.

"Tom, did I lose you?"

"How long have you known?"

"Since my father confessed all on his deathbed, with a warning and instructions on what to do if I was ever approached by the Irish."

Tom had nothing to say to that.

"How's Diane?"

Thankfully, Tom had something to tell me about my friend.

"She's in Upstate New York with a friend of mine who's taking care of her."

Thank God for that.

"And the charges against me? Where are you with that?"

"We're not done discussing your current situation."

We were.

I wasn't calling Saint.

"Tell me what you're doing to clear my name?"

"They have your DNA, Calli."

I knew they did. I'd stupidly broken a window.

"Don't feed me some line of bullshit. The rich and powerful have been getting away with murder since the beginning of time. The Agency cannot expect to send me out to do their dirty work but turn it off when I'm stateside. He was raping her, Tom. What did they expect me to do? Stand outside and call nine-one-one? Wait for the police to arrive while she endured more? Then watch him get off on some bullshit technicality because he's *rich* and *powerful*, which means he gets a free pass? I call bullshit on that. I saved the taxpayers money on a trial, and if by some miracle he was convicted, I saved them money housing and feeding that monster. They owe me a thank-you, not murder charges."

"I don't disagree, but . . ."

I stopped listening. My attention was pulled to the street below and the silver Maybach rolling to a stop at the valet stand. I would've preferred a sea-view room at the Park Hyatt, however, the room I was in with the view of the parking area was tactically the better option.

"I have to go. Amir is here."

"Twenty-four-hour check-ins," he demanded. "No excuses."

I swallowed my snarky retort.

I had work to do.

"Bye, Tom."

I disconnected.

Checked my hair on the way past the mirror and left my hotel room.

I did this wondering what Mason was doing, and if I called him to ask for his help, if I could keep my hands to myself.

Probably not.

I'd be begging him for a quick and dirty romp before the first twenty-four hours was up.

Damn.

◆ ◆ ◆

Mason Hughes
Downrange Ranch

"I think you're cheating," Ryan groused as he handed over three ten-dollar bills to Cat.

"Loser!" Fallon called out from the chair next to me.

I took a swig from my beer and for once kept my mouth shut. I was enjoying the show too much to interject.

The day was warm, the sun was shining, the sound of rapid gunfire *not* aimed at me was the perfect lullaby to help me relax.

"Rematch?" Cat offered for the fourth time.

Ryan nodded, and the shooters moved away from the match stage to the table with their ammo. Pete ambled out to the targets and placed stickers over the holes in the paper ones while Jack reset the steel.

"What's up with you?" Fallon asked.

"Nothing, why?"

"You've missed numerous golden opportunities to bust Ryan's balls, and you're sitting quietly."

"You've got it handled," I reminded him.

My friend narrowed his eyes.

"Are you sick? You never miss an opportunity to flap your gums."

"What are you, seventy-two? No one says that anymore."

"That's not an answer," he pointed out.

Maybe not, but I didn't have an answer for him. At least not one that made sense. Something had felt off since we'd come home from Mexico. Like there was a disturbance in the Force. Like there was unfinished business out there, and it was making me antsy.

"Just enjoying watching Ryan embarrass himself."

Fallon didn't look like he bought my excuse, but thankfully he dropped the subject.

Pete and Jack came back from cleaning up the range just as Cat was making her way to the starting box. The stage was simple, with a mix of paper and steel. Ryan should've been running circles around Cat's time. But true to her word, the woman was damn fast and accurate.

Jack stopped behind Cat, glanced around him, taking a visual account of everyone.

One could never be too careful when playing with guns.

"Range hot," Jack loudly called out. "Shooter ready?"

Cat's hand hovered just above her holster.

"Ready," she confirmed.

"Stand by."

A moment later, the beep of the timer Jack was holding went off. A millisecond after that, Cat pulled her Glock from her Kydex holster—the draw so smooth and so fast, if I'd blinked, I would've missed it.

She double-tapped the first paper target, ran to the next station, leaned to the side to get a clean sight picture of the steel, and plinked each of the five down lightning quick. Without lowering her weapon, she released a mag, let it fall to the dirt, tipped her Glock to the right while her left hand pulled a new mag from her belt. She shoved it in, straightened the gun, and resumed firing, executing a perfect combat reload.

"Damn, that reload was quick." Fallon mumbled my thought.

Watching her move through the stations was impressive as fuck. Every step she took purposeful, there was no wasted movement or breaths, and she counted her bullets like a pro, making sure she was never without ammo for the shots she needed to take.

Cat knocked down the last steel target, and Jack stopped the clock to call out her time.

"Fastest run yet," he proudly announced.

Cat tipped her head back and beamed a megawatt smile at her man.

An emotion I'd never felt before slithered up my spine and made my gut uneasy. An emotion that felt a lot like jealousy. It wasn't that I'd never had a woman look at me like that. It was that one had never looked at me with so much love and actually meant it.

Love was a bullshit farce unless it was Catarina Keys beaming a smile at her man. Then I believed it. Or it was Mia smiling at her man, Cole. Then I trusted it. Any woman beyond those two, I didn't trust or believe. Women were lying and manipulative and only loved a man until they got what they wanted, then they bailed.

My phone vibrating in my pocket pulled me from thoughts that were really memories I'd done everything I could do over the last two decades to forget. And I'd done a damn fine job of forgetting her but remembering the lessons she'd taught me.

Never again would I be someone's fool.

I yanked my phone free, glanced at the screen, and frowned.

A text from a number not programmed into my contacts.

I positioned the phone to read my face and opened the text.

What do you say about a trip to Abu Dhabi? I could use some backup.

The left side of my chest started pounding.

Just to be sure, even though I was fairly certain I knew who that was from, I texted back, Who is this?

CV

Calista Ventura.

Fuck me.

I shot back another message.

Are you safe?

Define safe.

Give me five minutes to get the team together. Answer me when I call.

Do women always bend to your orders?

I felt my lips tighten.

And just like in Mexico, I had an overwhelming urge to kiss the fuck out of her to shut her up. Unfortunately, she was on the other side of the world.

That's a show not tell, sweetheart. And I'm happy to show you when I get there.

What the fuck was wrong with me? I'd never in my life had the urge to kiss a woman to shut her up. Moreover, I was never happy to show a woman *anything.*

The feisty blonde with gemstone eyes and a death wish was a temptation I didn't need. A temptation that stirred something inside of me that was better left dead. A temptation that would test my control in ways I wasn't sure I could best.

Fuck.

I stood and shoved my phone back in my pocket.

"Yo, Pete, we need everyone at the big house. ASAP."

My best friend looked over at me, read my tone, and pulled out his phone to gather the rest of the team.

Looked like we were headed to Abu Dhabi.

Chapter One

"Don't be mad."

My gaze slid from the mirror, where I was watching myself unclasp my earrings, to the video call on my phone.

"That's never a good way to start a conversation," I told my . . . what was Atlanta? Not my assistant, not exactly my intel specialist, not my friend in the sense we shared secrets over cosmos and scheduled manis and pedis at the same time so we could gab and gossip.

Though she was a friend in the sense she helped me hide the bodies. That was, the bodies that needed to be disposed of. Sometimes it was better to leave the dead where they were, as a warning.

To say Atlanta was displeased I didn't call her after the DC situation was an understatement. She would've had the crime scene cleaned, and I wouldn't be on the hook for three men's deaths.

The authorities would and did call it manslaughter. I called it consequences. It would've been a lesson in 'no means no' if I'd left them breathing. Seeing as I didn't, and they earned their punishment by ignoring my friend's pleas for them to stop, in the end, their deaths were nothing more than justice. A savings for the taxpayers. The police should've been thanking me for taking three raping, low-life scumbags off the streets.

News flash, they weren't. And to further their ungratefulness, I now had a warrant—or warrants, as it were—out for my arrest.

I watched Atlanta pinch her lips before she rubbed them together. Something she did when she was trying to come up with the best way to spin news she didn't want to share but knew she had to.

"Just spit it out," I said and went back to my earrings.

"I texted Mason Hughes."

At her declaration, my eyes sliced back to my phone. "You did what now?"

With a long, heavy sigh, Atlanta attempted damage control. "I talked to Tom—"

"That was your first mistake," I interrupted her.

Atlanta rolled her eyes. Not because she didn't know I was correct. Speaking to Tom was always a mistake. He was a snake. And not just any snake. Tom was at the top of the deadly snakes we dealt with. The Black Mamba, if you will. I had no doubt he'd eat his young if it meant saving himself, and, seeing as that was the case, one day when the time was right for him and it served his purpose, he'd throw me under the bus.

Which meant he wouldn't think twice about throwing Atlanta into rush-hour traffic, nor would he blink at leaving her bloody, mangled body on the side of the road.

Actually, I wouldn't be surprised if he had a wake of buzzards at his command to pick clean the carcasses of those he screwed over.

"I happen to agree with him about this."

I had a sinking suspicion I knew what she'd agreed about. I also knew I did *not* agree.

"I wholeheartedly, one hundred percent disagree with Tom regarding Mason Hughes and Pete Young. What did you text Mason?"

A sheepish smile tugged at Atlanta's lips. "*I* didn't text Mason anything."

I gave her a moment to continue. When she didn't, I asked, "What does that mean?"

"You texted him. Well . . . technically, I texted him, but I did it using your number, and I kinda lied and said I was you. So I did but I didn't, since he thinks you texted him. And before I forget to tell you, I booked you a room at the Burj Al Arab for tomorrow's move. It's under a new alias, Lois Lane. I thought it went well with your journalist cover. Not that you're using—"

"You did what?" I cut off her rambling about covers as her betrayal burned through me.

This was why I didn't have friends. This was why I preferred to work alone. This was why I trusted no one. In the end, they always screwed you over.

"You're moving down to Dubai tomorrow."

I brought my hands up in front of me in a prayer position for no other reason than to stop myself from throwing my phone across the room. Over the years, I'd worked hard and learned to keep my temper in check. I wasn't the same angry, impatient young woman I was when I'd started this crusade. I'd learned self-control—unless my friend was being violated, then all bets were off—yet here I was, on the verge of blowing.

"Don't play games with me," I admonished. "Let's go back to the text you sent."

Atlanta flinched, and I knew she caught the angry wave of hostility coming at her through the phone. Not that I was trying to hide my anger or hostility, but it was good to know I hit my mark.

"Calli—"

"You overstepped."

"Maybe," she conceded. "But friends don't let friends make stupid decisions to save face. Friends don't let friends suffer from hubris. You're skating the line of 'in over your head,' and before you start to sink, which in turn will lead to you drowning, I stepped in—and okay, maybe overstepped, but goddamnit, Calli, you need backup. This isn't cartels in Mexico. This isn't kidnapped girls off the street. This is something else, and what it is, is next-level dangerous.

"You're dealing with Amir Bakir. If the man even catches a whiff you're not who he thinks you are, he will not think twice about slitting your throat. Your cover's solid, and back in Mexico, Ahmad Sindi didn't see you, but one of his guards on the island might've. Now is not the time to start taking unnecessary risks when you're so close to your endgame."

Atlanta wasn't wrong. Amir had a well-known mean streak. He was also a man who had money and power and an ungodly amount of both.

What made Amir more dangerous than the normal danger a psychopath would present was his background. He had no royal blood; he was not related to a well-respected tribal leader. He was what we'd call in America a desert rat. Born into poverty.

Growing up, Amir had less than nothing. He was a scavenger. Being that, he learned young the only way for him to get what he needed to survive was to steal it.

There was a saying: The most dangerous kind of man is one with nothing to lose. However, a better saying would be: The most dangerous kind of man is one who was born with nothing, grew up hungry, learned to steal, cheat, and lie, and found a way to use all he'd learned to move up the felonious ladder until he made it to the top.

Now that man knew what it was like to eat shit, and he would do absolutely anything to never have to eat it again. A man like that, who'd tasted the good life, had it all, wouldn't think twice about protecting all he'd amassed by any means necessary.

But still . . .

"That doesn't give you the right to go behind my back and do what you did," I pointed out. Then added, "And friends don't betray friends."

"Betray?" she whispered. "I didn't betray you. At worst, I went behind your back—"

"And betrayed me, Atlanta. You used your access to my phone to pretend you were *me*. Taking that a step further, you did it knowing damn good and well I wouldn't *want* you to do it. You listened to Tom and sided with him instead of respecting my wishes."

My statement was met with a stone-cold stare.

Something to know about Atlanta, not only was she a genius behind the keyboard, with great instincts and a knack for finding a thread that was never meant to be found, then unraveling it until she had actionable intel, she also had skills that made her scary deadly.

The difference between her and I was, she preferred to be behind the scenes, while I'd rather gnaw off my own arm than search the dark web for hours on end.

She was also a few years older than me and had been at the game a lot longer. She called her desire to step back from the field burnout. But I suspected there were only so many marks the darkest of souls could take before you became the very thing you hunted.

Before the kill was just as much for pleasure as it was for the greater good.

Was that where I was at?

Regret had never crossed my mind. Not even in the beginning. But there had been a tinge of remorse. Now, I felt nothing.

I was who I was. I did what I did. I was nothing more than a killer for hire—and I was damn good at it.

Except I'd left a mess in DC that said otherwise. So maybe I was as reckless as my friend Berta warned me I was. I'd allowed emotion to override my training. I hadn't followed protocol. My concern for my friend took precedence over cleaning the crime scene. Not a regret but a mistake. One I didn't plan on making again.

By the time I was done in Dubai, the world would be rid of Amir Bakir, and the women he sold would be free. That was, until someone else stepped up and took over Amir's trade.

It was a never-ending cycle.

"I'll give you this, Calista. I knew what I was doing when I went behind your back and texted Mason. I knew you'd be pissed. I also know you're not stupid, but you *are* stubborn. It was Tom's idea to call in Mason and his crew, and that alone would make you dig your heels in. I did what I did, and it was underhanded the way I did it. I don't regret it, and I'd do it again if it means at the end of this assignment you're alive to be pissed at me."

With that, she disconnected the call before I could tell her it was not Tom's idea to call in Mason. He wanted to call Saint 'Pete' Young. It was just that where Pete went, *Mason* went, and I didn't trust myself around the latter. If Tom had suggested anyone else, I might've considered it.

Not that my contemplation would've led me to accepting help.

Yeah, maybe I had a severe case of hubris.

On that thought, I went to the safe in the closet and pulled out my personal phone. While I was waiting for it to power on, I finished removing my jewelry. My makeup was one step below call girl—smokey eye shadow that made my blue eyes pop, full-cover foundation that made my skin look flawless even though it wasn't, and bombshell-red lips.

I couldn't wait to wipe all this shit off my face. Classy call girl—or one step down—wasn't my favorite look. However, I needed to play the part of wealthy madam. How Atlanta and Tom thought Mason and his team would fit into my cover, I couldn't fathom. I was here to buy women. I had a plan, and so far it was working better than I'd expected.

Men were men—dangerous or not. Tits, ass, and legs made them stupid. Package all of that in a tight dress, fuck-me heels, makeup that was classy but heavy . . . give them good hair, let them think they might get themselves some, and stupid becomes reckless.

I snatched my phone off the bureau, took a deep breath, and opened my texts.

It was time to see if I could instigate damage control.

Atlanta had helpfully programmed in Mason's contact information.

What do you say about a trip to Abu Dhabi? I could use some backup.

Who is this?

CV

Are you safe?

Define safe.

Damn, Atlanta was good. That sounded like something I'd say.

Give me five minutes to get the team together. Answer me when I call.

Do women always bend to your orders?

Great. Now she was flirting on my behalf. What was not great was the way my stomach clenched in anticipation. What was equally not great was the way butterflies were trying to squeeze through the clench.

I went to the next text, and those butterflies broke free.

That's a show not tell, sweetheart. And I'm happy to show you when I get there.

I pushed through the riot in my belly and looked at the date of the exchange.

It had been five days.

Five. Freaking. Days.

Shit.

I blew out a frustrated breath but couldn't deny that frustration was mingled with a fair amount of belly flutters.

Before I closed the text thread, I did another quick scan of the messages.

Fucking Atlanta.

Thankfully, the burn of her betrayal won out and singed those stupid butterflies.

I also had a voicemail notification. I didn't have to look to know who it was from.

Tomorrow. I'd deal with the voicemail and Atlanta and whatever trouble she'd caused tomorrow. Hopefully, it wasn't too late to call Mason and tell him not to come. Five days was a long time, but if I was lucky, I could still stop him before he rallied the troops.

I knew my hope was for naught, and that was proved true when the knock on the door came.

No, not a knock—banging.

Shit.

Chapter Two

"Jesus, brother, you planning on breakin' down the door with your knuckles?" my teammate Fallon Harris quipped from beside me, as I continued to bang on the unanswered hotel door.

Unanswered seemed to be a theme with Calista Ventura.

I stopped banging on the door, exhaled through my teeth, and tried to pull up my nonexistent patience.

"Seriously," Pete, my other teammate, grumbled from his position on the opposite side of me. "Give her a minute."

I'd already given her five fucking days to answer. Waiting another minute might shove me right over the edge.

Logically, I knew I had no right to be pissed. I had no claim over the woman. I'd only spent a couple of hours in her presence, and during that time, conversation was scarce. Beyond that we'd shared eight texts, and I'd left one unreturned voicemail.

So maybe I did have a logical reason to be pissed. She'd requested backup, then didn't pick up her phone when I called—like I said I would—then taking that a step further, she'd disconnected her number.

So, yeah, fuck yeah, I was pissed. Not only because she'd ghosted me, but in an effort to track her ass down, I had to call CIA Officer Tom Washington. A man who'd proven to be shady and underhanded. Not that there were many spooks who *weren't* shady and underhanded. It was just that Tom Washington was more so. I didn't trust the man, which meant I had to play telephone tag with Shepherd Drexel, our hacker, to confirm Tom's intel. Something else that pissed me off.

Shep was the best at what he did, but when he felt like being a pain in the ass, he gave you the runaround before he answered a call.

By the time we had confirmation, I was worried something had happened to Calista. Which necessitated another unpleasant call to Tom, who told me not to worry about the disconnected number, that this was normal operating procedure with Calista, and she'd check in when she had time.

For a man who, a few weeks ago, went all out to get my team to Mexico to rescue her from a cartel before she was trafficked, his lack of concern for her in the present told me not only was he shady and underhanded, he was also a motherfucker.

I lifted my hand to resume pounding when the door flew open.

And there she was. Or at least, there was a woman who closely resembled the Calista I remembered, only this version of the woman was not in dirty jeans and a T-shirt. She was in a clingy little black dress that hit mid-thigh and showed a goodly amount of cleavage. But it wasn't her perfect tits that had my attention, or her long-ass legs that gave a man unhealthy ideas. It was her glossy blonde hair that was swept up, exposing an elegant neck I had the sudden urge to taste.

"About fucking time," I snarled, and pushed inside.

Calista wobbled back a few steps, and that was when I noticed that on top of the sexy-as-fuck dress, she was in a pair of strappy heels that weren't fuck-me shoes, they were something else altogether. It didn't help that her toes were painted a soft, feminine pink, which was an in-your-face contrast to the devil red painted on her lips.

I was studiously ignoring that mouth of hers. There was only so much a man could take before he snapped.

"Mason," she whispered. I couldn't decipher if that whisper was shock or fear or a little of both. If I was a betting man, I'd say shock. I doubted there was much Calista feared.

Fuck me.

Her. That dress. Those shoes. The hair. Those lips. The sexy column of her throat. All of it together, plus the way she whispered my name, had me rethinking my abstinence.

"Disconnected your phone, babe," I unnecessarily told her, as I kept pushing my way in farther.

Calista stopped her retreat and asked, "What?"

I didn't stop my advance until I was close. So close I was in her space, and the smell of her perfume wrapped around my senses. It wasn't flowery and sweet like a woman would wear. It was spicy and alluring, like something a siren would wear. It was meant to entice. You had to be close to smell it, but once you did, it held you captive. It was the kind of perfume a man wanted to have linger on his sheets.

And it pissed me right the fuck off.

"Told you I was going to call," I reminded her. "Told you to pick up when I did. You didn't, you disconnected the number."

"Disconnected—"

I was too deep in my anger to process the question in her tone. "Disconnected," I growled. "What the fuck, Calista?"

"Step back."

That wasn't a whisper, it was a sharp demand.

I ignored it and pressed on. "You called for backup, then ghosted me. Again, what the fuck?"

"I didn't call for—"

Seriously? The woman wanted to play word games?

"Honest to God," I snapped. "Called. Texted. Same shit."

Calista's eyes lit up, the blue deepening, then through gritted teeth, she bit out, "Step. The. Fuck. Back." When she was done punctuating every word, I stood my ground, earning me a scowl and squinty eyes.

"Maybe we should start over," Pete suggested, reminding me we weren't alone.

I'd taken one look at the woman, lost my head, and hadn't even heard the door close. Actually, I'd forgotten Pete and Fallon were with me.

I took a step back, lost her smell, but the full effect of the dress and shoes took its place. I wasn't sure which was worse. What I *was* sure of—this woman was trouble. Trouble and sin. She'd lead me astray if I wasn't careful.

Belatedly, I took in the room.

It was a hotel room—nothing special. Walls, carpet, furniture, bedclothes, padded headboard, all cream. No color except for the angry woman in black standing in the middle of the room. The view was of the parking lot. I could understand that strategically—her wanting to see who was coming and going—but still, the view totally sucked.

"Pete's right," Fallon said. "You already know him and Mase. I'm Fallon. Nice to meet you."

I didn't miss the humor lacing my friend's introduction.

"Fallon," Calista returned, then transferred her stare to Pete. "It seems there's been a mix-up. I'm sorry you've wasted a trip. I'll see to it that you're reimbursed for your travel expenses."

Mix-up?

What the fuck?

"Woman, I can read—"

"I'd hope so," Calista interrupted. "Unless Pete's now hiring illiterate baboons on top of assholes."

My jaw clenched, and I fought to find a retort that sounded less the asshole she accused me of being and more professional. This woman meant nothing to me. Literally nothing. My reaction to her was on me. It wasn't her fault seeing her in that dress had awoken something in me I'd long ago killed.

There were plenty of attractive women in the world. Hell, I couldn't escape a shift behind the bar of the Dirty Plank without women hitting on me. Never had it crossed my mind to pull one of those women into the office, yank up her skirt, bend her over my desk, and fuck the bad attitude right out of her. Or in Calista's case, tear that fucking dress off, toss her on the bed, and spend the rest of the night exploring all those sexy curves before I fucked her to within an inch of her life.

My reaction to her had to be because I'd been worried she was in trouble. I'd spent my adult life protecting people. First in the Navy, then in recent years rescuing women and children from abuse. That had to be it. It had nothing to do with Calista being gorgeous, nothing to do with those lips, those beautiful eyes, hips, legs, and girly pink toenails.

It took longer than I was proud to admit to pull up my self-control and will my body's reaction to her to recede.

Much calmer, I told her, "Your text said you needed backup."

"Right. About that." She blew out a breath. "I didn't send that text. Atlanta did. And I doubt my phone is disconnected, though I don't use my personal cell when I'm on a job, so I can't verify."

"Who's Atlanta?" Pete asked before I could.

Calista glanced around the small room. "Would you like to sit down?" She motioned to two chairs in the corner.

I'd do jumping jacks if it meant she hurried this along and answered Pete. Instead of a smart-assed comment, I stepped aside, allowing my teammates to maneuver to the chairs. I kept my feet . . . and my distance from Calista.

Both men sat. Calista leaned her hip against the dresser and crossed her arms over her chest, shoving her already impressive cleavage to new heights. I bit back a groan and the string of obscenities that were begging to break free and tore my gaze away from the woman next to me.

Before I could prompt Calista, Pete repeated, "Who's Atlanta?"

"My . . . assistant."

Calista's pause gave me, well . . . pause.

"Are you sure?" I asked.

"Sure, I'm sure," she snapped, drawing my attention back to her.

"Well, you don't sound sure," I pointed out.

"So your assistant has your personal phone and texted Mase?" Fallon inquired skeptically.

Her eyes darted to the phone on the dresser, then back to Fallon. For a woman who had dubious ties to the CIA, and those included undercover work, she sure did suck at thinking on her feet—and not giving herself away.

"Seriously?" I grumbled.

"Seriously, what?"

My gaze shot to the phone before returning to Calista. "Christ, woman, you don't look at the phone in question when you're trying to convince someone it's not in your possession. Or did you skip that chapter in *Spies for Dummies*?"

Her beautiful blue eyes narrowed. No, they narrowed dangerously.

"This is good," she mumbled.

"What's good?"

"You being a dick. It knocks you down a few notches on the hotness chart."

"Only a few?" I quipped.

Calista smiled sweetly before her eyes swept down my body. "Actually, you barging in here acting like an asshole knocked you down a few rungs. You being a dick just makes you flat-out unattractive."

Ouch.

I heard Fallon snort. Calista went on like she didn't hear him. "No, Atlanta doesn't have my phone, but that doesn't mean she can't send texts from my number since obviously she did. And it's not disconnected, she just made it so when Mason called, it's disengaged."

"And Pete and Fallon and Aiden and Ryan and Jack and Catarina?" I asked, naming all of my teammates.

With a shrug, Calista answered, "She's thorough."

"Your assistant's a hacker," I surmised.

"Among other things," she vaguely confirmed. "I only found out about the texts a few minutes before you knocked." With a tilt of her head toward the phone, she continued, "I got my phone out of the safe to read the messages." Calista's lips pulled up into another deceptively sweet smile. Her eyes roamed my face right before she went in for the kill. "You must've skipped more than a few chapters in *Seduction for Dummies* if that's your idea of flirting."

I covered my laughter with a grunt because damn, the woman was quick with a comeback. Which posed a new problem. If there was one thing I found more attractive than a pretty face with great tits and ass, it was a pretty woman with a good sense of humor.

Calista Ventura had it all—great legs, tits, ass, pouty, full lips, slender, delicate neck, gorgeous eyes, beautiful face, and wit.

An octet threat.

Fuck my life.

"Okay," Pete started, and I didn't miss the humor wrapped around that one word. "So the real question is, why would she send that text asking for backup?"

Gone was the fake smile, and in its place was a carefully crafted mask of indifference.

"Tom and I had a disagreement about how this job should go. Atlanta sided with Tom and went behind my back to do his bidding."

Now we were getting somewhere.

Chapter Three

I wasn't sure who I wanted to kill first: Atlanta or Tom.

The unfortunate truth was, I was used to Tom screwing me over. Another unfortunate truth was, I needed him. Tom Washington was nothing more than a means to an end. And that end was near. It was so close I could taste it. Like that first lick of the tart cherry ice pops my mom used to make when my sister and I were kids—the flavor exploding on my tongue, sour and sweet and cool and refreshing. Something to be savored on a hot summer day.

The taste was nearly identical, but instead of sour, there was a blend of bitterness with that sweet. Bitter memories that damn near consumed me the closer I got. Bitter reminders that no one had been able to save my sister. The bitter reality that my beloved mother might still be living and breathing, but she was a ghost—totally lost to me.

The only sweet that would come from this story's end was vengeance. But that was saccharine—fake, false, manufactured. Not that I wouldn't take it, and glory in the punishment I planned to unleash.

Nothing would ever bring my sister back to life. Revenge wouldn't make me miss her less nor would it erase the horrifying things that were done to her or the way she'd died. The bottom-line truth of it was, my sister was discarded like a piece of trash on the side of the road after she was brutally used and abused—and someone was going to die as penance.

And I knew who that someone was. The last thing I needed was too-hot-for-his-own-good Mason and his buddies screwing it up. I didn't need backup. I didn't need counsel. I didn't need opinions. I needed to focus.

"Speaking of Tom."

I leveled Mason with my best bland stare and waited for him to say more.

"When was the last time you spoke to him?"

That was not where I thought Mason was going. "Why?"

"Call me curious."

"Call me uninterested in satisfying your curiosity."

Piercing green eyes locked with mine. This was better. This was something I excelled at. This was something I could do all day. I loved a good stare down. And it would seem by Mason's unflinching gaze, he did as well.

It took five seconds—yes, I counted—for the silence to break. However, it wasn't Mason who broke it, it was Fallon. "Are you two really going to stand there and have a staring contest?"

Mason arched a brow. I remained still with my face carefully set to bored.

"Fuck. I hate games," Pete muttered irately.

With my eyes still fastened on Mason, I matched Pete's irritation when I told him, "So do I, and I hate being toyed with."

"Good, we have that in common. Mase asked because when he called Tom—"

"You called Tom?" I asked Mason, forgetting about the stare down.

The ass smirked before he answered. "I got your text. Tried to call, your line was disconnected, so hell yeah, I called Tom. He told me not to worry and you'd probably check in with him soon."

Meddling asshole.

I rolled my eyes to the ceiling and kept them there while I attempted to get myself under control before I lashed out and gave away too much.

"Are you counting?"

I rolled my eyes back to Mason. "What?"

"Counting. I heard some people count in their heads to find self-control."

I hadn't been counting, but now that my patience was slipping further, maybe I should've tried that. "I could count to a hundred and still want to dick slap you."

Mason tipped his head to the side and smiled. "Dick slap?"

"It's like a bitch slap except what you give a dick."

That smile turned wicked. "Kinky." He winked.

"Oh for fuck's sake, I'm not saying I want to smack your dick. I'm saying you're a dick and I want to slap you."

"You're the one who brought my dick into it."

Good God, why was I engaging?

I flipped him a middle finger to concede the conversation. I'd rather discuss Tom than Mason's dick. As disturbing as that was, I wasn't going to dissect why speaking about a man I loved to hate was better for my mental health than thinking about Mason's boy parts.

"Now you're just trying to turn me on," Mason quipped.

"If you two are done with the Al and Peggy show, maybe we can get down to business," Pete suggested.

That sounded like the best idea I'd heard all day.

But first . . .

"I've got better hair than Peg Bundy," I pointed out. "And I'm not nearly as rude."

Mason's lips quirked. "But you admit you're rude."

I closed my eyes and did that counting thing Mason suggested. I got to six and abandoned the useless recommendation.

"You're enjoying this," I noted.

With a shrug of his broad shoulders, he made no reply. Which I guess *was* his reply, just the nonverbal kind. He was having fun talking me in circles and would gladly stand there all night and continue the annoying banter.

I had better things to do. That was, if showering and crawling into bed without dinner was considered better.

"Listen, I'm sure you all are tired after a long travel day, and I'm exhausted. How about we meet tomorrow for breakfast and I can properly apologize before you catch a plane back to the US. Like I said, I'll make sure your travel expenses are covered."

"Good you brought that up again. We booked the Royal Suite," Mason shared. "It's like the Presidential Suite, but with four private terraces instead of three."

Goddamn Tom and Atlanta.

"Let me guess, you flew here first class too?"

"Do I look like I fit in economy?"

No, he didn't. But I would love to see the big dumbass squished into economy. With his broad shoulders and tree-trunk legs, it would be an uncomfortably tight fit. Hopefully it would cause him back pain that lingered for days. The kind that made it hard to sleep. And a charley horse. Yes, there would be something so satisfying about seeing big bad Mason Hughes with a charley horse the size of a Clydesdale.

"Why are you smiling like that?" Fallon asked.

I hadn't realized I was.

"I was imagining Mason scrunched into a tiny airplane seat, wondering if it's true a long flight can cause a blood clot, hoping it does," I partially lied.

"Vicious." Fallon chuckled and stood. "I like it."

At least someone appreciated my sense of humor.

Pete followed Fallon and took his feet. "Breakfast. Nine."

I made the decision to allow Pete to get away with his grunted directive in the interest of getting the three hulking beasts out of my room.

"Sure," I fibbed.

Mason's eyes narrowed on me, but he kept his trap shut for once.

I told myself I wasn't disappointed the sparring match was over as I watched them walk to the door.

What could I say, I was as good at lying to myself as I was to other people.

It was easier that way. Nothing good came from telling the truth.

Truth was like sex—the root of all evils. It was a weakness.

Sex had killed my sister.

The truth had stolen my family.

Now if I could just get Mason and his crew gone, I could get on with why I was in the UAE.

Vengeance.

It was mine.

Finally.

Chapter Four

"Are we going to discuss what happened down there or are we going to pretend the air conditioning wasn't broken in Calista's room." Fallon stopped and snapped his fingers. "Wait, it wasn't the AC, it was you and Calista and fire sizzling—"

"Do you hear yourself? Fire sizzling. Did you lose your balls somewhere? Grow a vagina? Hit your head?"

I was actually impressed Fallon waited until we'd taken the elevator up to the top floor and made it into our room before he started giving me shit. If heckling and shit talk was an Olympic sport, he'd be a gold medalist. But fire sizzling, that wasn't his style. Normally he went straight for crude and obscene.

"Since you asked, my balls are in fine working order and have been used in the last decade, unlike some tight-assed . . . what'd she call you? Oh, right—dick."

"I didn't ask, and I don't want to know what you've been using them for."

I glanced over at Pete, who was already sitting down at the dining room table that was bigger than the one in my condo back in Imperial Beach. The eight white leather high-back chairs alone probably cost more than the cheap full set I'd bought from Ron's Discount Furniture. The table looked suspiciously like African blackwood. Which meant the table cost more than my couch, big round chair—which the salesperson called a cuddler—my bed, and my dresser combined.

"Which one of you is taking first shift guarding Calista's door?" Pete asked, not looking up from his laptop.

Thankfully, Pete had opted for work rather than participating in Fallon's fuckery. If Fallon was a gold-medalist shit talker, Pete was a master at stirring the pot.

"Right. Got it. We're pretending there wasn't enough sexual tension between Mase and the hot chick with the gorgeous legs and sexy shoes to make a monk reconsider his vows."

That hit way too close to home.

A dangerous growl slipped out of my throat before I could swallow it down.

My mistake was all Fallon needed to push his luck. "Bet that dress would look a fuckuva lot sexier on the floor next to my—"

"You're done," I ground out, uncaring what that gave away.

The damage was done. Fallon smelled blood, and like the shark he was, he was already circling his chum. With a smile I wanted to punch off his face, he declared, "I'll take first shift."

That worked for me. There was no doubt Calista was going to bolt and bail on breakfast. But she wouldn't run until she was positive the coast was clear. Which meant she wouldn't do it in the next three hours Fallon was posted on her floor, in front of the only bank of elevators and stairs.

"Before you go, Tom sent a full mission brief."

Christ, what a douche.

Mission specifics were good for us, but it was a betrayal of Calista's trust. It would seem the woman didn't have anyone in her corner who was loyal.

"That shit's whacked," Fallon rightly noted. "First her assistant went behind her back, and now Tom's throwing her under the bus."

"I'm sending it to your phone," Pete told him without injecting his personal opinion. Though I knew my friend, so he didn't have to. Pete valued loyalty just as much as I did. "Something to keep you busy while you're guarding the exits we all know she's not going to use until dawn breaks."

"Why do you think I want first shift," Fallon said as he headed to the door. "Mase is the one who pissed her off. He can deal with the angry hot chick when she finds him at the elevator during her escape."

With a flick of his hand over his shoulder, the door closed behind him.

Pete looked up from his laptop. "What's in your head?"

Without thinking, I asked, "Come again?"

"Calista."

Fuck.

This was the double-edged sword of brotherhood. One side loyalty and trust. The other, history and knowledge. I should've known Pete would call me out. That's what brothers did. They didn't let shit slide—not when it was important.

"Pete—"

"Oh hell no." His declaration was like the strike of a hammer. "You don't lose your mind with women. You don't care enough to get pissed and bang on doors or get in the face of a woman—"

"I get in Mia's face all the time," I reminded him.

My defense was lame—Mia wasn't just a woman. She was Pete's little sister. She was the third in our trio. I'd known her since she was a scrawny teenager with pimples. There were only two people in this world I trusted with every part of me—Pete and Mia.

There were only two people I loved, down to my soul—Pete and Mia.

Their other sister, Camila, had a piece of my heart, I'd do anything for her, but being two years younger than Mia, six years younger than me and Pete, she hadn't tagged along like Mia had when we were younger. Not to mention, where Mia was ballsy and a tomboy, Cami was shy and quiet and girly—extremely so.

"Mia doesn't count."

I shrugged, not wanting to have this conversation, but also not wanting to lie to my best friend. I had no defense for my behavior, no ready explanation for my anger, no excuse for why I reacted to Calista the way I did. There was just something that pissed me off about the woman.

Not that I was the kind of man who would give the feeling time and consideration—I'd long ago learned my lesson when it came to women; feelings and emotions were pointless.

I'd never again give a woman my trust. The exception was Mia . . . and possibly Jack's woman, Catarina. Cat had proven she was skilled, and she made Jack happy—*really* happy—and seeing as Jack was far from dumb, he wouldn't've fought so hard for the woman if she wasn't trustworthy.

But, there was a difference between trusting someone with my life and trusting them with my emotions. I trust Cat with my life and keep my secrets to myself.

It was always better that way.

No weaknesses.

No vulnerabilities.

No lies.

"You're right," I conceded. "I lost my cool because I thought she gave us the runaround. If her story checks out, I won't be pissed anymore."

"Distrusting prick," he mumbled under his breath.

Sleep. I needed to sleep off this shit mood, and when I woke up, I'd be in a better frame of mind to deal with the sexy Calista Ventura.

"You look ridiculous."

My observation was met with Fallon's middle finger. He unfolded out of the chair that was far too small for his large frame, rolled his neck, and groused, "I'm too old for this shit."

"Too old to pull watch in a luxury hotel?" I chuckled.

"Too old to pull all-nighters," Fallon corrected. "This shit was a lot easier when I was twenty."

He wasn't wrong. Not that I'd admit I had a kink in my neck and a knot in my back from lying on the couch to catch a nap. Hell, when I was twenty, I wouldn't've needed the nap.

"Pussy."

He ignored my jab and hit the call button on the elevator. The doors slid open, and with another salute with his middle finger, he disappeared into the lift.

I didn't bother with the chair. When Calista opened her door, she'd find me standing there.

Okay, so, the two hours of sleep I'd managed hadn't gotten rid of my shit mood. There was just something about the woman that made me want to push her buttons, rile her up, and piss her off. And there was something, again, I wasn't willing to process.

My shoulder had just hit the wall opposite Calista's room when the door swung open and a pair of blue eyes collided with mine.

Furious blue eyes.

Good.

"Going somewhere?"

"Seriously?" she seethed.

"Seriously," I taunted, and pushed off the wall.

She'd changed out of her dress, washed her face clean of the makeup she'd had on earlier, and instead of the complicated updo, her hair was in a ponytail. The jeans, tee, and sneakers did nothing to detract from her beauty. If I was being honest, her natural beauty was far more appealing than the made-up version.

What hadn't changed in the hours since I last saw her was her frown and sparking-with-fury eyes. If anything, those eyes burned brighter.

I stepped closer, and last night's perfume still clung to her skin. A tactical error on my part, but it was too late to back down now. Too late to brace against the impact of her beauty. Too late to rethink not taking the first shift so Fallon or Pete could deal with her sneaky, lying fine ass.

"Where are we going?" I asked calmly, when I was anything but.

"We're not going anywhere."

I waited for the lie—her attempt to bullshit me with some excuse of a hankering for a middle-of-the-night snack or her needing to switch rooms because of some fictitious reason.

No such lie came.

"I'm going downstairs to catch the taxi I called." She pushed forward, but her suitcase remained wedged in the door. "Step back."

"I'll save you the trouble of going to the lobby. Your taxi's been canceled."

Not giving away a single emotion, she lifted one shoulder. "I'll walk."

"Correct, you will. Right back into your room."

"All right, hotshot, I'm really trying to keep my cool and not make a scene in the hall of a fancy hotel in the middle of the night. But I'm done with this shit. Get out of my way. And by that, I mean go home and butt the fuck out of my business."

That wasn't going to happen.

"You've got two choices. Turn around and move back to your room on your own, or I'll *put* you back in your room."

Like a temptress luring me to my death, she curled her lips into a seductive smile. "You forgot one, Mason. Choice three. That's where I knee you in the balls and you spend the next few weeks recovering from testicular retrieval surgery. That is if they can find them after I shove them up your ass. Now, get out of my way."

Without warning I dipped forward, my shoulder connected with her stomach, and I heard the whoosh of oxygen leaving her lungs.

As I kicked her suitcase back into the room, her fist connected with my lower back. I welcomed the pain. I welcomed her anger. I welcomed anything that made the *something* I was feeling go numb.

Pissed off, I could deal with. The attraction, I could put aside. But the way my insides heated when I was close to her, I couldn't. The way my body reacted to her scent was foreign. The way I felt when those siren eyes locked with mine, and my first thought was that I wanted to drown in them, was so out of character, I was beginning to wonder if I had a brain tumor.

I was three feet into her room when I felt her hand curl around my belt. "Are you going to give me a wedgy?"

Before she could answer—or worse, tug my cargos up my ass—I set her on her feet.

"You're un-fucking-believable," she growled.

It had been a long time since a woman had said that to me. Still, I replied, "So I've been told."

"That's what all men say. Then they get down to the deed and it's nothing but disappointment and fumbling."

"Sounds to me like you've picked the wrong men to take to your bed."

A pretty pink crept up her neck, and damn but I liked that I could make her blush.

What the fuck was wrong with me? I was playing with fire, but I couldn't stop stoking the embers.

"Are you always such a dick?"

"Is there a reason you're always bringing up my dick?"

She rolled her eyes and amended, "Are you always such an asshole?"

"Nope."

"Unbelieve—" She cut herself off with a shake of her head and started again. "Are you saying it's me that brings out the dic—asshole in you?"

I had no answer to her question, but she absolutely caused my unruly dick to jump to attention by reminding me that despite not being used in a very long time, he was still functioning and fully on board with pinning Calista to the bed and fucking her breathless.

"What I'm saying is, you're not leaving. We're going to go over your assignment and make some adjustments."

"Adjustments?" Her tone was cool and composed, but her eyes gave away her rage.

"Overall, the mission is sound. With a few exceptions."

She slowly closed her eyes, tipped her head back, and I watched her mouth move.

"I see you took my advice and tried the counting thing."

"Six, seven, eight," she said out loud, but finished with, "I could kill you and be done with your annoying ass."

"I've been told it's a nice ass."

Her eyes popped open. "I'm being serious."

"You're wasting time," I argued. "We've got three days before your mission starts."

"How do you know that?" she fumed.

I didn't bother answering. She knew exactly how I knew.

Calista turned her back on me while mumbling, "That motherfucker."

I didn't hate the view of her ass in her tight jeans, but I preferred looking into her eyes when she spoke. They didn't lie.

"Why?" she asked.

And maybe it was better I had her back, better I didn't have to look her in the face while I struggled to come up with a suitable answer.

"Why what?" I feigned ignorance to buy myself more time.

"Why are you doing this? I explained I didn't send the text. I apologized for the inconvenience. I told you I'd cover expenses. You and your team are off the hook. Actually, you were never *on* the hook. You can go on your merry way and forget this ever happened."

I wished it was that easy.

"You need backup."

That wasn't a lie, but that wasn't the reason I couldn't do the smart thing and get the hell away from her.

"I don't. And you guys being here is going to screw everything up."

A familiar sensation started at the base of my spine and licked its way up. An awareness that had saved my ass many times. The intuition in my gut that shit was about to get real.

"What aren't you telling me?"

Calista turned, leveled me with a hateful stare, and shoulder-checked me as she passed.

“Everything,” she snarled as she stomped her way to the bathroom. “Be gone by the time I’m out.”

The door slammed behind her.

I went to the bed, arranged all the pillows in a pile on one side against the headboard and plopped my tired ass down.

If I was going to wait out this latest drama, I might as well be comfortable.

I was nothing if not patient.

Chapter Five

The stubborn asshole was still in my room.

I'd been lying in the empty bathtub with nothing but towels to cushion my neck. My ass was sore, I was angrier than I had been in recent years, and part of that anger included my lack of access to a weapon.

I could go out there and challenge the prick to a fistfight, but he'd best me before I could kill him. Sure, a few solid punches to his handsome face would make me feel better, but it wouldn't solve my problems.

I needed him gone. Him and his busybody friends.

Fucking Tom.

I was going to kill him too. I no longer cared that I needed him alive to work his magic and get my DNA and prints to magically disappear so I could reenter the US without a warrant for my arrest. I didn't care that my father had respected the man. That was just another lapse in his judgment. That and not getting my mother into a program when she turned to alcohol to numb the pain of losing my sister.

I wanted this life to be over, and I was close.

This would be it, then I'd tell Tom I was no longer available to be his personal assassin and go about my life. I'd find someplace quiet. I'd never look at a gun again. The only time I'd ever hold a knife would be when I was chopping vegetables. Which reminded me, I needed to add watching cooking videos to my post-CIA-contract-killer life. Wherever I was going, I would for sure not have internet or a phone.

Okay, I needed the internet so I could watch my cooking videos. But no phones and no email.

I wanted to be totally off-grid—with my internet. I'd grow a garden and live out the rest of my days talking to birds and wildlife and pretend they were talking back. I'd forget I had a dead sister, a dead father, and a mother who hadn't been coherent enough to have a real conversation in a decade. I'd never utter the name Tom again; hell, I wouldn't even think it. I'd change my name and call myself . . . nothing.

That's what I wanted—nothing. I wanted to sink into my nothingness and be left alone.

But I had to finish this first. Then I'd have everything, which would mean I could have my nothing.

One more kill.

Okay, not one more, there'd likely be a few more, but only one of those mattered.

Everything I'd sacrificed had led me here. All the black marks on my soul would be worth it. I knew there'd come a time when I'd have to pay for my transgressions. When I stood in judgment to a higher power, I'd accept my damnation. I wouldn't plead or beg for salvation.

I was irredeemable.

Apparently, I was whiny and self-indulgent as well. Instead of worrying about what I was going to do after and plotting Tom's murder, I needed to strategize.

Getting rid of Mason wouldn't be easy. Ditching him and his friends would take too much time. Maybe I could use him to my advantage.

I had a rock-solid cover—rich and powerful madam who was on the hunt for fresh talent to add to her stable.

It wouldn't be out of the realm of possibility I'd have bodyguards with me.

Actually, it would be weird if I didn't.

I'd already followed Amir Bakir to two expensive dinners with potential buyers. You would think it would be the buyers trying to—for lack of a better word—woo Amir. But that wasn't the case. Amir liked to show off his wealth; it was him treating the buyers to an evening of excess. The extravagance was nauseating, but the bottom-line truth was, they each had a security detail with them.

Then last night, when Amir met with Ahmad Sindi, he, too, had an entourage. I still didn't understand the dynamic between those two—were they equals, or did one of them hold more power than the other? Ahmad the kidnapper, and Amir the man who provided vetting and a lavish venue to sell Ahmad's merchandise.

Of course, Ahmad wouldn't be the only seller at the auction.

The ever-present gnawing in my stomach clawed its way to the surface. I had a bad feeling Tom was going to pull his normal underhanded bullshit. This wasn't the usual kind of assignment he sent me on. My role was twofold: secure an invite to Amir's sick-fuck party and relay the details to Tom, and verify Ahmad was back in Abu Dhabi.

Tom had assured me he had a team on standby for the takedown, that the women would be taken care of. But something about that didn't sit right. If he had a team close, and he was worried about me, why not send one or a few of the Ground Branch commandos to back me up? Why Pete and his team?

Unless Tom was lying, and he had no plans to actually shut down the auction.

Another reason I was ready to walk away—the lies, the double-crossing, the subterfuge. Tom would spin the deception; he'd cite some bullshit about the mission being fluid and targets changing.

But one problem at a time.

Bodyguards, that would work.

Then after Amir and Ahmad were taken out and the women were freed, Mason and his friends would leave.

And I'd be free to finish *my* mission.

Perfect.

Problem solved.

I rose in the bathtub, stepped out, and went for the door. I gave myself enough time to take a deep breath before facing the big, stupid, nosy, sexy jerk.

God, how was it possible to be attracted to a gigantic pain in the ass? Was this what normal people felt—temptation and desire and pissed-off-ness all swirled together? If so, I was glad I wasn't normal, happy to be the outcast, ecstatic to be the only forty-year-old virgin on the planet who wasn't a nun or saving herself for marriage.

Maybe it was time I took up masturbation. Dust the ol' cobwebs off and banish all thoughts of Mason Hughes and his stupid face. It had been years since I'd tried the frustrating, never-coming-to-fruition self-pleasure route. But that was before I'd met Mason and had something to fantasize about.

I clenched my thighs and rested my forehead on the door. What would it be like to kiss Mason, to feel his lips on mine, and other places besides? And those big rough hands, what would those feel like on my skin, on my breast, down there?

I closed my eyes and willed away the images I had no business conjuring up.

"You okay in there?" Mason's question had me jumping back from the door.

It also reminded me, I had work to do.

No more fantasizing about . . . anything. No lips, no hands, no penis.

"I'm thinking," I called back.

"About?"

How good your mouth would feel on my breasts.

Lord, I needed a lobotomy.

"If it's worth dismembering your body or if I should leave it in one piece for your friends to bury."

I heard his deep, rumbly laugh through the door, and damn but the sound made me shiver.

"I want to be cremated," he told me.

"Really?" I asked, opening the door to find him lounging on the bed.

His shoulders rested on a pile of pillows against the headboard, long legs straight out, ankles crossed, hands resting on his stomach, eyes trained on the door, waiting. Nothing particularly sexy about the pose, but so totally sexy all the same. I had to swallow a groan and remind myself I seriously disliked Mason Hughes.

"Dead's dead. Just burn my body and toss the ashes."

My gaze hadn't left his hands, or more to the point, his very thick fingers.

I was too transfixed to reply, so he went on. "I take it you want to be put in the ground."

"No." I shook my head and repeated, "Dead's dead. Just burn my body and toss the ashes."

Not that I'd have anyone to claim my ashes or visit a grave. Two-thirds of my family were gone, and with the state my mother was in, she wouldn't be able to find her way to the cemetery. I knew because two-thirds were buried, and she never visited. Not that I was in a position to judge. I'd only been to my Lili's grave twice—first when we put her into the ground, and the second was the day we laid my father to rest. Or maybe I'd laid him to rest, and my mother just sat there next to me, comatose.

"Calista?"

"Yeah?"

"Look at me, sweetness."

My gaze snapped to his.

"You okay?"

What the hell was wrong with me? First dirty thoughts, now I was letting my guard down thinking about crap I had no business thinking about.

"Fine," I scoffed. "Your dirty boots are on my bed."

"So?"

"So? I don't want to sleep in a bed—"

"You're not staying in this room alone," he interrupted me. "We have—"

It was my turn to interrupt, and inform him, "I'm not part of a 'we.'"

"You are now."

Shit. I kind of was.

"Okay, hotshot, here's the deal. I don't do teams and I don't do partners, but I thought about it, and since you're here and it'll help my cover, you, Pete, and Fallon can act as my security."

With a smooth lift of one eyebrow, he asked, "You don't do teams?"

"No."

"Thought you had a hacker assistant."

"I do."

"You don't consider her a part of your team?"

After the stunt Atlanta pulled, I wasn't sure I considered her anything. But that was for another day. "I work alone."

Mason's gaze went from perusal to scrutinizing. His study of me was intense and uncomfortable. An anger-fueled stare down was one thing. Mason observing me like he was reading my deepest, darkest secrets—no.

"I get that," he finally said.

I didn't see how that was possible when he was literally part of a team.

"I don't think you do," I stupidly mumbled.

"You can't be part of a team without trust. Tom's as untrustworthy as they come, and it doesn't sound like the hacker chick is any better."

For some reason, even though Atlanta went behind my back and I wasn't sure I could forgive her, I didn't like hearing Mason call her untrustworthy.

"I don't agree with how she handled the situation, but she's had my back a lot over the years."

"Yeah?"

"She's the best investigator I've worked with. She never fails to get me what I need when I need it, and some of the time she's a step ahead of me and predicts what I'm going to ask for. She helped train me for fieldwork, and when she did, she didn't go easy on me. She'd kick my ass, and before I could drag myself up off the mat, she'd tell me an enemy wouldn't pull punches, so neither would she. But even with all of that, I still don't know if I'll ever trust her again."

"Justifiably so."

This was one of those times when I wondered what a normal person's response would be. Someone who'd lived untouched by the atrocities I'd seen. Someone who didn't have a dead sister and blood on their hands. Someone who hadn't dedicated their life to killing as many evil men as possible.

In a moment of sheer idiocy and curiosity, I asked, "Do normal people forgive?"

Mason's eyes flashed with what looked like panic before he blinked it away.

"I don't have the first fucking clue what normal people do. I just know what I do."

My curiosity turned morbid when I pushed for more. "What do you do?"

"I don't give anyone my trust. They can't break what they don't have."

Wise words to live by. "Smart."

Mason shifted, yanked out a pillow from behind his back, and tossed it next to him. Why did he have to look so damn good in my bed?

"Stick with me. I'm full of good ideas."

He looked more like he was full of delicious mistakes.

"So you say."

"You look dead on your feet," he noted.

He wasn't wrong, but screw him for pointing it out. "Thanks," I said dryly.

"Come lie down."

And that was when I found myself blinking so fast I was worried I was going to have a seizure.

"What?" I was worried my question came out as a squeak. My suspicion was confirmed when Mason smirked.

"I don't bite."

"Well, I do." Inwardly, I cringed at my retort.

"How about we save the biting for later and you come lie down and rest. We have a busy day tomorrow."

There was no way I was getting in that bed with him. "I have a better idea. You go back to your room, and I'll rest when you're gone."

"I don't trust you not to bail."

That was fair. After all, he'd caught me mid-bail.

"I've changed my mind since then and come up with a new plan. One that includes you being my bodyguard, so I won't be ditching you."

Mason's gaze latched onto mine. His mask slipped and showed me the lethal man beneath the veil. Weirdly, I felt more comfortable with the real Mason.

"I still don't trust you."

"Good, we have that in common," I returned. "I don't trust you either."

"You shouldn't."

It was his quick honesty that had me walking to the foot of the bed and toeing off my shoes.

I put a knee to the bed.

Was I really doing this—crawling into a bed with a man I didn't know, willingly lying down beside him, willingly putting myself into a vulnerable situation?

I totally needed a lobotomy.

When I made it to the pillow, I dragged it to my front and held it to my chest like a feathery shield and laid my head on the mattress. My hip was teetering on the edge. If I did manage to close my eyes, I hoped I wouldn't move or I'd fall off the bed.

I was on my side, facing Mason. He was still on his back staring at the ceiling.

"Thank you," I whispered.

"For what?"

For telling me the truth. For not doing what everyone else in my life did and try to manipulate me. For not watching me crawl into bed.

"For being honest."

Chapter Six

"I already miss America," Fallon grumbled, and shoved the last of his beef bacon into his mouth.

From the ugliest brown leather low-back chair I'd ever seen, Calista smiled. "At least you get to go back to the States."

Pete was watching Calista balance a plate on her thighs while she cut into her waffle. He hadn't taken his eyes off of her since we'd arrived at the suite. Not that I blamed him. The woman was stunning even sleep deprived with purple shadows under her eyes, but that wasn't why my friend was keeping an eye. He was sizing her up, looking for anything that revealed what she was thinking, weaknesses, lies.

I didn't need to look. I'd already found her tells. Her fingers lightly drummed the outside of her thigh when she was thinking. Her left eye twitched ever so slightly when she was annoyed and trying to conceal her irritation.

If she had more, I'd find them, but not by watching her eat. She gave them freely when I pissed her off, and in some perverse place inside me, I enjoyed pushing her buttons. I liked that she didn't back down. I liked that she wasn't afraid to shovel shit back at me. She gave as good as she got and didn't bend.

"About that," Fallon ventured. "Those warrants are still valid."

Calista's smile broadened. "Checked up on me, eh?" She took no offense at the intrusion.

"What's taking Tom so long getting the charges dropped?" Pete inquired.

"Tom does what Tom does." Calista shrugged. "His excuse is the DNA I left on the scene and the men I killed were power brokers in DC. You know the game; the story the media spun was a home invasion and triple homicide of three good men. The public is outraged and wants justice. Their allies want my head. Tom says he's in a tight spot."

Calista had already served justice to the public and to her friend, who was being violated by three pieces of shit who'd died too quickly. Calista had shown mercy by simply ending their lives with a bullet. I would've taken my time and gotten creative.

"But . . ." I prompted.

"But Tom doesn't *want* my name cleared. He wants me on my back foot, beholden to him. He likes holding the strings, forgetting I hold the scissors and cut them anytime I want."

I don't do teams.

I wasn't lying when I told her I understood. With the people she surrounded herself with, teamwork would be impossible.

"Tom's a douche," Fallon rightly announced.

Pete set his empty plate on the coffee table in front of him. "Tom's a necessary evil."

My best friend wasn't wrong.

The world needed Toms—men with no moral compass or compulsion to prioritize loyalty to a singular person. Men who did the unspeakable for the greater good. Men who lied, cheated, manipulated to maneuver the desired outcome. Men with no limits or lines not to be crossed.

I just didn't like that Tom used Calista as a tool to achieve his goals while at the same time manipulating her.

"At least the man doesn't pretend to be something he's not," Calista agreed.

I wondered if she was thinking about Atlanta. That particular betrayal had to have stung. If anyone I worked with went behind my back and did something as shady as pretending to be me, I'd cut them out after I made my displeasure known.

"He's an authentic douche," Fallon amended.

"That he is." Calista once again smiled. This one almost looked genuine, but it lost some of its luster when she went on. "One could say he's always on brand. He'll do whatever he feels he needs to do for mission success. Even if the mission he's selling is bullshit."

"And you think this mission is bullshit?" Fallon pushed.

"I don't know." She shrugged. "And that's not me being evasive, it's the plain truth. I know he wants the location of the auction. I know he wanted confirmation Ahmad was home. I know that he told me he'd send in a team to take down Amir and Ahmad and get the women. But what he tells me and what he does are two different things."

"You think he'd leave the women behind?"

Calista's gaze swung my way. The look on her face said it all, yet she still answered my question. "He would do anything to further his agenda. Like say Atlanta gets her hands on the guest list and he finds a bigger target that could yield him intel on other HVTs. He'd leave those women behind to play the long game."

"If Tom doesn't order the auction to be hit, we'll pull in our team," I told her, not bothering to run my declaration by Pete first.

There was no way in fuck we'd leave women behind to be sold.

"After the official invitations are extended, there will only be forty-eight hours before the auction," Calista informed me.

There was anger and sadness in her tone, but it was the hope I heard that threw me. Did she really think we'd walk away before ensuring the women were safe?

Of course she did, and why wouldn't she, given who she worked for—or with. I still didn't fully understand their relationship. With effort, I refrained from rehashing old ground and reiterating what a piece of shit Tom was.

"Before I call the team to spin up, Shep called," Pete announced.

Calista frowned, Fallon perked up, and my gut tightened.

Shep calling Pete could be anything from an update to a favor that could swing from taking out an enemy to helping overthrow a small government.

The guy was a wild card.

"What'd he want?" Fallon asked.

"He has a proposition."

Pete's ominous answer had me adding my half-eaten breakfast to the table next to his plate. "What kind of proposition?"

Pete's gaze landed on Calista even though I'd been the one to ask the question.

"The mutually beneficial kind. He's offering us use of a penthouse in downtown Dubai, which would help Calista's cover and offer us more security."

"I'd ask how he knows I need to be in Dubai today, but I can guess," she grumbled.

"The catch?" Fallon challenged.

"There's a woman—a senior girl in Bur Dubai who needs an exfil. Shep needs us to find her and make sure she makes her flight."

A 'senior girl' was a prostitute who was in a slightly elevated position. She was in charge of watching the less-experienced girls and reporting back to her pimp if a girl stepped out of line.

Tap. Tap. Tap.

Calista's fingers were drumming on her thigh.

"Pure Shep," Fallon mumbled. "Only he could manage to find a prostitute who just so happens to need safe transport in a city we haven't even been in for twenty-four hours."

Shepherd Drexel might've been the one man on the planet who gave me a shiver of fear. If he wanted to, he could systematically ruin your life. There'd be nowhere you could hide from him, no hole deep enough to keep you safe. If he wanted your life—he'd take it. And he wouldn't do something as easy as putting you in the ground; he'd keep you alive like a mouse to play with.

"Bur Dubai?" Calista inquired. "Is she a massage girl?"

You couldn't walk the streets in that area without seeing hundreds of business cards littering the ground. All of the cards were advertisements for 'massages.' Phone numbers you called to order a prostitute, in the sense the pimp would tell you what back alley or storefront to go to. The prostitute would then take you to a nearby apartment, where you'd get off, then get robbed.

I couldn't find it in me to feel bad for the men who were divested of their money and jewelry after they paid for sex with a woman who was there against her will. The women weren't actually prostitutes. They'd been forced into sexual slavery.

Women who'd been lured to Dubai with promises of employment as maids, cooks, nannies, but when they arrived, they were in debt to the people who'd funded their visas and travel expenses. The debt plus interest was worked off by taking as many johns a night as they could, and when the girls didn't perform, that's when the senior girl stepped in.

It was humanity at its worst.

"Yes. She was brought here from India. Her family wants her back."

Calista eyed Pete skeptically, and I knew why. The unfortunate truth was, in most cultures, the woman would be ostracized. She'd be seen as used, filthy, unworthy. The woman would find no help healing from the trauma and abuse. No love and comfort.

"Shep spoke to her father. He's promised she's welcome and will be brought back into the family."

Calista's fingertips once again tapped. "And Shep's sure the woman will be safe?"

"He wouldn't send her home if he wasn't positive," Pete assured her.

"Where does she work?"

"Meena Bazaar."

I picked up my phone off the coffee table and pulled up a map of the area. The Bur Dubai district was across the Dubai Creek, close to Port Rashid and north of Jumeirah. The area was mostly Pakistani, Indian, and Bangladeshi.

"It would be a stretch Amir Bakir would step an Italian-loafered foot into that district, but he could have scouts or associates in the area. Us being seen there would be a risk, especially Calista," I pointed out.

"Amir wouldn't be caught dead in the red-light district. That's below his station, and he thinks common prostitution is foul," Calista returned. "But he does have people who notify him if a girl worthy of his attention is in play."

The drumming started up again, but there were only a few taps before she leaned forward and dropped her plate on the table.

"I can wear a shayla to cover my hair and neck," she decided. "Modest clothes will cover my body. I have brown contacts. I can't do much with my face, but in the cover of darkness, I should be fine. When does Shepherd need this woman picked up?"

No hesitation, Calista was all in.

"Tonight. Shep has a helicopter on standby to get her out of the UAE as soon as we can get her to a helipad."

Fallon let out a low whistle. "Doesn't give us much time to plan."

"We've had less," Pete reminded him.

"True," he agreed. "But that's us. Not us with a strap."

Calista's left eye twitched, and I couldn't hold back my chuckle.

That twitch turned into squinty eyes. "Something funny?"

"Yeah, you," I told her.

Another twitch, and my smile couldn't be helped either.

"What's funny about me?"

Seriously, the woman was hot when she was pissed and going toe to toe with me.

"Just find it amusing Fallon called you a strap, and you immediately went into that pretty head of yours and started plotting murder. For the record, you need to leave him in one piece. He wants a casket and the whole nine yards. It'd help if Pete and I didn't have to collect body parts when you're done with him."

"Figures a guy dumb enough to piss off an assassin would want a funeral. Bet he wants 'Amazing Grace' played on the bagpipes while a roomful of mourners blow sunshine and tell stories about how kind and generous he was."

I also found it hilarious she was talking about Fallon like he wasn't in the room while staring me dead in the eye when she admitted she was a gun for hire.

No prevarication.

No hiding who she really was.

No using words like 'allegedly.'

No shame.

No bullshit.

No games.

All things I respected.

All the more reason to get this job done and get the hell away from her before my control slipped.

"Yes on the bagpipes, no on 'Amazing Grace.' And I *am* a kind, generous person," Fallon returned with a smile.

He was kind and generous unless you crossed him or someone he cared about, then Fallon Harris was ruthless and demonic.

"What else would bagpipers play? 'Scotland the Brave'?" Calista quipped.

"'Thunderstruck.'"

Of all the topics Calista could've possibly hit on, she had to stumble onto one that would lead to me wanting to poke my eardrums with ice picks.

"What are the chances?" Pete muttered, mirroring my thoughts.

"There's this hot chick on YouTube who does rock 'n' roll covers. I've set money aside to have her flown to my funeral," Fallon said while pulling his phone out of his pocket.

Here we go.

Calista looked at me and asked, "Is he serious?"

"About the money? No clue. About the hot chick who plays covers, yes. And now you get to sit with him for the next hour and watch video after video. Good luck, sweetness." I stood and snatched the plates off the table. "To save my hearing, I'm going to take a shower. Be back so we can plan tonight."

I didn't miss Fallon and Pete staring at me. Further, I didn't miss how their eyes followed me into the suite's full kitchen, and I only lost their attention when I stepped into the bedroom.

I was hoping a nice long, hot shower would get my head straight.

If not, I was fucked.

Chapter Seven

I decided, for my peace of mind, I was ignoring the looks Fallon and Pete were exchanging. I was also ignoring what it felt like waking up next to Mason. I told myself I didn't sleep next to him, I'd rested. There was a difference between sleeping and resting—right?

And I absolutely wasn't thinking about Mason calling me sweetness. That was a full stop, do not pass go, lock up in box right next to childhood memories that were too painful to think about.

"How'd you hook up with Tom?" Pete asked.

Like he didn't know.

Pete seemed close to Shepherd, and anyone who ran in our circles understood Shep knew all. That knowledge made a lot of powerful men and women nervous. Some might say his ability to find out things he shouldn't put a bull's-eye on his back. Rumor had it, that was why he stayed in the shadows and moved around a lot, never staying in one place long enough to be discovered.

It was a smart play on Shep's part. If I was an omniscient god of intelligence gathering, I'd hide too.

"Is this a test?" I asked back. "To see if Tom and I have matching stories?"

"Fair assumption, but no. I know the story he told us, but I believe less than ten percent that comes out of his mouth."

I could only imagine the bullshit story Tom told. Likely it was one that cast him in a good light and me like the reckless vigilante.

"Did you know that my grandfather on my dad's side cleaned money for the Irish mob?"

Pete arched an eyebrow. "Tom mentioned it but said you didn't know anything about your father's past."

"I didn't. But when my dad got sick and he knew he was going to die, he confessed. He told me to be careful, and if I was ever approached by anyone, I was to tell Tom. My dad also told me how he really knew Tom, and that he was an informant. Tom didn't know I knew all of this until . . ." I trailed off.

"Until," Fallon prompted.

Fuck it.

In for a penny . . .

"Until last week, when Tom and I argued. He wanted me to call you." I gestured to Pete. "I was adamant I wasn't going to do that. Tom pushed, and I got annoyed and told him he'd paid his debt to my father and I didn't need his protection."

"Right. So that explains your father's connection to Tom, but how did you get involved?"

"Does it matter?" I evaded.

"No."

I waited for Pete to say more. To push or probe or, my favorite, manipulate me into giving more than I was willing to give. But he didn't, and maybe that was his tactic—silently acquiescing. Luring me into a false position of power. Allowing me to think he'd surrendered, knowing I'd feel comfortable to share since I now had the upper hand.

"Smart play," I told him.

He didn't insult me by denying his game.

"After my dad died and my mother got . . . worse, I asked Tom for help finding the man who took my sister."

Pete nodded as if he understood, though I knew he didn't. He had two sisters, both of them alive and healthy. He didn't have a mother who was lost to her grief and didn't bother to try and pull herself out, even though she had another daughter who needed her. He didn't have a father who'd done whatever he'd had to do to keep his family safe, and in the pursuit of that safety made a deal with the devil.

Now he was dead, and I'd inherited Tom.

Lucky me.

"Did he?" Fallon rejoined.

"No. He refused, so I went in search of him myself using my connections as an investigative journalist. Tom caught word of what I was doing, tracked me down, told me to stop. We had words. And I went my merry way and continued fumbling into the underbelly of society." I paused to fight back the shiver that threatened to rack my body at the memory of being taken. It was dumb luck Tom had been close before I was transported out of the country. "I found trouble, and when I still refused to stop, Tom agreed to help."

"Agreed?" Pete contested.

I had to hand it to the guy, he was smart, intuitive, and didn't bother with bullshit. If I was in the market for friends, I could see myself liking this guy. But I didn't do friends. I was never in one place long enough to develop anything that minutely resembled camaraderie.

"Agreed might be a gross overstatement. More like he took me under his wing and trained me under duress. Then he introduced me to Atlanta and, together, they made me who I am."

Made me who I am?

Lord, that was lame.

"Berta respects you," Pete told me.

Berta Lanza, my fairy godmother. I'd met her while I was investigating the atrocities happening in her country for a story I was writing. The femicide rate in Honduras was appalling. But there in the midst of tragedy and evil, the purest woman I'd ever met worked hard to do what she could for her people. A woman with a golden soul, to whom I was eternally grateful.

"She's a good human. The best the world has to offer. Tom and Atlanta trained me, they gave me the skills I needed. But Berta . . . she gave me soul, she gave me purpose. She showed me what it truly meant to be selfless."

"No disrespect to Berta," Fallon interjected. "She's everything you said she is. But to some people, she's not that."

Fallon was correct; to those who harmed her people, to those who raped the land, who killed Honduran women just because they were women, to them, she was the Angel of Death.

"The duality of man," Mason said, as he made his way back into the living room.

Hair still wet, a fresh black tee that molded to his chest, forearms on display, tan cargo pants, and socks on his feet, no boots. I had to remind myself he was an obnoxious asshole when he wasn't being . . . Sweet wasn't the right word, neither was gentle, and he'd never been kind . . .

Civil, that was the word. He was a gigantic ass when he wasn't being civil.

But he was a damn good-looking jerk.

"Berta is both empathy and cruelty," I added. "It's up to the person which side of the coin they see."

Mason's lips twitched. "Tom almost found himself on the wrong side of that coin when he showed up in Belize while we were meeting with Berta, and she found out you'd been missing for three weeks and Tom hadn't called her and was playing games instead of sending in someone to get you."

That was a lot to unpack for so few words.

"Tom knew exactly where I was and what I was doing. He knew I'd planned to get taken by Carlos Quintero. I needed intel on someone, and I knew the best way to get that was to let Carlos's men grab me. Now, I didn't foresee being driven across Mexico and taken to an island to wait for my buyers to pick me up . . ."

The air in the room was suddenly icy cold, which made the heat behind Mason's words boom across the space like a thunderclap.

"What the fuck?" Mason exploded.

Um.

I didn't understand his question.

"What the fuck, about what?"

"Mase—"

"Let's back up a second," Mason went on, like Pete hadn't called his name. "Tom knew you were in Juárez to allow a drug dealer and pimp to kidnap you?"

"Ah, yeah. That was the plan. Tom put the word out to some of his sources I was in the area. I made myself an easy target and was picked up."

The room went from icy to a whole nother dimension of arctic. The kind of cold that seeped into your bones and threatened frostbite. The kind that was so cold it burned the skin. And that freeze-out was coming solely from Mason. His fury blanketed the suite. With every breath I took, his anger filled my lungs.

This time when Mason spoke, his words were abrasive, scratchy, and dangerously calm. "Are you fucking crazy?"

My temper flared to life. I didn't answer to Mason or anyone. I was in charge of my life. No one told me what to do or how to run my investigations. I didn't need permission from anyone. And I certainly didn't ask for or need Mason's opinion.

"I don't know what your problem is—"

"My problem? Woman, you put yourself in unimaginable danger."

The danger wasn't unimaginable. Not for me and not for the men in the room. We were all well acquainted with the dangers that lurked, and we were all willing to put ourselves in front of it.

"Hi, Pot, I'm Kettle, nice to meet you," I volleyed.

"I'm not a fan of sarcasm."

Annoyed with his attitude. Pissed off that Tom and Atlanta had screwed me over. And now that I was saddled with this big beast of an asshole and his friends, I lost the last fray of my temper.

Wondering why I was still sitting in the small chair like a naughty child in time-out, I surged to my feet. Not that it did much by way of bringing me eye level with him, but at least he no longer had the dominant position.

"You know what *I'm* not a fan of?" I shot back. "You."

Pete and Fallon were still sitting. Fallon's gaze was happily ping-ponging between me and Mason like he was watching a tennis match. Pete didn't look happy about anything, and he wasn't watching the Calli and Mase show; he was staring at his feet.

"Right back at you, sweetness."

"Look at us, that's two things we have in common. How about we not find out if there's a third and use this as the perfect opportunity to part ways."

My suggestion was met with a growl.

"Sorry, I don't speak dog. Was that your agreement?" I asked sweetly.

Fallon snorted from the couch. "As entertaining as this is, we have an op to plan and only a few hours to plan it. Someone get Mason one of the thirty-five chocolate bars he picked up at the airport, so he can concentrate."

"You bought chocolate at the airport? It's five hundred degrees outside. Who eats melted chocolate?"

"Mason does. He'll lick the wrapper if he has to," Fallon informed me.

"The op," Pete prompted.

Pete's reminder was the perfect segue I needed.

"You don't need a *strap*, and I don't need you. So I assume you have tonight handled all by yourselves, then you can go home, and I can get back to why I'm here."

In Fallon's defense, he did look a little sheepish when I reminded him he'd called me a strap. I couldn't know if he'd meant it as an insult, insinuating I was dead weight strapped to their team, or if it was nothing more than a turn of phrase. Either way, I was no one's burden.

"Did you get the intel you were after in Juárez?" Pete asked.

"Sure did," I told him. "Now, if you'll excuse me, I have shit to do."

"You're not leaving."

Was it possible to be so angry your vision hued red—actual red with blurry dark spots? Before that moment, I would've said no. I would've said allowing yourself to get incensed to the point of hazy vision was a weakness to be snuffed out. Rage was a symptom of loss of control. But there I was, fuming and seeing red, all because of Mason and his proclamation.

"Actually, I am."

I skirted the table but didn't get far when Pete stood.

"What Mason means is, you're a smart woman," Pete wrongly paraphrased. He'd said I was fucking crazy, and he meant it. "You know us being here only strengthens your cover, and we can use your help tonight. No doubt the woman we grab will be scared. She's been living in hell for three years. She'll need a woman's touch to smooth the way. So we're all leaving here, going to Shep's penthouse, and planning tonight. Like Fallon pointed out, we only have a few hours, so we best get moving."

My suitcase was sitting by the door. I could grab it and go. I could rid myself of the irritation and focus on what was important—meeting Amir Bakir for dinner, securing an invitation to the auction, passing the intel to Tom, and then finally avenging my sister.

All I needed to do was put one foot in front of the other and walk out.

Yet my feet stayed where they were.

"What intel was so important you'd risk your life for it?"

Anything that got me one step closer to killing the man who stole my sister from me.

"There's a lot of intel floating around out there that would be worth risking my life to find."

Mason tipped his head back and stared at the ceiling. I didn't need him to say a word to know I was taxing his patience.

Same, friend, same.

Chapter Eight

The woman was downright infuriating.

Berta Lanza's words from several weeks ago played in my head on repeat.

Calista is a brave woman.

Calista has made it her mission to bring awareness but also to rescue and return victims home. Much like what Saint here does. These women need a champion, a savior, and she has a beautiful soul, so she's decided that savior will be her. She reminds me of you, Catarina. Mia too. Brave. Strong. But not as smart. She wants to save the world, not just those she can.

Not as smart.

I had no doubt Calista was smart, but she was dangerously stupid with her safety.

What the hell had she been thinking, making herself a target, purposefully getting taken? For what, information? Jesus fuck, she could've been killed. She could've been raped.

Had she been?

My mind raced through every interaction I'd had with the woman. No hollow, haunted eyes, no recoiling from men who were much bigger and stronger than her, no timidness, jumpiness, anxiety. Of course, just because I hadn't seen any signs didn't mean shit.

No, she had to have escaped that cruelty. I wouldn't allow my brain to contemplate the alternative.

I raised the palms of my hands to my eyes and pressed hard in an attempt to vanquish the horrific thought.

When I dropped my hands, my gaze went back to the view in front of me. From the window, the world's tallest skyscraper stood proud. The Burj Khalifa, UAE's latest claim to power. Below, the famous fountain was inactive. Later, the crowd would gather and watch what was now considered the world's largest water shower.

Dubai was famous for a great many things—all of them a facade.

All of them hiding the truth.

All of it built by slaves.

Not that polite society liked using that word. Society played moral gymnastics to make the world around them more palatable. Well-meaning intellectual types liked to distance themselves from uncomfortable realities. They played word games: forced labor, hazardous working conditions, unpaid services, servitude. It freed them of the inconvenient guilt of enjoying the luxury built by poor, desperate, and beaten-down men.

When in truth it was fucking slavery.

There was no way to pretty up the actuality. But we did that now too. Your truth. My truth. We warped the truth and made it subjective. We hijacked words, changed the meanings to fit the narrative. We called women and men and fucking children being kidnapped and sold human trafficking, exploitation, instead of calling it what it was—sexual slavery. Because it was less offensive to hear.

The longer I stared out the window at a building that was built by slaves, the more my disdain grew. A beautiful skyline, luxury, money, all hiding the truth—the vile, revolting, disgusting truth. Right now, as I stood in the extravagant display of wealth, there were women and men and children down somewhere in that city being raped. Unspeakable trauma being inflicted.

Fuck.

I turned my back on the window, unable to stomach my own thoughts.

The need to hunt down, maim, kill every man who dared to harm the innocent was a living, breathing beast inside of me. A monster I didn't bother to control. The people who perpetrated those atrocities didn't deserve mercy.

I wondered if Calista felt the same way I did. Not that it would excuse her for putting herself in a position where something precious could've been stolen from her in a way that would forever mark her . . . but it would explain her asinine behavior.

Christ. The thought made me murderous.

I bowed my head and blew out a breath. I had five minutes to pull my shit together and meet Pete, Fallon, and the woman who was driving me insane back downstairs. The woman who was currently in the bedroom next to mine with nothing but a wall separating us and a shared balcony that connected the rooms. This was torture. Pure fucking torture.

The two-story penthouse was cavernous and disgustingly opulent. The wall-to-wall marble floors throughout the apartment extended into the bedrooms. The thick rug under the bed protruded just enough for your feet to hit plush carpet, yet it did little to purge the cold and uninviting feel. There was nothing—from the gold trim on the furniture to the teal-green walls to the ugly brown silk comforter—that fostered warmth. Nothing in the room made you want to come in here after a long day and relax.

I hated everything about this room and the penthouse in general. I'd take my condo in Imperial Beach with my view of the ocean over this monstrosity any day.

With a final exhale that did nothing to quell my loathing, I started for the door. As soon as I stepped into the hall, I nearly ran into Calista.

"Sorry," she muttered, and tried to move past me.

I did that. Made her want to avoid me, since I'd been a dick to her again. I didn't want to be an asshole, I just couldn't figure out what it was about her that made me want to bang my head on the wall, or toss her over my shoulder and lock her away so she couldn't make shitty decisions with her safety, or kiss the living fuck out of her to shut her up.

"How's your room?" I asked, as if I had the right to speak to her after I'd been a monumental prick just a few hours ago.

Those pretty eyes flared.

Yeah, sweetness, I get it, my audacity knows no bounds.

"It's an in-your-face display of wealth."

My lips twitched at her description mirroring my own.

Which spurred me to ask my next question. "How do you like the view?"

Her grimace said it all, but still she answered. "You mean the view of the city built by slave labor and corruption? It's repulsive and makes me want to track down every land developer and stab them in the heart for exploiting people from around the world who came here with the promise of opportunity to better the lives of their families. How's yours?"

"Same, sweetness."

She tilted her head a fraction and narrowed her eyes.

"With one slight difference," I continued, before she could unleash that runaway mouth of hers and call me a much-deserved name. "Disembowelment is far more painful than a quick and easy blade to the heart."

Calista nodded. "You're right. And while I don't mind mess, cutting someone open from throat to groin to remove their innards takes too much time. My way is quick and efficient."

Fuck but I liked this woman.

"Fair."

I gestured for her to precede me down the hall.

"Scared I'll shove you down the stairs if you go first?"

I hadn't thought of that, but now that *she* had, I realized I was off my game and needed to focus, because Calista would absolutely shove me down the stairs or over the balustrade.

"Just being gentlemanly."

She gave me an unconvinced look before she skirted around me and started down the corridor.

"I don't believe that," she noted.

As crazy as it was, it was the truth.

"I don't care what you believe."

She huffed a cute, annoyed breath as she clomped down the stairs. Her red Vans squeaked going from the solid white treads to the gold-veined marble in the foyer.

"Good thing it doesn't rain here or this floor would be slippery as fuck."

"Huh," she mumbled.

"You don't agree?" I asked.

"No, I was thinking almost the same thing but about getting out of the shower, wondering how many people have courted a concussion in this place because they didn't dry off their feet."

I hadn't bothered checking the bathroom in my suite, but now I'd make sure there were ample towels to put on the floor.

"This place sucks," I grumbled.

"Agreed."

With every agreement, I felt something tighten in my chest. I didn't want to have similar thoughts and opinions as the woman who drove me insane. I wanted her to be a raving, stuck-up diva with a bitchy personality. Instead, her only flaw was reckless abandonment for personal safety, and if I was being totally honest, I couldn't fault her for that when I put myself in danger all of the time, as did my teammates—and I didn't get in *their* faces when they did.

Why the fuck was I thinking about this?

Christ, I had a serious problem.

Thankfully, before any more opinions could be shared, thus me finding out I had more in common with Calista than I was comfortable with, the living room came into view.

"You look ridiculous," I told Pete.

The stark-white couch he sat on was absurd. The seats were deep, but the back was so low, it stopped at the middle of Pete's back. He looked like a giant. I glanced over to the matching couch and cringed.

"I'll give you a hundred bucks if you give me your chair," I propositioned Fallon, who was sitting in the only chair in the room.

"Nope. I scouted this chair before you idiots went up to check out the bedrooms."

Sure enough, Fallon's backpack was resting on the floor by his feet.

"I hate you," I grumbled, and moved toward the hobbit couch.

"You hate that I'm smarter than you," he quipped.

He was probably right. Though I blamed Calista. If she hadn't muddled my head, I would've scoped out the living room before going upstairs, and my ass would've been sitting in the comfortable chair.

Calista's gaze went from couch to couch. Unsurprisingly, she made her way to the one opposite me and sat next to Pete. This had the unfortunate consequence of being in my direct line of sight.

"Shep sent over a full report. There's not much in there that's useful," Pete started. "Kiara Das, nineteen—"

Calista startled and glanced over at Pete before interrupting, "How long has she been here?"

"Three years."

I knew Calista did the mental math when her head twitched.

"She was sixteen," she whispered through gritted teeth.

I kept my gaze planted on her as Pete went on. "She came to Dubai with a group of women to be cleaners. There's no record of any of them working at any of the hotels or record of them being paid."

"How'd Shep find Kiara?" Fallon asked.

"Dumb luck. He was tracking . . . name redacted," Pete said, and rolled his eyes. "He got a hit on his guy here, and Kiara was with him, so he ran her. Her family filed what's equivalent to a missing person's report in Odisha, where she's from. Of course, Shep hacked the records and contacted the father to get more information. The father told him about the other girls and the service that hired Kiara. Shep dug around some more. No hits on the others, but he's still looking and hoping Kiara will give him a lead."

"Do we have a clear image of her?" Calista queried.

"Passport photo and a still from the footage Shep used to run the facial rec. It's a clear shot. She's thinner, hair's longer, but it's her. She has a mole on the corner of her right eye."

"So what's the plan for tonight?" Fallon asked.

"Simple and stupid," Pete shot back.

"You have the number for the massage service," I guessed.

"Yeah. I'll call and find out where the pickup spot is, and we'll move in."

Simple and stupid.

There was no reason to overcomplicate things when we had a phone number to call that would lead us right to the girl.

"What about muscle?" Calista asked.

"From what Shep could find, Deepak Bashu, aka Sparkle, runs a crew of ten, with twenty girls working for him. But that's not confirmed."

"Sparkle?" Fallon repeated. "Where the fuck did he come up with that, and who told him Sparkle was a good street name? At least go with something like Killer or Blade or Pimp Daddy. Christ, what a tool."

"Pimp Daddy?" Calista scoffed.

"What? I heard it used on TikTok."

Calista's gaze slowly slid in my direction. When she had my attention, she made one of those big-eye faces women make when they find something . . . Hell, I don't know why they make the bug eyes, but I've seen the servers at the Dirty Plank do it plenty.

"I think your buddy has found himself on the wrong side of TikTok if Pimp Daddy's coming up on his algorithm," she stage-whispered.

"What? I use it to watch my bagpipe vixen."

"If you say so." She pinched her lips and gave me big eyes again. "But if you tell me you only subscribe to the Naughty by Nature website for the articles, I'm not going to believe you."

Pete chuckled. I was too busy staring at her to make a sound.

"Never heard of it, but now I'm interested in how *you* know about a website that leads with naughty."

"Research," she shot back with a wink.

I was not going to think about Calista poking around the internet on naughty websites. I was not going to think about why I wanted to kick my friend in the dick for being on the receiving end of Calista's wink. And I absolutely wasn't going to think about why I found that playful wink so sexy.

Christ, I must be coming down with a brain infection.

"Let's get this shit done." Pete nabbed his phone off the cushion next to him and started stabbing at the screen. "I want to order up a woman from a sleazy fucking pimp like I want a hole in my head."

No more than the rest of us wanted to hear the call, but it was a necessary evil.

Pete put the call on speaker.

Five rings later, a heavily accented male answered, "Hello?"

"I found your card," Pete said through clenched teeth. "I'm looking for a massage."

"Yes, brother, come tonight."

Calista's head twitched. Twice now. A new tell. I didn't have to guess what that small tic gave away. Bloodshed would be imminent.

Nice.

Once again, I liked the way the woman thought.

Pete's jaw clenched. "How much?"

"One shot, eighty. Full service, two hundred."

There was commotion on the other end of the line, people talking, the sound of traffic, music.

The asshole was walking down the street conducting business like he wasn't selling the services of girls he'd forced into sexual slavery.

Visions of stabbing him in the throat danced through my head.

"Where?"

"You know Meena Bazaar?"

"Yes."

"Beside Atheryat on Al Fahidi. Will you come?"

Christ, I wanted to bury this asshat.

And by the disgusted lip curl Calista had going on, she seemed to be in agreement.

"What kind of girls?"

"Pakistani, Indian, Russian, Thai. You take your pick. You get good service."

"I'll be there."

"Good, brother."

With that, Sparkle the pimp hung up.

"That easy?" Calista asked with a frown.

"That easy," Pete confirmed.

Nauseatingly easy. Hundreds of men would call that number every day. Some would show to pick a girl, some would call another number, find a better price, and head to whatever location that pimp controlled. That easy. Every day. Hundreds of times a day. Three sixty-five. And when one pimp was taken out, another would be put in his place, but the girls would never leave the streets.

"The Atheryat building houses retail shops and a restaurant," Fallon announced, looking down at his tablet. "Corner of Seventy-Fourth and Al Fahidi. There's an alley on the east side of the building. Multiple entrances to the building next door. Bottom floor is a perfume shop and shoe store. Top floors are apartments."

"Other entrances to access the apartments?" I asked, pissed at myself I'd left my tablet in my room.

"One on the east side on Seventy-Fourth Street. None on the backside. But there are businesses back there. It's not an alley or a street. A car or motorcycle could pull in, but it's a dead end, approximately two hundred meters, and connects back to Sparkle's alley."

Pete was staring with narrowed eyes—his normal thinking face—at the dark screen of his phone. Calista sat silently beside him with her gaze fixed on her red sneakers. A desperate need to know what she was thinking churned in my gut. A curiosity that would only lead to trouble, yet I couldn't stop the question from spilling out of my mouth.

"What's on your mind?"

"The girls."

That was the generic answer; we were all thinking about the girls. That's why we did the work we did. Long after we left this world, the war would continue, yet we willingly marked our souls for the ones we could save. What seemed like small victories were in reality monumental to each woman, man, and child we pulled from the bowels of hell.

"What else?" I pushed.

Calista abandoned the study of her shoes and lifted her gaze.

"I'm wondering if it will ever stop coming as a surprise. My sister was taken . . . not like these women, by someone she knew. He took her, gave her away, and she was sold, then passed around. I've lived this for so long, yet I'm still shocked. Right out in the open. Business cards passed out with phone numbers to call. It's easier to order a woman than it is real bacon and a martini."

She wasn't wrong.

"It never stops coming as a shock, sweetness, because it's fucking shocking and disturbing."

She nodded but didn't look convinced.

Chapter Nine

Simple and stupid went out the window when we were dropped off three blocks down from the location Pete was given.

Shep had arranged a driver. The man looked like he wasn't a day younger than a hundred and seventy-five. His English was impeccable; so were his manners. There was something about the kind old man that made me want to whisk him away and force him to retire someplace far from here.

On the drive over, he explained he'd worked with the "American" before. I thought he was referring to Shepherd as the American, but as it turned out, he worked with more people than just Shep. "Worked" didn't mean he accepted money. He offered his taxi services for free transporting women to safety. He reminded me of Berta. Good and honest and noble, trying to do right in a country he loved. Trying to right wrongs that were not his.

But that wasn't what derailed the simple and stupid strategy to get Kiara. It was Mason changing up the plan after we'd already hashed it out back at the penthouse.

It was simple—Pete was going to the alley. Fallon and I were going to use the side entrance to get into the building and wait inside for Pete to hopefully bring Kiara in. If she wasn't in the alley, Pete would leave without picking a girl. Then thirty minutes later, Mason would come into play and go to the alley to look for Kiara. If she still wasn't there, Pete would come back later and try again.

Simple.

Or it would have been if Mason hadn't decided *he* was going to accompany me into the apartment building, and Fallon was going to take his place looking for Kiara. This led to a minor squabble between me and Mason. I didn't like last-minute changes, especially when they were made with no explanation. But I didn't need one. I knew he'd switched places because he didn't trust me to have Fallon's back.

"You're not to be outside of touching distance," Mason demanded.

Now I wanted to kick Mason in the balls for not trusting me to do my job and for being a bossy twit.

"What? You mean I can't do a skip-dance in the street?" I asked as I fiddled with my dusty-rose shayla that was already damp, making sure my neck was still covered. "This is torture."

Mason glanced over at me. "You could go back to the penthouse."

"Bet you'd like that."

His jaw clenched under the scruff of his not-yet-full beard, but full enough it was more than a five-o'clock shadow and sexier than I wanted to admit.

"I would."

Gah. I was going to cause the man bodily harm before the night was over.

I decided now was a good time to ignore him and start paying attention to my surroundings. The street was packed despite how late it was. Late and hot as hell. The sun setting had barely put a dent in the temperature and did nothing to touch the humidity. If the sweat rolling down my back and between my boobs was anything to go by, it had to be pushing ninety.

Shop signs were lit up, and streetlights cast a white glow over the dirty sidewalks. I couldn't take a step without seeing a massage card—on the ground, stuck on parked cars, taped to the light poles.

They were everywhere.

All in English.

Spa and Massage: fifty-percent-off special.

Oil Massage, facial, body scrub: call now.

Massage Therapy: special rates.

Phone numbers boldly displayed.

There had to be hundreds and hundreds of them. Every-fucking-where.

People all around me hustling on the sidewalks, crossing the street, standing in front of shops and sitting at outside tables of restaurants, and hardly anyone paid attention to those massage cards.

There was bumper-to-bumper traffic, horns honking, roadwork being done.

Everything looked normal, but there were thousands of men and women being held against their will in these hotels, apartments, in the backs of stores. Thousands in this district alone.

In my stomach, a lethal cocktail of fury and hate bubbled.

The enormity was such that we were powerless to stop it. The best we could do was save a few . . . but there would always be more.

"Sweetness." Mason's gruff voice pulled me from my thoughts.

"What?" I snapped.

"Calli . . . honey, look at me."

Calli?

I dragged my gaze away from the disturbingly normal movements of those around me and looked over at Mason.

"Everything's going to be all right."

"No, it won't. It'll never be all right. We'll never be able to make it all right."

He nodded. "You're right. But tonight we're going to make one young woman safe and return her to her family. Think about that instead of wanting to murder every person who walks by us."

"How'd you know I was plotting murder?"

"You're glaring at every person who passes us, and you're holding my hand testing my bone density."

I was holding his hand?

I flexed my fingers and, sure enough, I was.

When the heck did I grab his hand? I loosened my hold, but he held strong.

Neither of us spoke the final two blocks.

And when we passed the alley, I kept my eyes trained on the concrete in front of me, not trusting myself to look.

I didn't want to save one girl tonight. I wanted to save them all.

There were sisters out there who were missing them. There were mothers and fathers and grandparents.

"The shops on the bottom floor are vacant," Mason mumbled.

I glanced over, and there was nothing but trash in the vacant spaces.

"That's helpful."

"Yep."

Mason guided me around the corner. Unlike Al Fahidi Street, 74th was desolate. There were parked cars, but the street was empty of people. I glanced across the street opposite the Atheryat building. There were businesses, but they were all closed.

I wasn't ready for Mason's sharp tug on my hand. I stumbled forward, and before I could right myself, he spun me around and shoved my back against the building.

"What—"

Mason leaned closer. "Shh."

What the hell?

"Move, brother," a man said from behind Mason.

Shit, now I knew why the businesses were closed. After dark, this was Sparkle's block.

"In a minute."

"Now. Move."

"I'm just getting a taste, big man. I'll be done in a minute."

Mason was pressed close, completely shielding me. I could feel the tension in his body. His muscles bunching and coiling, readying to strike. I reached into the pocket of my loose-fitting linen pants and wrapped my hand around the handle of my custom-made retractable knife. I blew out a breath and relaxed.

"Move," the man repeated from up close.

I glanced over Mason's left shoulder and saw the man's hand come up—but before I could draw my knife from my pocket and warn Mason, he was already on the move.

Lightning quick, Mason shifted and delivered a brutal jab with his left fist to the man's throat, followed by a right hook to his jaw.

The man dropped just as two more men came around the corner. Both of them looked at the man on the ground, then at us, and started yelling in Hindi.

Simple and stupid had officially gone to shit.

"It's all good," Mason muttered.

Apparently his definition of all good significantly differed from mine.

"Do you know what they're saying?" I asked.

Mason didn't answer. The larger of the two men rushed him. I stayed against the building, doing my best impression of a damsel in distress. My acting skills must've been impressive, or the boy-man in front of me—who looked like he was underfed and hadn't had proper nutrition at any point in his life, causing his growth to stunt—underestimated me because I was a woman. I was five-seven and was looking the guy in the eye.

He reached out and grabbed my wrist. I let him pull me away from the wall, still playing the 'I'm a scared girl, please don't hurt me' card.

I really didn't want to have to kill the boy-man. He looked like he'd barely kissed his teenage years goodbye. Not that that meant anything. The guy who took my sister had been twenty. But there was a sadness in this kid's eyes that made me hope he'd go down easy.

The grunts and thuds of fists hitting flesh reminded me I needed to drop this kid before someone else came around the corner.

"Please don't hurt me," I begged.

"Come."

"Just let me go."

The kid stepped closer to me and yanked my arm. I used the force of his tug to slam into him and pulled my other hand out of my pocket.

With my fingers still tightly wrapped around the handle of my knife, I swung and hit him square in his ear. Before he recovered, I landed a front kick to his gut and followed up with a perfectly placed uppercut.

The kid didn't even stumble before he pitched sideways and went down.

Thank God for glass jaws.

I pocketed my knife and made my way to Mason.

He was straddling his opponent, pummeling his face with no signs of stopping.

"Mase, he's down."

Like he didn't hear me, he continued his beating.

"Mason. Enough. We need to move."

Suddenly, Mason pulled out of his trance and looked up at me.

The lighting was shit on this side of the building, but I still saw the green of his eyes—wild and raw and furious.

"We need to move the bodies," I told him.

He did a top-to-toe scan of me and stood.

Without speaking, he pulled zip ties out of his pocket and handed me two.

It took me seconds to roll my undersized attacker to his stomach and zip his wrists together. I moved to his ankles and did the same, making sure I tightened them as much as possible to cause maximum pain. Just because I didn't want to kill him didn't mean I wouldn't be happy inflicting as much damage as I could.

I was reaching for the guy's back pocket to check for an ID, phone, something, when Mason grabbed my arm.

"Not without gloves."

Damn, that was a rookie mistake. There could be drugs, including fentanyl in his pockets.

"Where are we taking them?"

"Bottom floor."

I didn't get the chance to ask Mason to elaborate before he turned on his boots and stalked away. I didn't want to be impressed when

Mason bent and hauled the mangled-face guy off the ground and hoisted him over his shoulder—but I was.

I didn't have that option available to me, so I rolled my guy to his back, prayed I wasn't going to get a flesh-eating disease when I grabbed him under his sweaty armpits, and, mostly bent over and walking backward, dragged him in the direction Mason was going.

I was looking over my shoulder to watch where I was going. Again, I didn't want to be impressed, but with one vicious kick to the door, it flew open.

Damn, that gave new meaning to the term 'door kicker.'

Pulling dead weight was harder than it looked, even when the weight wasn't much more than your own. I tried to keep the huffing and puffing to a minimum when I towed my cargo through the rickety door that was hanging haphazardly off its hinges.

"Keep sharp," he told me as I passed.

"Where to?" I asked, ignoring his insult. I might not have been able to hoist a man over my shoulder or kick in a door, but I wasn't an idiot.

Mason moved deeper into the dim space and unceremoniously dropped his haul. With a thud and bounce, the guy hit the ground, producing a plume of dust mixed with some bacteria I was sure I didn't want to think about.

"Seriously," I complained, and choked back a cough.

"Stay here."

Mason disappeared, leaving me in the darkened, germ-infested, empty storefront. With only the streetlight coming in through the window, I could make out overturned furniture, boxes, miscellaneous trash, and broken shelves. The place creeped me the hell out. I reached back in my pocket and fisted my knife.

The silence was starting to get to me when I heard footsteps. Not the kind when someone was trying to sneak up on you. The loud, angry kind of a beastly jerk.

He put his first attacker down next to the other two.

As annoying as it was, I waited for assface's orders.

Like he had superhuman eyesight, he moved around the room riffling through boxes. Moments later, he came back with a shiny black shirt with gold paisleys on it. The thing was hideous in the dimly lit room; it would be downright offensive in the light.

Understanding dawned.

I pulled out my knife and held it out to Mason. "Here. Use this."

Mason didn't accept my knife. He used his hands to tear the fabric.

Well, okay, then—show-off.

Two more rips and he handed me a strip.

I got down on my knees, happy I wasn't attached to these pants, because I would be throwing them away after tonight. No amount of detergent would be enough to disinfect them. I tied the makeshift gag around my guy's head, wishing I could grow new hands so I could throw these ones away. The boy-man was sweatier than I was, and that was saying something. I was the one with a headscarf, and I was pretty sure I was having a hot flash, seeing as the lake of sweat between my boobs had turned into a hot tub.

Was I old enough for a hot flash?

Mason was done with his two by the time I was done.

Did I say show-off . . . ?

"Everything go okay when you went back out?" I asked.

"Yes."

Great, not only was Mason being a jerk again, he was being a monosyllabic jerk.

The guy had the whole Jekyll and Hyde thing down to a science.

"You're like a box of chocolates," I mumbled under my breath.

"Come again?"

"You never know what you're gonna get. Nice Mason. Dick Mason. Reassuring Mason. Bossy Mason."

"Are you done?"

"I'm sure I can come up with more if you'll give me a minute or two."

"Should I order you a latte, too, while we wait for you to remember more ridiculous quotes from stupid movies?"

Someone was testy.

"I was needing a minute to remember your other personalities, since there seems to be so many of them. Not movie quotes. But are you saying that *Forrest Gump* is a stupid movie?"

"Not the whole movie, just the parts with that bitch Jenny in them."

"Jenny wasn't a bitch—"

"You're right, she wasn't just a bitch, she was a total piece of shit who took advantage of Forrest until she used him up, then she ran off, fucked who she wanted, smoked what she wanted, and injected shit into her body until she made herself sick. Then when Forrest did something good for himself, her manipulating, selfish ass crawled back so he could take care of her kid."

The kid was Forrest's, too, but I ignored that.

"That's awfully judgmental."

Mason's body turned to stone, and his face twisted into a scowl.

"I'm judgmental as fuck, and people who tell you they're not are lying." Mason paused and stepped closer. "You're judging me right now, thinking I'm an asshole because I called Jenny a bitch. You're judging me because I'm honest enough to admit I judge the fuck out of every person who comes into my orbit.

"I protect my peace and my boundaries. If I deem someone's character unacceptable, I don't allow them close. But just because I don't want a certain behavior in my life doesn't mean it's wrong. It just means it's not right for *me*. And there's where everyone gets it wrong—no one has the right to shove their judgment down someone else's throat. That makes them an asshole, and if they take that further, it makes them a piece-of-shit tyrant.

"Do not mistake me, Calista. I judge, but I will be the first one to call out an asshole who thinks their beliefs or opinions should be shoved down anyone's throat." Mason yanked his phone out of his pocket, stared at the screen, and finished with, "Pete's approaching the alley. We need to get upstairs."

"You're right. I was judging you. I think you're an asshole, and not only because you think one of my favorite movies is stupid."

"Right."

I followed Mason to the far back corner of the abandoned shop, where there were two doors. According to Fallon, one of those doors should exit into a passageway that connected all of the stores, as well as had access to the apartments. Thankfully, that access was stairs. There was zero chance I was getting into an elevator in this run-down building.

The mere possibility of getting trapped in a small space with Mason was out of the question.

Chapter Ten

I never should've switched places with Fallon.

I shouldn't've let my need to have Calista close override my good sense. But the thought of Calista being out of my sight while we'd be surrounded by dangerous men had the potential of giving me an ulcer.

Then she had to go and mention the one movie I hated. This after we'd had a little scuffle. It wasn't the fight; Calista had handled herself better than I'd thought.

It was hearing that fuckwad tell fuckwad number two to grab Calista and get her to the car that had me spiraling.

She was not safe in this city. Women in general were not safe.

All it would've taken was one thing to go wrong, and Calista would've been dragged away.

And instead of dragging her ass back to the penthouse to get her safe like I wanted to, we were ascending stairs into another unknown situation, with more dangerous men who wouldn't think twice about snatching her.

"Stay sharp," I told her as we approached the door at the top of the stairs.

"That's the second time you've said that to me in the last five minutes," she groused.

Obviously she had no idea what those men on the street wanted.

"Do you speak Hindi?"

"No. Do you?"

"Speak it, no. Understand enough to get by, yes."

I pulled out my phone and shot off a text to Pete that we were in position.

He'd knock on the door once as he passed if it was clear for Calista and me to enter, twice if we were to hold, and three times if he needed backup.

Now we waited.

"What'd the men say when they saw us?"

Smart.

"Nothing worth repeating."

There were a few moments of silence before she pressed. "It was about me, wasn't it? That's why you beat the hell out of the guy instead of just knocking him out like you did the first one."

Fuck.

"Like I said—"

"I don't get you," she interrupted. "You're like this big gruff asshole superhero. You don't like me—"

"I never said I didn't like you."

Thankfully, that shut her up. The woman was too smart for my mental health.

The stairwell was quiet. No sounds coming from the other side of the door. No beds banging on the walls from sex. No groans or screams. Either this building was soundproof, or something wasn't right.

"Something's wrong," Calista whispered, even though moments ago she was speaking normally.

Why did she have to be so fucking remarkable? No, she was astute. She had good instincts. That wasn't remarkable; that was skilled and good at her job. She didn't impress me. I didn't find it wildly attractive she could read a situation.

Absolutely none of that was filtering through my mind while I pulled up Fallon's text thread and tapped out a message.

It's too quiet here. Where are you?

At the end of the alley. I have eyes on the target. No prize yet.

Holding position.

Copy.

"What are you thinking?" Calista asked.

"Fallon's got eyes on Pete. No sign of Kiara yet."

"What if what's behind that door isn't the first floor of the apartments?"

Fucking Shep and his favors.

"What do you mean?"

"What if it's the lobby or the laundry room or more retail space?"

This wasn't the US; space was at a premium. It wouldn't be wasted on laundry or a lobby. Not in this area. But damn if she wasn't on to something.

"Six stories," I started, and closed my eyes to picture the building from the outside. "Eight individual balconies on each level. The first floor doesn't have the same balconies. It has a gallery with chain-link fencing from the knee wall to the overhang roof. I thought it made sense, that enclosure to keep the girls locked in, and it does, but they don't take johns to that floor."

"So you're thinking that's where he keeps the girls when they're not working?"

"Yeah."

I reached into my back pocket and fished out my lockpick kit. Two seconds later, the shittiest lock I'd ever worked was cracked.

"That was easy," she drawled.

I knew the life she lived, the business she was in. She didn't need the lesson. Still, I educated. "No passport. No money. If they do get out, where are they gonna go? The police? Authorities are bought off. Ask a tourist for help? What are they gonna do? These women are stuck in a way they'll never get unstuck, and they know it. So they don't try to escape because if one of them is brave enough to try, she'll be brought back and made an example of in front of the others, then she's back out a few hours later, beaten to shit, taking cock, but she'll do it fucked up. The lock is symbolic, not functional."

"How evil does a person need to be to . . ."

She didn't finish that statement, and I understood why. Just saying the words made acid churn in your gut. The mere thought of what these people were forced to do, what they endured night after night, day after day, was too much to comprehend.

I replaced my kit for my phone in my pocket and sent another message to Fallon.

On the move. Look up, first floor fenced in. We're moving up a floor.

Copy. Still no prize.

I put my phone away and relayed, "No Kiara yet." I twisted the doorknob. "Stay—"

"Sharp," she hissed. "Warning. Next time you tell me that shit, I'm gonna show you how sharp I can be and shank your ass."

Shank.

Goddamn, she could be cute.

I beat back my smile and nodded.

Slowly, I pushed open the door.

I barely had it open a few inches when the smell knocked the breath out of my lungs. I heard Calista's gasp, felt her moving behind me, likely adjusting her shayla to cover her nose and mouth. Not that the fabric would hide the stench, but I got the sentiment.

I pushed the door open a little more. Stained mattresses on the floor and cots came into view. Crumpled sheets, small piles of clothes, but no women or guards.

Slaves didn't get the day off.

With a nod, I stepped over the threshold, holding the door for Calista. Her hand tapped mine, I moved, and she slowly and gently closed the door.

The room was filthy. Filthy in a way it would never be clean. The putrid smell of sweat mixed with desperation and depravity coated the air. Human waste intermingled with the misery.

The impulse to burn the building to the ground and free the ghosts that haunted these walls was hard to fend off.

"Do you have matches?" Calista sneered.

Good Christ, it was like this woman shared my brain.

"Come on," I grunted, and carefully maneuvered around the trash toward the door farther down the wall.

No lock on this one.

I took a moment to listen for any sounds behind the door, but in the silence, all I could hear was the cries of the women who'd been trapped in this room. Their grief. Their fear. Their souls keening.

"Mason?" Calista's voice cut through the quiet.

The doorknob was sticky. I knew it was too much to ask that the tackiness was from grape jelly, but still I hoped.

Like the first, this stairwell was lit by one light bulb at the base; it illuminated just enough to see the steps and the door at the top.

My phone vibrated.

With my clean hand, I reached back to grab it, then, one-handed, I unlocked the device and read the message.

No prize. We're taking a walk. Be back in thirty.

I tilted the screen so Calista could read it.

"Damn," she whispered.

"My hands are dirty. Take my phone and respond."

She'd just slipped the phone out of my hand when the door at the top of the stairs opened.

Calista immediately fisted the back of my shirt and yanked it while she shuffled back. I held the door as it closed, turned, and followed Calista back to the other door.

We slipped back into the first stairwell, and I kept the door propped open a crack with my boot.

"Tell him we're back in position one with company. No backup yet," I whispered.

I watched as Calista tapped out the message.

Holding at position one. We have company. No backup needed.

On standby.

Copy.

"Want me to keep this?"

"Yeah."

Calista shifted behind me and down one step. I went back to the crack in the door, hoping I could see or hear something.

It took a few moments before I heard a door opening, then closing. The crying was next. Then rapid-fire Hindi.

I was catching bits and pieces, enough to understand someone had hurt whoever was speaking, but not enough to paint a full picture.

A second female voice told the first to stop crying and clean up.

"Krpaya, Kiara."

Please, Kiara.

Calista's fingers curled into the waistband of my pants before I heard her short nails clicking on my phone's screen.

Then in English, "You know. I have to tell." The voice sounded pained. That had to be Kiara. "Clean."

"We'll take them both." That came from behind me.

Of *course* Calista would want to take both. One girl was going to be hard enough to control and smuggle out of the area.

I turned my head, leaned down, and at the same time, Calista leaned forward and crowded me. Once I had her ear, through the fabric I whispered, "Text. We have the prize plus one. Side entrance now."

She started nodding after the word *text*, and by the time I got to *now*, she was doing it rapidly.

Simple and stupid, famous last words.

My attention went back to the two women. Kiara was telling the crying girl to hurry and clean. Her pleas were frantic now. As a senior girl, she would be responsible if the other girl didn't get back on the street. She'd be punished. I could practically feel Kiara's fear.

We needed to hurry. As if on cue, Calista tapped my shoulder.

I looked back over my shoulder while at the same time, Calista was coming up on her toes. Her mouth collided with my jaw. Instead of flinching, her lips brushed over my cheek.

It was not my proudest moment. Neither was it reasonable how my body reacted to her lips on me. But there it was, a flash of awareness. A spark that if stoked would blaze wild and out of control. A flicker that needed to be doused immediately, and it didn't help when Calista's whisper came out breathy.

"Fallon said two minutes."

Jesus. Fuck me.

"We're gonna have to be quick. You grab the smaller of the two."

I felt Calista stiffen, and I knew she wanted to give me shit but settled on lifting her right hand and presenting her middle finger.

Seriously. I liked this chick.

I covered that up with a scowl, jerked my head toward the door, and didn't bother counting down. Calista didn't need it. She'd follow me in, and when she did, she'd take care of business.

That was a mistake. I should've counted down and reminded myself what I was walking into. Not that a three-second pep talk would've done shit to prepare me for the sight before us.

The girl, I mean *girl*, was fucked up—torn lip, blood smeared from her chin up to her swollen eye. Hair matted with either blood or something else I wasn't going to allow myself to think about, or my earlier restraint would snap, and I'd burn this motherfucking building to ash.

Kiara gave a squeak of shock when she saw us. I scanned her face, looking for the mole that would positively identify her. The three inches of makeup caked on her face made it difficult, but there under the layers of foundation was the mark.

Calista was already pulling the injured girl to her side by the time I got in front of a trying-to-make-a-run-for-it Kiara.

She opened her mouth to scream, my hand went over her mouth, and I swung her up into my arms. Christ. She weighed nothing. A skinny bag of bones.

"Move."

But I didn't need to order Calista to get her ass downstairs. With her arm around the girl, she was dragging her to the door.

Kiara struggled in my arms.

This was the worst part—the struggle. It wouldn't matter what I said to her, she was too scared to hear, too traumatized to comprehend I was there to save her. That her nightmare was ending, and the struggle to heal was on the horizon.

I let Calista go in front of me, leaving a few steps between us in case Kiara kicked or punched so she wouldn't hit the other two women.

Calista was almost at the bottom when the girl came out of her stupor and fight-or-flight kicked in. She swung her fist in a wide arc, clocking Calista on the side of the face. Her head barely moved with the impact.

"It's okay. You're safe," Calista cooed.

The girl tried again, but this time Calista had cleared the stairs, caught the girl's wrist, twisted to face her, dipped, and hefted the girl onto her shoulder in a modified fireman's hold I was shocked as shit she could maneuver.

The tiny girl didn't give up and whaled on Calista's back as she made her way through the derelict store.

"You good?" I called out.

"Sure."

Her voice sounded tight and determined, not in pain, so I refrained from telling her to put the girl down and contain her until I could pass Kiara off to one of the guys, who were hopefully waiting for us outside the door.

"Almost there, Kiara," I murmured. "You're safe now."

As expected, she didn't acknowledge me.

My heart rate ticked up when I heard muffled yells and moving on the ground, until I remembered the three assholes we'd zip-tied.

Almost there.

The mangled door came into view. Next I saw Fallon outside the door, standing guard. He didn't wait for Calista to get to the door; he rushed inside, pulled the girl off Calista, and took off running.

"Go."

"You first," Calista returned, catching her breath.

"Go!"

Her head snapped up, she shot me a glare, then took off out the door.

Hot, humid fresh air slapped me in the face. Or at least it was fresher than the stale body-odor stench in the building. I'd take the dirty city air and be happy.

Pete came up beside me at a jog.

"Two blocks north. Al Satwa Road. Want me to take her?"

"I got her."

I glanced up the block and saw Fallon and Calista. Her much smaller legs trying to keep up, Fallon taking a slower pace than normal so he didn't lose her.

I wanted her by my side.

"Sorry, Kiara, I'd uncover your mouth, but I can't have you screaming."

Pete jumped off the sidewalk to get around a group of tourists staring into a closed shop. Thankfully, this street was mostly empty, or we'd be fucked. But what was more fucked was, none of the men looking into the store said a damn thing about me running with a woman in my arms. Didn't yell for help. Didn't so much as spare me a glance.

This world was fucked.

Al Satwa Road came into view. Less than fifty meters. A silver minivan came to a screeching stop at the corner right in front of Calista and Fallon.

"Pete—"

"That's our ride."

Fallon must've relayed the same information. Calista opened the sliding back door and waved Fallon inside. He shook his head and waved for her to enter. Her head turned. With laser precision, our eyes locked.

I wanted to yell and tell her to get her ass in the van but didn't want unnecessary attention. We were twenty yards away from hijacking two victims and getting them to safety. I'd yell at the stubborn woman later.

Finally, Calista crawled into the van. Fallon followed. A few seconds later, I did the same, falling into a seat with Kiara now fighting in earnest. Pete slammed the sliding door closed. As soon as he did, I craned my neck to see Calista in the back seat. At some point, her shayla had come loose and was hardly covering any blonde.

Whatever I was going to say to her died in my throat when her gaze lifted and tormented blue eyes found mine.

The van shot forward into traffic.

An elbow landed in my solar plexus.

I removed my hand from Kiara's mouth, and as soon as I did, she screamed—a loud, piercing shriek that could wake the dead.

Fuck. I really hated this part. Hated that it was me who was now causing this woman fear.

"Call her father," Calista said softly. "His voice will calm her."

"Pete—"

He didn't let me finish. "On it." But before he made the call to Shep to tell him we'd secured Kiara and get her father's number, he turned and took a picture of the defeated girl on Fallon's lap.

Kiara was going home to her family.

The other frightened girl needed to go somewhere. Pete would offer to put her on a plane with Kiara, or he'd make other arrangements. But last night was the last time they'd sleep in the putrid room knowing that the next morning, they'd be forced to live a nightmare.

Chapter Eleven

Thankfully, we were staying in a penthouse. Not only was the shower huge, it also provided unlimited hot water, or at least enough that the water hadn't begun to run cold after forty-five minutes. Bad for the environment, which was why I didn't push it, even though I could still feel the grime and misery on my skin.

Some of it should've dissolved when Kiara spoke to her father on the phone, and her fearful tears had turned into ones of relief, then gratitude. More should've leached away when Kiara told the girl—whose name was Mira—we had saved them, not taken them to give them to someone else. Her tears had, too, turned into ones of relief.

That was, until the hospital had come into view. Then both of them turned hysterical.

It was Kiara who'd explained that Sparkle had told them under Islamic law, prostitution was an offense punishable by lashings. He also told them they'd be taken to a prison camp and would never be released. The girls believed this with such certainty, it required another phone call to Kiara's father for him to explain no one was going to put them in prison or harm them.

A very kind older female doctor had looked over Kiara and Mira. She didn't try to separate them, or me from them, while she tended to Mira's face. She didn't do a thorough examination; it was a very brief look at both to make sure there was nothing that needed to be taken care of immediately. That also should've washed away some of the helplessness I felt.

It didn't.

Neither did walking with them out to the back of the hospital, where a Bell 429 helicopter was waiting to take them to Bahrain.

Seeing Kiara's wobbly, scared, brave smile did nothing but make me heartsick.

Seeing Mira's face clean only made her look younger than she had when it was caked in blood. Seeing that made me want to throw up. I didn't ask how old she was because I didn't want to know. My soul could take no more.

I needed a reprieve.

I only had a few days before I'd walk into a different kind of hell. There would be no trash or horrendous smell of decay.

This new hell would be glamour and lavish trappings.

I finished drying off. Grabbed the white satin robe I'd set on the counter and pulled it on. I didn't know who it belonged to, but I was helping myself, even if it only hit me mid-thigh and was a size too small.

I avoided my reflection in the mirror as I exited the bathroom. I didn't need to see the hollowness—I felt it. It settled in my bones.

Why do I do this to myself?

How much longer can I do this to myself?

I ignored the bed and continued to the balcony door. When I slid it open, there was nothing but a whisper. I'd stayed in some expensive places, and never had a door been so quiet.

When I got to wherever I was going, I wanted whisper doors. I wanted nothing but silence. No girls with haunted eyes. No more blood. No more tears.

I walked to the railing and looked down. Way up high, the world looked so far away. That was what I wanted—to be far away from the world, from evil.

"You doing okay?" Mason's rough voice gave me a start. "Sorry. Didn't mean to scare you."

I turned to face him and immediately wished I hadn't.

He was lounging on a chaise. Bare chested. Eyes glued to my legs.

I looked back at the fountains below and contemplated jumping. I could make my escape less dramatic and go back into my room.

"Sorry to disturb—"

"Adrenaline or overtired?" he asked.

Neither.

I was afraid of what I'd see in my dreams.

"Maybe both," I lied.

"There's another lounger," he offered.

I glanced back over at him and his bare chest with a dusting of hair over his pecs. A perfectly formed happy trail disappeared beneath the elastic band of his track pants.

Yeah, I really should jump and put myself out of my misery. Obviously I'd finally cracked. Something had to have broken inside of me. This kind of attraction was not right. No one wanted to jump on top of a man she wanted to punch in the face more than seventy-five percent of the time she was around him and beg him to do naughty things to her. Especially a woman who has never had anything close to naughty.

Unless getting to third base in high school was considered naughty. Then I'd been naughty.

But nothing after that.

"I should—"

"Come sit down, Calli."

Before I could talk my feet out of obeying Mason, they took me to the chaise next to his. Instead of sitting, I stared at the tan cushion.

"I don't bite, sweetness. You can sit."

"I seem to remember you telling me that when you tried to get me to sleep with you," I told him as I sat.

"Tried? I seem to remember waking up next to you."

I carefully tugged the edge of the robe down, painfully aware I hadn't put on panties.

As sad as it was, this was the most undressed I'd ever been around a man. I crossed my ankles, clenched my thighs, and stared at my toes.

Mason cleared his throat. "You did good tonight."

I didn't want to talk about tonight. Or what was going to happen in a few days. Or sex slaves. Or the state of the world.

"Where do you live?" I asked.

The silence that ensued had me glancing over at him.

He was doing that Mason thing again, where his eyes took in every detail, looking for the smallest element he could note and file away. Every microgesture. I was too tired to put in the effort of hiding who I was.

"Not tonight," I whispered. "Don't study me. Don't look for my tells. Don't analyze my every word and movement. Tonight, right now, I just need to be as normal as I *can* be. I want to forget the evil, vile, wicked things people do to each other and sit up here and pretend it doesn't exist. I want to be Calli. I want you to be Mase. I want to pretend we didn't zip-tie and gag three monsters earlier. Though, before I forget them, I hope rats have chewed off their balls and have moved on to eat their eyeballs. I just need to forget everything. Just for a few hours."

"Okay, Calli."

He was giving in. Relief flooded.

"I live in Imperial Beach, in a condo a few blocks from the beach."

"Is it peaceful?"

"Yeah, baby."

"I'm glad you have that."

Even though Mason was mostly a dick to me, he was still a good man who did good work. He deserved peace.

"Where do you live?"

"Nowhere."

"Nowhere?" I didn't miss the disbelief in his tone.

He'd told me more than once he didn't trust me, and he obviously thought I was evading, not telling the truth.

"Nowhere," I confirmed. "I have some stuff at my mom's house, old keepsakes from high school that people keep until they've moved them enough times, they wonder why they have them and throw them away. When I have downtime, which isn't often, I do a short-term rental or stay in a hotel. I do have a storage unit in Phoenix and one in Charleston. Not furniture or anything personal. Clothes, shoes, cash, IDs, things like that."

"You didn't mention staying with your mom during your downtime," he pointed out.

I hesitated, but not for the reasons I normally would. There was nothing about my mother that was normal. But if I took a pass on his question, he might get up and leave me out here alone. And for once in my life, I didn't want to be alone. Feel alone.

"I avoid spending time with her as much as possible."

There.

Answered.

"Why?"

Shit. Goddamn.

"She's a drunk. I can deal with her when she's tipsy. I can mostly deal with her when she's drunk. I cannot handle her when she's three sheets to the wind, crying and carrying on about Lili and how I should've stopped my sister from going out with her boyfriend."

I slid my gaze back to the high-rises, not wanting to witness his judgment. I knew it was coming; he'd said it would. Though in fairness, he was clear he didn't shove his opinions onto other people.

Did he think I was an asshole for abandoning my mother? Did I? Some days, I could reconcile not visiting her by convincing myself I'd set boundaries. Other days, it was harder to sate the nagging in the back of my mind I'd left her alone in her grief.

The days when the guilt held me hostage, that was when I *judged* her, convicted her of not handling her pain the way I thought she should by punishing her with my absence.

Shame was a fickle bitch. Regret a prison. When they came together, they were an agonizing tornado of irrational emotions. I was caught in a never-ending cycle of self-loathing and guilt.

And I was a hypocrite.

I'd judged Mason from the time he'd stepped foot in my hotel room. I judged my mother and thought she was weak. Mason was right—and that pissed me off. I judged people every day.

The rumble radiating from Mason pulled my attention back to him. "She blames you?"

"Of course. I was with her at the mall with her and her boyfriend. He wanted to leave. I wanted to stay and meet up with some friends, so they left me there."

I could almost feel my sister's last hug in front of the Claire's Boutique. I could smell the flowery lotion on her skin from Bath & Body Works. I could see her cute red tank top and matching flip-flops.

I didn't watch her walk away. I'd turned and hustled to the food court where I knew my friends were.

If I had known that would be the last time I saw her, I would've watched. I would've hugged her tighter. I would have told her I loved her. But I didn't.

"Why don't you like the movie *Forrest Gump*?"

Mason's jaw clenched, his shoulders stiffened, his abs contracted. I'd never seen a man turn to stone before my very eyes. It would've been fascinating if he didn't look like he was about to come out of his skin.

"Never—"

"Jenny reminds me of someone I knew. Selfish to the core."

I wanted to know more, but just that tidbit of information looked like it cost him to say out loud. I knew better than most some things were better left unsaid, left in the dark, left alone.

Maybe *I* was that something—better left alone with my scars.

"You were a journalist." I wasn't sure where Mason was going with this, but it was outside of the normal I wanted tonight. "Do you miss it?"

I turned back to the city lights. In any other city in the world, I would've thought the cityscape was beautiful. I would've marveled at the engineering. I would've wanted to take the glass elevator up to the top floor of the world's tallest building. But the view was spoiled knowing who'd built those buildings and the conditions they'd worked under. The pain and corruption.

"I've always loved writing," I admitted. "My mom used to read my short stories."

The constant ache of sorrow throbbed in my heart. Good memories that were bittersweet. Memories I never allowed myself. They only served to make all the ones after Lili disappeared worse. My parents had been loving. We'd been happy. As far as I knew, we were just an average, normal family. My father had kept his secrets hidden. Maybe I should've been angry at him, but I wasn't. I was grateful. He'd shielded us. He'd given us normal. He'd lived with the burden and never let it touch me or my sister.

"Yeah?" he prompted.

"I think I was around eight when it started. 'The Boy Who Stole the Bike.'" I couldn't stop my smile. "It was a mystery. A bad one, as the title gave away who stole the bike. But my mom pretended like it was the best story she'd ever read. When she was done with the five handwritten pages of junk, she asked me to write her another one. Once a week, I'd give her a badly written story, and once a week, she'd act like I cured cancer.

"They got longer and longer, I learned how to develop characters. And that's when I truly fell in love with storytelling. For a few hours every night, I could be someone else. I could feel what they felt. I could solve problems that weren't mine. I wanted to write mysteries or maybe fantasy. Create worlds where dragons existed, fanciful beasts with claws and rows of teeth. Heroes who were larger than life, heroines who were strong—who slayed those dragons. But I knew being a novelist was a long shot, and I needed to pay my bills, so I went into journalism. I still got to write, just not fiction."

Now I lived in that world, where monsters were real and there were no immortal heroes to swoop in and eradicate the villains. I couldn't bend reality and go back in time and save the girl. I could write every day from now until my last breath on earth, and the story wouldn't be complete.

Lili's story had run out of pages. It had abruptly ended in the middle. There hadn't been a hero to save her. Just *The End*.

"Not romance?" he teased.

I shrugged away Mason's question. I'd shared enough. "I guess even back then I didn't believe in happily ever afters," I lied.

I *had* believed.

"I think you're lying."

His accusation held no heat, merely calling me out on my bullshit.

If nothing else, Mason was honest.

"Wouldn't be the first time. Won't be the last."

As long as we were on the topic of romance . . .

"Have you ever been married?"

"No."

"Still looking for the future Mrs. Mason Hughes?"

"Fuck. No."

Well, that was firm.

"What about you? Still looking for the future Mr. Calista Ventura?"

"Fuck. No."

I heard him chuckle but didn't take my eyes off the view. I didn't want to see him smile. I didn't want to see how that handsome face transformed when he laughed. I'd had enough for one day.

"Do you ever get tired of your own thoughts?" I asked.

"Come again?"

I could feel his eyes on me. I could also hear the click of Mase turning back into Mason the watcher.

"You're getting ready to analyze me. I can feel your scrutiny. We're in a judgment-free bubble, remember?"

"Did you hear that on social media? The 'we listen, and we don't judge.' Hate to tell you, but the faces gave it away—every nose scrunch, every wide-eyed response, every jerk of the shoulders—they judged. We used to associate judgment with discernment and intelligence. Somewhere along the way, we've changed the meaning. It's no longer thought of as common sense and the ability to read a situation and make judgment calls on the outcome.

"If I were to judge you on a good deed you did, and draw the conclusion I thought you were a kind, thoughtful person, that would be okay. If I saw you kick a puppy and thought you were an asshole who deserved to be punched in the head, some people would think that was okay. But if I saw someone behaving in a way I found personally abhorrent, that would be wrong. That would make *me* the bad guy for passing judgment. That would make me the dick, even if all I did was distance myself.

"What it is, and what I am, is honest. I could not give the first fuck if someone thinks I'm an asshole. I don't give any consideration to what people think of the job I do, how I do it, or their judgment on the matter. We—you and I—do important work. We save lives, and I don't give a fuck who judges how I go about doing it. If they don't like it, they can get their asses off the couch and do it themselves. They can breathe the misery. They can listen to the pleas for help. They can put themselves in harm's way for a stranger in need.

"Straight up, Calli, I've already judged you, and you shouldn't give a shit about my opinion of you. You should know who you are and what you believe in and that you are good down to your soul. And fuck whoever thinks otherwise.

"So with all of that, explain your question so I can give you my honesty."

I wasn't sure I wanted his honesty.

I wasn't even sure I could articulate my thoughts.

"Never mind."

"You're pissed because I laid it out," he guessed wrongly.

"No. I just don't know how to explain it. I'm tired. I'm worn out. I don't know if I can continue doing this—any of it. I don't know if I have anything left. I'm broken. But in my head, I keep going back and forth. There are more Kiaras and Miras out there who need help. If I stop, what happens to them? I'm exhausted, and I'm exhausting myself with all the thoughts that run through my head that I can't turn off." I closed my eyes and sighed. "I'm tired of thinking."

"The easy answer is—stop. Recognize the lives you've saved. Remember the two girls who are now on their way home. The honest answer is—there will always be more. Whether you're in the fight or not, there will always be another Kiara and Mira. You can do this until there is nothing left inside of you, and that will not change. You cannot break yourself on a quest that will never end."

"You're right," I whispered. "But I don't know how to stop."

I thought of the man who'd taken my sister.

One more.

I kept telling myself, just one more and I'd be done. I could go and find my peace. What were a few more marks when I was already slashed to hell? I bore no physical scars, but my insides were shredded. I was already ruined, so why stop now? There were more people I could help.

I was worthless. They were worth saving.

God, my life was exhausting.

I was floating.

Weightless.

Had I jumped?

I jerked awake and found myself in a pair of strong arms.

Mason's strong arms.

My cheek was resting on warm flesh with a view of pecs with a dusting of hair. I wanted to touch it, so I did. My palm went to his chest, and sleepily I brushed over the swell, noting the texture—coarse over smooth. It was interesting, not how I thought it would feel. My fingers grazed his nipple. It tightened immediately, as did his entire frame.

Oh. My. God.

"Calli." I felt the vibration.

My resulting shiver was unconscious and one I didn't fully understand, but I wanted to feel that rumble again. I wanted my body to tremble. I wanted to feel something other than nothing.

My thumb brushed over his pebbled nipple again. This time I felt *his* tremor as it worked its way under my hand.

"Sweetness, wake up."

He thought I was asleep.

I had amnesty. I could explore and there'd be no repercussions.

So I took full advantage and slowly touched everywhere I could. Down to his abdominal muscles. They jumped and flexed under my fingers. Unable to go lower with him holding me, I ventured up. Back over his pec, his nipple, the apex of the throat, over to his collarbone, his shoulder, in and around to the back of his neck. All the while committing the feel to memory. If this was my chance to feel a man's body—no, Mason's body—I wasn't going to forget a single moment.

Before I could finish my examination, I was moving again. This time I was falling. My fingers curled tight until my shoulder and hip touched the soft mattress.

Not falling. Mason was putting me to bed. Before he could see I was awake, I closed my eyes as he untangled himself from me. A soft, cool sheet was pulled over my legs. Mason wasn't putting me to bed, he was tucking me in.

I ignored the sweetness of that and kept my breathing even. The sheet dropped on my shoulder, my hair was brushed away from my face, and warm lips pressed on my temple.

"Faker," he whispered.

Damn it all to hell.

I felt him move away. I didn't hear the door close behind him, but I wouldn't. Still, I knew he was gone.

Only then did I allow myself to smile at a very good memory I would replay so often, I'd keep it alive. I'd never forget the warmth, my shiver, his tremor. It was the closest I'd ever felt to someone, and I'd need that closeness to keep me company.

Chapter Twelve

Unsurprisingly, Pete was already awake, dressed, and caffeinated by the time I made it to the kitchen.

"Coffee's made."

He sounded too happy.

I grunted.

"Hurry up and get some of that in you so you can shake off your grouch-ass mood. We've got work to do."

Coffee wasn't going to touch my mood.

Not this morning.

Not after feeling Calista's hands on me—her soft, tentative touch. It was fucked, but once I realized she was awake, I wanted to tip her head back so I could see her eyes when she touched me. I felt her shiver, but I wanted to see the accompanying look.

Did the blue of her eyes deepen with lust? Did her face go soft with desire? I wanted to know almost as badly as I wanted to know if her nipples had pebbled under that flimsy satin robe. I hadn't trusted myself to look; that would only lead to me needing to find out if she was as wet as my dick was stiff.

Her pretending to be asleep had been torture. I'd stupidly given myself permission to allow her hand to move on me freely. It was nothing more than lightly skimming my chest. I could categorize the whole episode as juvenile. But it hadn't felt innocent, and not just because I hadn't been with a woman in a long-ass time. Though I could use that as an excuse as to why I got myself off in the shower, remembering how her thumb had felt teasing my nipple.

Christ.

I had to stop this shit. What was next, I'd beg my way to second base and get some side-boob action? I was a grown fucking man jerking off to the hesitant touch of a woman. I had far better memories of past experiences.

Fuck.

I shoved the carafe back into the machine harder than necessary.

"What'd I miss?" Fallon asked as he came into the room shirtless and with his hair still wet.

"Put on some fucking clothes," I growled.

"Someone needs to crawl back into bed and roll out on the right side."

"If you think that someone is me, you can shove your opinion up your ass right after you put on a shirt."

Fallon's eyes moved to the stairs. When they came back to me, he smirked. "I warned you one day this whole 'I don't fuck empty pussy' would make you snap."

My already clenched jaw tightened.

It pissed me off he was right. I *had* snapped.

Though it didn't have anything to do with lack of sex and everything to do with a woman who had driven me to the brink of insanity. The vulnerability she'd shown me last night was now at the top of the list that made me insanely attracted to her. Her bravery was just under that. Her desire to right wrongs was closely under *that*. Her smart-ass mouth and the way she wasn't afraid to give as good as she got were also on the list.

Which meant her pretty face, great tits, and long legs weren't even in the top three things that made Calista irresistible.

So, no, it wasn't sex or the lack thereof or the intensifying need to have her that made me finally snap.

But fuck if I didn't want her hands on me again, this time while my hands were on *her*.

I ignored Fallon's comment and his bare chest, opting to pull shit for French toast from the fridge rather than giving him more ammunition to piss me off. Besides, I had no say. Calista wasn't mine.

I set the carton of eggs and bread next to my untouched coffee, spied my stash of chocolate on the counter, and detoured. The bowl could wait, but the kataifi, pistachio, and milk chocolate couldn't.

"We gotta go over Calista's op," Pete unnecessarily informed me. "Us being here as muscle is a good cover both for her and for us."

This had already been discussed, so I didn't know why Pete was bringing it back up.

"Right," I prompted around a mouthful of God's best creation.

"Also, Shep got Jack, Catarina, Gavin, and Aiden on a flight. They're on their way. Ryan's staying back," Pete announced.

A twinge of guilt soured the chocolate as I swallowed both down. Instead of being out on the balcony with Calista last night, I should've been helping Pete arrange travel for our team, or at the very least stayed downstairs while he briefed Shep and the guys.

"When will they be here?" I asked.

"A little after twenty-three hundred."

The penthouse had five bedrooms with only one currently available, which meant we'd have to double up. Jack and Cat would obviously share one; that left Aiden and Gavin to bunk with me and Fallon. Pete would sleep on the floor in the kitchen before he'd share a room with someone.

Without permission, my mind wandered to Calista and her bed and what it would be like to sleep next to her again.

Maybe a little forced proximity is what we needed.

Christ, where the hell had that come from?

Needing something to do to purge my mind of all things Calista, I tossed half the chocolate bar on the counter and went in search of a bowl to start breakfast.

"Why do rich people insist on buying shit that feels like it's gonna break?" I asked as I pulled a bowl from the cupboard.

"It's called china, you uncultured idiot," Fallon piped up.

As gently as I could, I set the bowl on the marble countertop. And Christ, what was it with all the damn marble? "I know what it's called, but does it have to be so thin?"

"I believe it's also called delicate, not breakable shit," Fallon helpfully corrected from his place across the kitchen.

"I hope you spill coffee down your front and burn your chest and your—"

"I swear on all things holy," Pete interrupted our bickering. "It's like the two of you are twelve."

"If we promise to be good, can we have dessert, Daddy?" Fallon quipped.

"I can come back later," Calista said from somewhere behind me.

I craned my neck to see her staring at Fallon, wide eyed.

Shirtless asshole.

"You might wanna close your mouth, sweetness," I suggested.

Angry blue eyes sliced my way. "My mouth wasn't open," Calli snapped.

"Can you not piss the woman off and make breakfast?" Fallon asked. "Or piss her off, but do it out of the kitchen so *I* can make breakfast. I'm starving."

"If I have a say," Pete started. "Stop pissing off the woman and cook. Your French toast is better than Fallon's eggs."

Throughout this, Calista's gaze swung to each man as he spoke until coming back to me with a brow winged up in question. "You cook?"

"Believe it or not, sweetness, I am self-sufficient."

"In more ways than one," Fallon muttered.

I quashed my smile at the last second. "Go bother someone else."

"C'mon, that was too easy."

Calista glanced around, waiting for someone to fill her in. "What was easy?"

"Nothing, darlin'. How'd you sleep?" Fallon smartly changed the subject.

"Fine."

The word snapped out of her mouth a little too quickly. I would understand why a few seconds later as she turned to busy herself with the coffee maker, but not before I saw the pink hit her cheeks.

Faker.

Suddenly, I was in a better mood. She knew that *I* knew she was feeling me up while feigning sleep, and that blush was proof I'd been right. Not that I needed it, but it still felt damn good getting it.

And the pink.

I'd take that too.

"While Mase makes us breakfast, let's go over your op," Pete suggested. "Tom sent us over some intel on Amir Bakir and his operation, but I'd like to hear your take. But first, you should know our team's en route. They'll be here late tonight."

I turned just in time to see Calista's flash of relief before she covered it with a frown.

"Of course he did," she sneered, even though she already knew Tom had sent us the information on her operation.

"Amir offers his facilities for a cut of the sales, but he doesn't provide the women. Part of the service he provides also includes vetting, though his idea of screening the clients is verifying they have the money to purchase. Am I understanding that correctly?"

With her mug of coffee in hand, she leaned against the counter next to where I was working and nodded. "Yes. He only provides the location. From what I've gathered for this auction, Ahmad Sindi will be the largest supplier. There's also a Russian, Sergei Volkov, who is rumored to be bringing women to sell. However, Atlanta hasn't been able to confirm."

Ahmad Sindi.

I dropped the fork I was using to beat the eggs and gave Calista my full pissed-off attention. "The same Ahmad who flew to Mexico with his men to pick you up?"

"One 'n the same."

Her nonchalance only served to piss me off further.

"So your cover's blown before the operation even begins," I noted.

"Ahmad didn't see me. I wasn't using my real name in Mexico, I won't be using it here, and no pictures of me were taken. All Ahmad knew was there was a blonde-haired, blue-eyed woman of Irish descent for sale."

She was hiding something. There was no way Ahmad would personally fly to Mexico to pick up a random woman.

"It's like she thinks we were born yesterday on a turnip truck with 'stupid' tattooed on our foreheads," I mumbled.

"Actually, I wasn't thinking that, but now that you mention it—"

"You're sure your cover will hold?" Pete cut in before she could finish her insult.

"Yes."

Without further pushing, Pete went on, "Opening bid for this auction will start at two hundred thousand."

Fallon whistled. "Do you have an idea what the bids will close at?"

"I had to authenticate I had a million in currency and another five hundred thousand in assets I could liquidate if needed."

"Tom's report said Amir hosts these auctions once a year," Pete went on.

Okay, so, no one else was going to back me up and call Calista out on her bullshit.

"Yes. That's why it's important I get an invitation."

"What do you know about the Russian? Tom's report didn't mention him."

Calista's gaze stayed studiously locked on Pete when she answered, "Next to nothing. He's notoriously cautious. Think Putin on steroids. From the limited information Atlanta could find, his security team is generational. The post is passed down from father to son. There are some rumors that say Sergei has a hand in picking who his guards will marry and reproduce with, ensuring the next generation to serve him is strong and loyal. Tom has been tight lipped about Sergei, so either he doesn't know anything more than what Atlanta's found or he doesn't want *me* to know."

I thought back to our earlier conversation, the one that sparked Pete to call in the rest of the team, then I thought about Calista's relief when she learned they were on their way. It wasn't surprising she didn't trust Tom, but was there more she wasn't telling us?

Of course there was. The woman was like a vault. Finding the right combination to get her to open up changed from conversation to conversation.

"You said you were worried about Tom not taking care of the women," I reminded her. "Do you think he could be protecting Sergei?"

Her eyes slowly journeyed back to me. When they landed, she looked less than pleased I'd gone down the Sergei line of questioning. Which was a clear indication I'd hit a nerve.

Now the question was, would she outright lie?

"I told you, I don't know what Tom's planning. I do know something feels off. And if Tom thinks he can bait a bigger fish, he will. That means he'll scrap the mission, call off his team, and follow a new lead. I don't disagree Sergei needs to be taken out of the game. I do disagree that should be done at the expense of the women."

"If Tom calls off the mission, our team will be in place," Pete reminded her.

Calista lifted her mug to her lips and drank. What she didn't do was acknowledge Pete.

I don't know if I have anything left. I'm broken.

Her words from last night hit me square in the chest.

Next came a one-two punch in the gut.

If I stop, what happens to them?

I'm exhausted.

I had yet to recover when she said, "Within the next forty-eight hours, I'll get a call with a time and location to meet Amir. This is his idea of an interview. What it'll really be is him showing off his wealth. Which we know means power. The last two times I followed him—"

"You followed him?"

She continued like I hadn't spoken. "He took Maxwell Lancaster to an exclusive invitation-only club at the Rixos on Saadiyat Island."

"Doesn't the crown prince own a private residence at the hotel?" Fallon inquired.

"Correct. A show of wealth, power, and connection. Amir took Samuel Allard to the Michelin-starred Al Muntaha inside the Burj. I didn't make it all the way up to the twenty-seventh floor, and I've never eaten there, but I know you're not leaving there without spending three thousand dirham before wine and champagne. Then they spent the rest of the evening at the Skyview Bar. Another show of wealth, but Samuel isn't of the same buying power as Maxwell, so he's got in-your-face money but not show-off money."

"Alcohol is illegal unless, of course, you can afford to drink it," Fallon mumbled.

"Calli!" I barked. "You followed him?"

"Geez, hotshot, what do you think I've been doing here? Sitting on my thumbs playing cellphone games in my room all day? I also followed Ahmad and Amir."

"Just pointing out it'd be hard to play on your cellphone if your thumbs were up your ass."

I growled at Fallon's stupidity.

Calista shook her head and commented, "Don't be a smart-ass. You knew what I meant."

"Actually, I didn't. I've never had a thumb up my—"

"My foot's gonna be up your ass if you don't butt out," I grunted.

Fallon lifted his hands in surrender.

Calli looked like she wanted to kick me in the nuts. The threat of physical violence looming in her blue orbs shouldn't have been so appealing, but it couldn't be denied the woman was gorgeous when she was riled.

"Yes, Mason, I've been following Amir," she said dryly.

Suddenly, my teammate Jack Donovan's face flashed in my mind. A memory of us in a warehouse in Honduras, him looking both frustrated and constipated.

Good God, was I turning into Jack?

The guy had bitched and complained about how Catarina had no sense of self-preservation. If memory served, he was so pissed, he'd told her he was going to redden her ass for being in Honduras unprotected. At the time, I'd laughed.

I owed him an apology for finding his misery a source of entertainment.

Now I was wondering if this was some sort of karma.

"Are we in another Mase-Calista staring contest or are we gonna eat in the next century?" Fallon asked.

She was not mine, I reminded myself.

Her choices were hers.

It was not my place to say a damn thing.

I shook my head and went back to cooking.

"So you're waiting for your call?" Pete prompted.

"Yeah. Amir will take me out like he did the others. After our meeting, he'll either give me an official invite to the auction or deny my entry."

"What's the backup plan if you don't get an invite?" Fallon inquired.

"That would be a question for Tom. I told you, my only part in this is to get the invite, get the location of the auction, and report to Tom. He'll have a Ground Branch team move, or one of his other shooters move into place to take out his target."

Yeah, I really needed the full story on how she'd become one of Tom's 'shooters.'

But that was a question for later.

Before I could ask about Tom's plan for the women, Pete did. "Who's supposed to be handling the women?"

"He told me he has an NGO coming in for the girls. Former Special Forces. The organization's called Lighthouse."

"Mason will be your shadow when you meet with Amir," Pete informed Calista.

"He might not let me—"

"That's a deal-breaker," I interrupted her. "Your personal protection doesn't leave your side. If you show weakness, he'll pounce and won't take you seriously. If you demand his respect on this issue, he'll give it."

"That was almost as condescending as last night's 'stay sharps,'" she noted.

I wanted to remind her what *wasn't* condescending about last night, but I'd never break her trust, so I settled on finishing the French toast.

"Fallon will stay close as well, and I'll play driver," Pete finished, as if our exchange didn't happen.

"Once you have the location for Tom, your part's done," Fallon circled back. "Where does that leave you?"

"Leave me?"

"Where are you going next?"

Fuck.

I hadn't thought of that. In a few days, this would be over, and Calista would be gone.

Gone from my life.

"I don't know. Until Tom clears my name, it won't be the US."

Fuck. Would she quit? Would she go someplace quiet and find her peace? Would she leave and go write the mysteries she never got to? Would she leave all of this behind—leave *me* behind?

My chest felt like it was going to cave in. A pressure so heavy it felt like my heart was struggling to beat.

Fuck.

How the hell had this woman gotten under my skin . . . and how did I work her out?

Chapter Thirteen

"Are you still mad at me?" Atlanta asked in my ear.

I turned off the faucet. My shower would have to wait. I made my friend wait until I sat on the ridiculous tufted bench that looked and felt like silk—but I hoped it wasn't, since I still had on my sweaty workout gear—in the ridiculously lavish bathroom.

"Yes."

"On a scale of one to ten, how mad?" she pushed.

A few days ago, I was at a ten. Now that I'd spent time with Mason and my worst fears had come to fruition, I was at a six hundred and ninety-one. Though in the rare times he was sweet, that number ratcheted up significantly. When he was being his normal jerk, it lowered. So I figured it was best to average it out.

I didn't share this with Atlanta.

"Is there a reason for your call?"

"You mean other than to ascertain where my friend's head's at and if she'll ever forgive me for having her back and doing the right thing, even if it meant going behind her back because she was being stubborn?"

I clenched my jaw. Another indication I needed to quit. I was losing patience, and with that my ability to suppress my emotions. I couldn't hide my anger from Mason. I couldn't hide my irritation. I couldn't hide my reaction to him in whatever form that came. It was dangerous and reckless and very careless.

"Yes, other than that." I was proud my tone came out bored.

"I'll tell you if you promise you'll only be at a level three and you'll work on forgiving me."

"I make no such promise."

I heard her laugh, and I wondered where she was. What she was doing with her life other than gathering information for the CIA—unofficially, of course. Like me, she was a ghost. We received orders, we executed those orders, we collected our pay, and we waited for the next order.

Did she have a man in her life, did she have actual real-life friends, did she go to the grocery store like a normal person, did she own a house or car? I knew next to nothing about Atlanta, because that's how people who did the work we did stayed safe. We didn't form connections. We didn't divulge secrets that could be used against us.

"Jason Anderson landed in Dubai thirty minutes ago."

My heart rate ticked up.

This was it.

He was here.

"Tell me," I prompted, uncaring I sounded like an eager five-year-old on Christmas morning.

"He has a reservation at the Bvlgari. Two suites. Arlo, Bodhi, and Archie are with him."

His three favorite guards.

Arlo Brown and Bodhi Lee were both ex-Australian Special Air Service Regiment. Archie Evans was ex-British Special Boat Service. All of them were deadly in their own right. Together, they were formidable in a way that meant no one in their right mind would go near Jason.

Luckily for me, I was not in my right mind.

I hadn't been since he'd driven away with my sister and handed her over to his father.

Was I supposed to be delivered too? Were Lili and I supposed to be a package deal? A two-for-one special to impress Big Boss Anderson?

"Predictable. What else?"

"Sources in Berlin say there's murmurings of a takeover. This being hostile from inside."

"He's got a traitor?"

I leaned forward, rested my elbow on my knee, and stared at the marble. On the surface, a traitor could be exactly what I needed. It'd be risky as hell, but if I could make contact, I could offer my services. I'd take care of their problem in exchange for access to Jason. However, that would do nothing to save the girls in his brothels.

"I hear your excitement, but no word on who the traitor is or confirmation. Sit tight on that and stick with the plan."

The plan. Right.

"You do realize with the shit you pulled, the plan's got a few kinks now. There is no way Mason, Fallon, or Pete will let me out of their sight. Mason will be glued to my side anytime I step foot out of this penthouse. And they've called in the rest of their team."

Hell, he'd checked on me three times while I was working out in the apartment's gym, even though if the front door was opened they'd all get alerts on their phones. I was good at sneaking around, but I wasn't Spider-Man and couldn't rappel down forty-two stories. Or I could, but not without my gear. I wasn't Tom Cruise and this wasn't *Mission: Impossible*.

"I already thought of that. New plan is, you read them in and they can help you—"

"Absolutely not. This is mine. *Mine*, Atlanta, and if you breathe a word to any of them about it, you'll find my red dot on your forehead—and that's a promise."

"You'd have to find me first, Calli. And just because they help doesn't make it any less yours. You can still pull the trigger, but you'd be safe doing it. There's no reason for you to go down with him."

Yes, there was. If it meant Jason was dead, I'd gladly go down with him.

"We've always known that was a possibility," I reminded her.

"Your endgame doesn't have to be the end of *you*," she argued.

Life was not a promise of longevity and happiness. There were no guaranteed days on this earth. There were no guarantees in life, period. I'd learned that when my sister lost her life. I'd learned it again when I lost my mother to grief. I'd learned that when I started working with Tom.

"Keep me updated on Jason's movements, and if you would, contact Tanner and confirm he has my kit ready. Also, in the Meena Bazaar, on the corner of Seventy-Fourth and Al Fahidi, there's a building called the Atheryat. It's run by Deepak Bashu, street name Sparkle. Work your magic, and get someone there to clean house and make it messy."

I heard Atlanta clacking away on her keyboard. "Does this have anything to do with the girl Drexel wanted?"

I had no idea how she knew what Shepherd wanted. And I didn't ask, first because she wouldn't outright tell me, which led to my second reason: I didn't want another lesson on how the underground web of information worked. Atlanta could get long winded when she blathered about dark-web chat rooms and encrypted this or that, and once she got started, it took forever for her to burn out.

Likely that was her intention—bore me to death so I stopped asking questions.

"Yes. We delivered two girls yesterday, but the others need to be taken care of."

"Consider it done."

"Thanks."

"Anytime, Calli, yeah?"

She sounded like she meant that. No, I knew she meant it. Putting aside the bullshit with the text messages, she'd always had my back, always came through in a pinch, and always offered her honesty. She didn't sugarcoat the truth.

"Before I let you go, can I ask you something?"

Shit. What was I doing?

"Of course."

I couldn't do it. I was too chickenshit to open up and ask what I needed to ask.

"Actually, I need to get back to my shower. I just got done with the gym when you called. We'll talk when I have more time," I lied.

Not about the shower. I needed one of those. But I'd never talk through my personal dilemma with her. I didn't know how, and I didn't want to learn. Transparency wasn't something I'd ever be ready for.

"No, we won't," she returned. "You'll hang up, add another layer on your already thick walls, and pretend you didn't ask to talk. And since you asked to talk instead of just talking, I know it's personal in nature. So I'll take a stab at it. Yes, you should have wild sex with the hot Mason Hughes. I have seen pictures of the man, and if you don't climb him like a tree and do nasty things to him, you are plum nutty.

"Also, yes, you should back away from fieldwork. We all, and I mean every single one of us who sees and does the things we do, need to know when it's time to quit. And that time for you is nigh. There comes a time when you can't come back from it. Before that happens, you need to step aside and allow someone else to take your place.

"Again, another yes, you need to tell Tom to take a hike and stop being his personal trigger puller. You're good, you're clean, you leave no mess. So far every hit has been righteous, but trust me on this, Calli, there will be a time he sends you out, and it will not align with your morals. He'll ask you to take out someone who's not a monster, but a pawn—and that, my girl, will mark you in a way that will keep you up at night.

"One more yes—you should stay pissed at me, because I betrayed the trust you gave me, and I know you don't give that freely. But I can live with anger. What I *can't* live with is you dead because your trust was more important than your life. I know you don't believe this, I get why, in our world, we are islands . . . but you're my friend. I respect you, I admire you, and you are the only friend I have, so selfishly, I'd like you to stay breathing."

That was a lot of yeses to a whole lot of questions I hadn't asked.

But somehow she'd nailed all but one question.

Not that I was going to ask about Mason, because there *was* no Mason. There could *be* no Mason. No matter how badly I wanted to climb him like a tree, I didn't know how to do nasty things to a man.

Though I had no doubt he'd know how to do all the nasty things and make them out-of-this-world pleasurable while he did them. He already drove me to distraction. I didn't need to offer up my virginity and add to the insanity. Not that he'd want to take a virgin to his bed when he could have experienced women to give him whatever it was he needed.

Gah. The thought of Mason and another woman made my stomach clench. Another reason to get this job done and get the hell gone.

"Is that why you stopped doing fieldwork? Did Tom give you an assignment that opposed your code?"

"Yes. So I found a way I could continue to help, but in a controlled way that didn't put me at odds with who I wanted to be."

Fucking Tom.

"You could too," she continued. "You don't have to be on the front lines. You could go back to being a journalist. I've read your articles and op-eds. You're a talented writer. In the field, you quietly take out a bad guy, and he's replaced within a day. But your words reach thousands. What if you inspire the next generation of warriors? And here's another what-if—what if you hang up your cape and give it all up? You're allowed to be happy, Calli. You're allowed to stop. You're allowed to put yourself first, and it doesn't erase the good you've done."

Give it all up. "It's annoying when you make sense," I complained. "But what's more annoying is I need to jump off the merry-go-round, and I don't know how. I keep going round and round with all these thoughts. It's tiring, and I don't know how to make them stop."

"Just jump off, Calli. It's that easy."

Just jump off.

Easier said than done.

"I'll figure it out after I'm done with Jason."

"What if you—"

"No, Atlanta. You were right with most of what you said. Dead-on right. But not with this. Jason Anderson is mine. He's the key to my freedom."

My peace.

"With most of what I said." I could hear her smile over the phone. "Does that mean you've already climbed Mount Mason?"

"Goodbye, Atlanta. Thank you for your help."

"Wait. Was it good? Did he—"

I pulled my phone away from my ear and disconnected. I didn't need any help provoking images of Mason or what he could do, which meant I didn't need my . . . friend asking questions I didn't have the answers to, though I could guess.

He'd be good.

No, he'd be outstanding.

But Mason wasn't for me.

And it sucked, because I wanted him to be.

Even if it was just once, I wanted to feel everything Mason had to offer.

Chapter Fourteen

I should've been in my room playing it smart. But instead I was out on the balcony, hoping Calista would show.

Hoping for more of Calli and Mase.

The last time I saw her, she'd been in the kitchen making herself a sandwich. Without looking at me, she'd told Pete she'd be in her room going over old intel on Amir Bakir and Ahmad Sindi and she'd pass on dinner.

I didn't believe her, but I kept my mouth shut and didn't call her out on it.

I'd waited until Fallon and Pete had left to go pick up the SUV Shep had secured for us to use. They'd do a sweep for trackers and take a drive around the city watching for a tail before they came back.

Calli and I would be alone for hours. Stupidly, I wanted that time with her on our balcony where, as she put it, we could be normal. No work. No evil bad guys to take out. No lies.

I didn't admit it to her last night, but I needed normal. I wasn't burned out or tired of my job like she was, but that didn't mean I didn't take full advantage of my downtime. The normalcy of working behind the bar of the Dirty Plank, drinking coffee off the back deck of my condo, going to the beach at night and using the rhythm of the waves to clear my head.

As much as I needed normal, Calli craved it, and I wanted to be the one who gave it to her. So there I was playing a dangerous game, waiting for her to show, hoping she was wearing last night's robe while at the same time hoping she'd found a snowsuit in the closet.

Her sitting in a lounger next to me with those long legs on display was an exercise in control.

Last night, I'd bested the temptation.

Tonight I'd have to dig deep—that was, if she came out and joined me.

Not interested in the view, I had my eyes closed when I heard the whoosh of the slider. With a smile, I opened my eyes but quickly hid my relief she'd come outside.

Her gaze and her feet immediately went to the chaise next to mine. My gaze ate up the view of her bare legs. It was time to dig and find my legendary control.

I gave her a few minutes to settle in before I asked, "Calli and Mase?"

"Yeah," she said softly.

I lobbed an easy question her way. "Favorite song?"

"I don't have a favorite, but I have a favorite album. Fleetwood Mac. *Rumours.*"

"No shit?"

"Something else we have in common?"

"Can't say it's my favorite, but it's in my top five."

I waited for her to ask her question, keeping my gaze on the skyscrapers that were now dwarfed in comparison to the Burj Khalifa.

But she didn't ask a question; she elaborated.

"Stevie Nicks is one of the best storytellers ever to live. Her breakup songs are golden, made better because Lindsey Buckingham had to sing harmony on the very fuck-you songs Stevie wrote. I want to be her when I grow up. Not that I want my man to cheat on me, but damn, she's brilliant. If I could only listen to one song the rest of my life, it'd be 'Dreams.'"

So she *did* have a favorite song.

And a damn good one at that.

"Though," she went on sheepishly like she didn't want to admit the next part. "They both were assholes and cheated." I heard Calli shift on her lounger and turned to look at her. "Beauty born from heartache."

Calli was staring right at me, but she wasn't seeing me. She looked miles away and lost in her head. I wondered if she was thinking about her sister—the ugly end to her. Nothing beautiful had come from Calli's heartache.

I didn't get a chance to ask. She continued down her morose path. "Look at Eric Clapton and the Beatles guy, George Harrison. Add in Pattie Boyd and you have an epic love triangle that inspired one of Clapton's best songs, 'Layla.' And I'm not a Beatles fan, but I can't deny Harrison's song to Pattie, 'Something,' is amazing."

She wasn't wrong. There was a lot of bed-hopping in the seventies and eighties. The music scene was rife with cheating and drugs and men taking women who weren't theirs under the guise of trying to find their muse—whatever the fuck that meant. I could argue Clapton's song "Tears in Heaven" was his best, though bringing up the death of the man's son would veer us down a path I didn't want to take us.

I didn't have to redirect the conversation—Calli did, bringing us full circle back to Fleetwood Mac. "Though Lindsey's 'Go Your Own Way' is an emotional sucker punch. A man accepting he couldn't give the woman he loved what she needed and loving her enough to let her go. On the other hand, that acceptance meant he didn't fight for her."

I didn't miss the loneliness in her tone, the whisper of what was left unsaid.

"Did a man not fight for you?" I asked gently.

"Never had a man, but I have a mother who let me go my own way and didn't fight for me or herself. It doesn't take a clinical psychologist to explain why that song hits me in the feels."

Never had a man?

What the fuck?

The woman was stunning, smart, and had a wicked sense of right and wrong. How had she never had a man?

I tried for levity and said, "Let me guess, 'The Chain' is your third favorite on the album."

"There are only forty-four original words in that four-and-a-half-minute song. In a world where people like to hear themselves speak so they use seventy-three words and a lot of filler to make themselves feel smart, instead of the ten necessary to get the point across, 'The Chain' proves it's about the quality of words, not the quantity."

I couldn't argue that, so I didn't. I moved on.

"Never been tied to a man?"

I saw the flinch, but no left eye twitch denoting irritation. Uncomfortable but not angry at the question.

"I've been busy. Never had time."

She'd had time. She just never made the time.

I wasn't going to ask about men she'd used to *pass* the time, because I didn't want to know.

"I know you've never been married and aren't looking to be, but have you ever been tied to a woman?"

I walked right into that motherfucking land mine.

"Yep, for four years."

Calli's lips parted and her eyes flared. "Wow. Four years is a long time to commit to a woman when you were clear there wouldn't be wedding bells in your future."

"Was there a question in there?" I taunted, for no other reason than to buy myself time to figure out how I was going to get out of the trap I'd laid for myself.

"Not if you don't want there to be. Calli and Mase and the cone of silence doesn't include having to share secrets that don't want to be shared."

Cone of silence.

That would imply trust.

Not that my relationship with Emily was a state secret, but I also didn't broadcast it.

"Tell me the truth why you've never committed to a man," I pushed.

Calista Ventura held my gaze hostage while she broke my heart. "Men scare me."

Fuck me. *Fuck me.* Fuck me.

"Do I scare you?"

Without hesitation, she answered, "No."

Thank fuck.

And fuck me sideways. Now I had to return the honesty.

"I met Emily when I was sixteen. She was fifteen. We dated until I was twenty. Then we broke up."

"Why?"

Christ.

"She cheated on me."

Seeing as it was a long time ago, the anger had long since fizzled out, but the betrayal still burned. Back then, I'd been naive. I'd believed Emily loved me. I'd believed her when she promised herself to me and only me. I'd believed her when she told me it was important to her that we wait to have sex until we were married.

All lies.

All bullshit.

The deepest betrayal.

"Now I kinda feel like an ass for talking to you about breakup songs," she muttered.

"It was twenty-five years ago, Calli. I'm not over here crying in my soup, sad my high school and college girlfriend cheated on me."

"Well, that's good news. I'd hate to tell you how lame I thought it was that you'd give twenty-five years to a woman who is clearly a blind and stupid idiot for throwing you away."

Christ, I didn't want that to feel good, but it did.

"No one serious after her?"

There had been a lot of someones. Lots of nameless, faceless, empty pussy that at the end of the night left me feeling like garbage.

I shifted in my lounger and took her in. All that shiny blonde hair, those incredible blue eyes, and I wished more than anything she was not sitting next to me. I wished she was anywhere but in the middle of an op in Dubai, exhausted and worn out. I'd give up my condo, my stake in the bar, my retirement, all my possessions in exchange for her being someplace else with someone special and this life having never touched her.

Cone of silence.

"Want some truth?" I asked.

"I want anything you're willing to give me."

Christ. A different me would take that statement and run with it until we collapsed into bed together.

That was not where I could go with Calista, or anyone.

"When I was with Emily, we were both virgins. I ended that relationship one. She did not," I told her.

Calli rolled to her side. The lapels of the robe slightly opened, exposing just enough of her cleavage to make my dick take notice but not enough to be indecent.

Fuck, she was beautiful, and I was an asshole.

"You were with her for four years."

I understood the question even if she asked it in the form of a statement.

"Her family was religious. She wanted to wait until she was married. I respected that and I loved her, so it wasn't a hardship. But, there I was at twenty, a virgin after I caught my pious girlfriend fucking a TA in her English class her freshman year of college."

"That's really shitty, Mase. I don't know what to say."

"Nothing to say. It was fucked she cheated. The end."

"So that was the end of you wanting to be in a relationship? She fucks you over and that's it for you? You just let her win?"

I smiled.

She shook her head, and confessed, "That sounded judgier than I wanted it to."

"Is that your way of admitting you're judgmental?"

"I never said I wasn't."

"Damn, you're cute when you get huffy."

Her eyes narrowed, and that was cute too.

"I feel like there's more to the story."

There was fifteen years more to the story.

"You sure you wanna know? It's a long story, and you look tired."

The prettiest pink rose on her cheeks. Better than the blush in the kitchen, because this one was all for me.

"Stop stalling, hotshot, and spill."

"Bossy."

Calli glared, and I hid my smile.

"The sad tale of my sex life," I started, unsure why I was willing to share any of this with her. "It took me a while to get over Emily, lick my wounds, and, now that I was single, figure out sex and what it meant to me. If I'd only been waiting because that was what Emily wanted, or if it was also something I wanted.

"I got over Emily, but I still wasn't sure about sex. Eventually I started dating. Met a girl, we hit it off. Date three, she's all over me. But I've never fucked a woman and I'm not sure, so I slow things down. Next time I take her out, we end up back at her house, she goes for it again. This time when I gently let her down, she asks me if I have erectile dysfunction. That relationship ends."

Calli was pinching her lips into two flat lines.

"Something funny?" I drawled.

"Nope. But erectile dysfunction. That's where she went with that? Bold on her part. I would've thought it was me and I was a shit kisser or had BO or something. I would not have gone straight to ED. Unless . . ." She trailed off and her eyes dropped to my crotch.

Which was unfortunate.

The bastard had yet to fully recover from the top swells of her tits being on display, and now that he had Calli's undivided attention, he thought it was a good idea to twitch.

Her gaze shot back to mine. But instead of the pink deepening like I thought it would, a sexy smirk tugged at her lips.

"Seems like it's in working order," she mumbled.

I could show her how well it worked.

Fuck.

Down, you greedy bastard. Calli is not for you.

And I was talking to my dick like a tool.

Focus.

"A few months later, I met another woman. I'm totally into her, she was sweet and shy and fucking pretty as hell. We've got two months into the relationship, I'm falling for her and committed to seeing where things are headed. I get to her work earlier than she was expecting, she's standing outside waiting for me, I approach from behind . . . and I hear her on the phone with one of her girls, telling her she doesn't know what's wrong with me. We'd fucked around, done everything but have sex, and she tells her friend she thinks I'm secretly gay and haven't come to terms with it yet. That ends."

"Gay? Seriously? These women are confident. I would've totally gone with I'm a shit kisser *and* the can't-give-a-blow-job route before gay."

The robe, the legs, the tits were torture. Hearing Calli say "blow job" was a new circle of hell.

To stop my mind from thinking about how her pretty lips would look wrapped around my dick, I went back to my tale of woe.

"The next chick lasts a month before I catch her with one of the guys I work with. Her excuse—women have needs and I wasn't fulfilling them. Fair enough, I get it, but at that point, I had no interest in mindless fucking. I'd waited as long as I had, I'd held out for the woman I thought I was going to marry, I could wait until I found the right one.

"It was number five who really taught me to never trust a woman. She played the long game, and she was damn good. I thought I'd found the One. Turns out all she wanted to do was fuck a SEAL. After she got what she wanted, she dumped my ass. I gave her my virginity, she got bragging rights that she bagged a Frogman."

Calli shot to sitting, her robe spilled open more, a hint of her nipple now visible. And it gapped at the juncture of her thighs, giving away she was wearing pink, lacy panties.

"Are you fucking kidding me? What's her name?"

"Calli—"

"Seriously, Mase, what's her name? I promise not to put her down, but the bitch needs to be taught some fucking respect."

I wanted to process that. I wanted her defense of me and my virtue to feel good, but I couldn't begin to process it when the more she spoke and gestured with her hands, the wider the opening in the robe became.

I slammed my eyes closed as the word *hell* took on a new meaning.

"Baby, your robe."

"Shit. Sorry."

I heard movement but didn't open my eyes.

Honest to God, there was only so much a man could take before his self-imposed rules flew out the window. I only had so much control, and the last threads were fraying. Soon I'd be on my knees in front of her, begging for a taste.

"I'm covered. Sorry again, and thanks for . . . you know, being a gentleman."

That wasn't gentlemanly, that was self-preservation.

Raw and desperate need to bury my face between her thighs was simmering too close to the surface.

"So, are you going to give me her name so I can kick her ass?" Calli asked, like my dick hadn't gone from hard to solid and I had actual blood in my brain to think.

"What name?"

"The girl who treated you like a pogo stick instead of a person with feelings."

I wouldn't mind Calli treating me like a pogo stick.

"Not worth you risking going back to San Diego when you have a warrant out for your arrest for triple homicide."

"Shit. I forgot about that."

Jesus. Only Calli would forget she was wanted for killing three men.

I pushed my head back on the cushion and laughed. When I finally got my hilarity under control and looked back at Calli, she was smiling.

A real smile.

Bright and blinding and so damn beautiful.

"You're a beautiful woman, Calista, but when you smile, you are downright gorgeous."

I heard her suck in a breath.

To break the moment we could not share, I went back to the rest of my story.

"The irony is, fucking a SEAL isn't some great feat."

Calista's smile fell. I wanted it back so desperately, I gave her more, knowing it would make me sound like a prick. I didn't trust myself with her. I didn't trust that if I had more smiles, more time in our cone of silence, more sharing of stories, I wouldn't fall for her. Top to toe, she was everything I'd want in a woman. And that was unacceptable.

"The bars around IB are packed with Team Guys who will gladly bang some Frog Hog skank in the bathroom or in the parking lot, and if she holds promise, they'll take her to their bed. But for me, I'd given that cunt something that meant something to me. Never again would I make that mistake. Emily broke my heart. Jennifer fucked me and left me. After that, I locked down my emotions and became what the women I'd dated wanted—a no-strings, good-time guy.

"I fucked my way through half the beautiful women in San Diego. I spent years having meaningless sex that, after, I showered off as nothing but a distant memory. I didn't bother with names because I wasn't going to remember them. I gave the bare minimum I needed to get a woman naked. I was known for how quickly I could get a woman off. My teammates thought it was a talent. What it was, was a necessity. The faster I got them off, the faster *I* could get off, then get the fuck out.

"Women are easy. Flash a smile, fuck her mind while promising mind-bending sex, and she'll drop to her knees. I didn't need the uniform or the Trident. I'd mastered the art of seduction. Truth be told, it's boring as fuck."

Unlike the other three times when I was done speaking, she didn't immediately provide commentary.

Mission accomplished.

Problem solved.

"I get that," she whispered.

"Get what?"

"Turning off your emotions and going through the motions. Using something painful as an excuse to be someone you were never meant to be."

Goddamn, fuck. There was more she needed to know.

"Calli—"

"Are you a football or baseball guy?"

"Sweetness—"

"Answer, hotshot."

"Football."

"Movie or book?"

"Book."

There was a long stretch of silence.

When I looked over, her eyes were closed.

I should've woken her up and told her to go to bed. Instead, I gave myself a few minutes to watch her sleep.

Using something painful as an excuse to be someone you were never meant to be.

Maybe I'd done that . . . or maybe I was just an asshole who stopped caring and started doing what I wanted, what felt good, and used the old, tired excuse that as long as both parties were consenting, there was nothing wrong with my behavior.

But Calista's whole life had been derailed.

This was not who she was supposed to be.

◆ ◆ ◆

I came awake when I felt the cushion I was on compress. I kept my eyes closed, wanting to know what Calli would do next. Her fingers brushing over my lips was not what I was expecting. My eyes came open and locked with blue. Ever so softly, her fingers glided over my cheek to my temple and back to the corner of my mouth.

"Calli—"

Her thumb pressed over my lips.

"I wish the world was different," she whispered so softly, I could barely hear her.

She traced my bottom lip with her thumb.

"You're a good man, Mase."

I wasn't, but I didn't tell her that.

"Calli—"

"Shh."

She leaned forward, bending deep, until her mouth hovered mere inches over mine.

I didn't dare move.

Indecision warred. I could feel it, see it in her eyes. She wanted something, was brave enough to come this far, but was now paralyzed by uncertainty.

"I won't move, sweetness. Take whatever you need."

It took a moment, but she closed the distance. Her lips touched the corner of my mouth.

My hands fisted at my sides. I held myself rigid while Calli slowly brushed her lips over mine. A barely there touch. I felt her soft tongue tentatively touch my lip. There, then gone.

She jerked back and stared down at me. I didn't understand the confusion I saw. I didn't trust myself to ask. If this was what Calli needed, I'd lie still and give it to her. But fuck, was it painful.

The next touch of her tongue was less tentative. I parted my lips and waited. Another touch, this one a sweep. Slowly, I licked the path hers took until our tongues glided against each other.

I swallowed my groan, but not my concern when she pulled away.

"Tell me what you need, Calli."

"I shouldn't've done that. I'm sorry."

"I told you to take what you wanted. But I need some guidance."

She sat all the way upright. "That was . . ."

If she said *wrong*, I was going to lose my mind.

She didn't finish her sentence. She stood, putting me eye level with pink panties. There was nothing I could do to hide my erection, so I didn't bother explaining the tenting in my track pants. But the longer she stood there staring down at me, the harder it became not to reach for her.

"That wasn't fair. I'm sorry."

"Nothing to be sorry for."

She swept her hand in the general vicinity of my hard-on.

"It'll go down," I told her.

After a cold shower and three jerk-off sessions.

"I should go to bed," she declared.

Fuck.

I wanted to get up, or at least tell her to stay, but I hadn't forgotten her telling me that men scared her. And while she said I didn't, I wasn't going to get up off the lounger while she was feeling vulnerable after she sort of kissed me. It was the softest, hardly there kiss I'd ever had, but it was sweet and sexy and all Calli.

"Night, Calli," I called to her back, as she made her way to the slider.

She paused before she went in and looked over her shoulder. "I'm not like those other women."

"What?"

"What happened just now, I wasn't using you. I just wanted to know."

Seriously, she was killing me. Calista was nothing like anyone I'd ever met, and she was nothing like some barfly who wanted nothing more than to get off.

"Know what?"

"What you tasted like."

With that successful parting shot, she disappeared into her room.

No question, this had to be karma.

This was my punishment for being a royal asshole.

Not that Fallon or Pete or any of the guys would ever know about my balcony time with Calista, but if they did, they'd have a field day with my misery.

A barely there touch of tongues had me tied so tight, it was going to be a bitch to get untangled. The fuck of it was, I was beginning to wonder why I wanted to get free.

Chapter Fifteen

"Calli, your phone's ringing," Fallon yelled over the music.

Crap.

I stopped the heavy bag from swinging and was working off my gloves on the way across the gym.

Fallon met me in the doorway. "Want me to answer it on speaker?"

I blew out a breath to calm my heart rate. I didn't need to sound like a sex worker while I took a call from Amir. "Yeah," I wheezed out.

Fallon slid his finger over the screen and put the call on speaker.

"Hello?" I greeted cooly.

"Zara Hawthorne?" a woman with a British accent asked.

Game time. Exit Calista Ventura, enter Zara Hawthorne.

My glaze slid to Fallon. His brow raised in question. I shook my head and answered the woman. "Yes. May I ask who's calling?"

"This is Mr. Bakir's secretary. He's asked I inform you dinner tonight will be at CÉ LA VI at nine. Do you know the Sky View hotel?"

"Indeed, I do."

As a matter of fact, I could see the buildings from my bedroom's balcony.

"Tower Two. Level fifty-four," she went on to explain. "Do you need a car sent to retrieve you?"

I caught sight of Mason making his way down the hallway toward the gym—toward me.

After last night's latest mental break, whereupon I thought it was a good idea to kiss the man, I'd successfully avoided him all day. Now I was stuck, with no avenue to escape.

"No, thank you. But if you could, please inform Mr. Bakir I will have my security detail with me. My driver will stay with the car; however, two of my men will escort me to dinner. They will be discreet," I finished, with my eyes locked on Mason's in warning.

His responding smirk told me we were in for a rip-roaring fight after I finished my call.

"That won't be necessary, Miss Hawthorne. Security is provided."

Mason's eyes narrowed.

I cleared my throat.

"That's a lovely offer. However, I'm a woman, as are you, so I think you will understand when I tell you my guards do not leave my side. If there is an issue with my personal detail joining this evening, please let me know within the hour so I can attend to other business."

"Yes, Miss Hawthorne."

Fallon disconnected the call and smiled at me. "Damn. Ice Queen Zara Hawthorne in the house. I was staring right at you and yet I was *still* wondering where our Calli went."

No sooner did "our Calli" come out of Fallon's mouth, Mason growled.

"Was that not to your liking, hotshot?"

"Wanna give us a minute, brother?"

Fallon handed me my phone. "Sure. I'll go get the popcorn ready. If Mommy and Daddy are going to fight, I need a snack."

"Please don't ever call me Mommy again," I begged.

"You sure? I looked up that website you mentioned." The man wagged his brows . . . actually wiggled them while he smiled.

I couldn't remember what website I'd mentioned, and I wasn't going to dig my current hole deeper, not that I had the chance before Mason growled again.

Oh boy.

Fallon started down the hall, and it was on the tip of my tongue to beg him to come back. Mason didn't look happy. After a full sweep of my body, he looked unhappier. I glanced down to see why he was frowning. Gym shorts and a sports bra and one boxing glove still on, the other under my armpit. Admittedly, that was gross. I was sweaty and shouldn't be shoving things in my armpit to hold them, but it didn't explain the frown.

"What's wrong now?"

"You're avoiding me."

I took a step back. Which was the wrong thing to do. That gave Mason room to walk in and shut the door.

Trapped in a room with Mason.

This was different. This wasn't our balcony. Our cone of silence didn't extend to the gym. Anything I said here could and would be used against me.

"Mason."

"Calli."

I could tell him I'd been busy all day going over files, but he'd ask me what files, and I didn't want him to know. I could lie and tell him I'd had a headache and lazed in bed all day, but he'd call me on it.

"You're right, I have been."

His torso swung back like I'd stuck him.

Which reminded me, I needed to take my gloves off and think of what I was going to do if Amir came back and told me dinner was off.

Tom would be pissed.

Tom could go fuck a duck.

I walked to the mini kitchen and tossed my glove on the counter, set my phone next to the glove, and got to work on the other.

"Why?"

Was he really going to play dumb?

"I didn't take you as obtuse," I told him, as I yanked off my other glove and tossed it with its match.

"Obtuse?" he asked from closer.

I turned around, not expecting him to be *that* close.

"Do you mind stepping back?"

He didn't budge.

Fine. He wanted to play it this way, I'd play.

In here, I wasn't Calli.

"I've been avoiding you because I don't like to admit when I've made a mistake. So I sulk, then, after I'm done, I face it and make sure I never repeat it. So now that you're here, I can face it and move on."

"Which part of last night was a mistake?"

I remained silent. He knew, and I wasn't going to be bullied into saying it.

"We're alone in here," he pointed out. "Cone of silence, sweetness. Tell me, which part was a mistake?"

Mason stared down at me.

I glared up at him with my shoulders stiff.

"Was you telling me your favorite songwriter is Stevie Nicks a mistake?"

Jerk.

"Me telling you something that only two other people know, was that a mistake?"

Only two other people?

He told me a secret-secret, not just something he doesn't want common knowledge.

Ho-lee shit.

"Mase—"

"Or was it you brushing your fingers over my lips? Or was it your sweet kiss? Because, baby, that wasn't a mistake. It was pure fucking torture, but trust me, I know a mistake when I make one, and that sure as fuck was no mistake."

I felt my face heat.

Torture?

It was that bad?

Fuck Tom and his op. Screw Jason Anderson, I'd find another way to take him down. I needed to leave. I could be in London in ten hours. Far away from Mason and my horrible kiss.

"Jesus. What the hell is going on in your head?"

"Nothing. I apologized last night, but that was before I knew it was torture. So I say it again, I'm really sorry."

I moved quickly to get around Mason. He moved quicker and grabbed me by my upper arm and hauled me to his chest.

"What's happening right now?" he asked.

"Nothing. I want to—"

"Explain to me what's going on."

"Let me go."

Instead of doing what I'd asked, he studied me in his Mason way. Meaning I had his full, undivided attention and his eyes were roaming my face. When they landed on mine, I knew I was in trouble.

"I see you misunderstood what I said. So let me rectify that."

No way in hell I wanted him to rectify anything.

"Let me go," I repeated.

He again ignored my demand and doubled down, tightening his hand around my bicep and pulling me closer.

"I told you most of the story last night, but I didn't tell you everything. That being, I haven't slept with a woman in ten years."

"I could guess that when you were clear on all of those women being nothing but—"

"No, Calli. I haven't fucked a woman in ten years."

I felt myself blinking—rapidly. I opened my mouth to say something but snapped it closed. When I reopened it, still nothing.

I tried again, and this time words came out. Unfortunately, they weren't very eloquent. "Um. What?"

"You heard me."

"How's that possible? I mean, I know how. But, um, why?"

"A smart man reevaluates his life choices when some rando tracks him down to tell him she's pregnant."

Mason has a child? Tom didn't include that in his dossier.

"You—"

"No. But for seven months until the baby was born, I was sweating bullets. Me and three other guys had to submit DNA for the who's-the-daddy lottery drawing. The kid wasn't mine, but it was the reality check I needed. Condoms break, and then I'd be stuck with a baby mama I didn't remember banging. But worse, my kid would be the result of a meaningless orgasm that, for me, had long ago stopped feeling all that great. After that scare, I haven't touched a woman."

Ten years. No sex.

Still, I had him beat. But I was thinking my condition was easier than his because I didn't know what I was missing.

Now might've been a good time to tell him my secret. But I wasn't ready. Maybe tonight on the balcony I'd find the courage to repay his trust by giving him something no one else knew.

"Do you understand?"

I wasn't sure why he cared if I understood his reasons for not having sex. That seemed like a rather personal choice, and from what I knew of Mason and by his own admission, he didn't give a shit what people thought of him or his choices.

But still, I whispered, "Yeah, I understand."

"No, Calli, baby, do you understand why it'd be torture, you sitting next to me in that robe with your long-ass legs? That my mind would go to how they'd feel wrapped around me. That first night, carrying you to bed, feeling your hands on my chest. Then last night, getting a good look at your tits after dreaming about what they'd feel like in my hands, in my mouth.

"Then I get your mouth and your sweet tongue, but I can't move. Can't touch you. Can't kiss you back. Can't give you what you were really asking for because if I make a move and take that too far and freak you out, I'd never be able to live with myself.

"Haven't fucked a woman in ten years, Calli. Haven't touched a woman either. Haven't allowed a woman to touch *me*. I feel the temptation of you in my dick. I wanted you to take what you needed, but, baby, it was the best kind of fucking torture given by you."

I stopped trying to get away and dropped my forehead to his chest.

I was the worst.

A tease.

"I'm so sorry. That wasn't cool of me to use you like that. Tempt you to do something you didn't want to do."

His hand let go of my arm and he slid it around my back.

Mason Hughes was hugging me.

Damn, that felt good. I couldn't remember the last time someone hugged me. Maybe my dad before he died. My mom in one of the rare times I saw her when she was only drunk and hadn't slipped into blitzed.

"Did it seem to you like I didn't want to be there? I got a mouth, sweetness, I know how to use it. If I didn't want you touching me, I would've said something."

I bet he did know what to do with his mouth.

I really wanted to find out all the ways he could use it.

Now, that was completely off the table, and not just because I was a pathetic virgin and wouldn't know what to do with a man like Mason. If I were ever to try sex, it'd have to be with a geeky IT guy who had less muscle mass than me and wouldn't care if I fumbled my way through the experience.

"What's on your mind?" he asked the top of my head.

I wasn't going to tell him about my impending sexcapades with my imaginary geek.

"I'm embarrassed. And I have to admit that, last night, I wore the robe again because I caught you staring at my legs the first night, and it felt good. It felt normal, instead of the skeevy way men usually stare at me. It felt clean and good, and I wanted to feel that again. I didn't think about how selfish it was."

"It wasn't selfish."

"It makes me a tease, Mase. And that's not cool."

I felt his body shake against mine. Stupidly I pushed closer, hoping to absorb more of Mason. More memories to take with me when I lost him.

"I'd tell you you're the best kinda tease, baby, but I know you'd take that the wrong way, so what I'll tell you instead is, I didn't mind. And if I have a choice, it'll be you in the robe on our balcony again tonight. If I had another choice, it'd be you sharing my lounger, taking from me whatever it is you need with the knowledge you're safe to take it. You want to be the only one touching, touch. You want to kiss me, kiss me. You want more, we'll talk. But Calli . . . you *have* to talk to me, not run away."

"You'd let me kiss you?"

"Fuck yeah."

"Touch you?"

"Anything above the belt, it's all yours. You wanna go lower, we'll have to discuss that."

Safe.

He'd make it safe for me to touch.

To kiss.

I lifted my forehead off his chest. As soon as I did, I caught his green eyes staring down at me.

He was serious.

Dead-ass serious.

He'd bend his rules for me.

Ten years, no women by his own vow, and he'd let me touch and kiss him.

"Mase—"

My phone ringing cut off the rest of what I was going to say.

He gave me a squeeze and stepped back. "You need to answer that."

I twisted, grabbed my phone, checked the caller ID, and answered, "Hello?"

"Miss Hawthorne," the British woman greeted. "Under the circumstances, Mr. Bakir will make an exception for you. One guard may accompany you into the dining room. The others must be discreet and not enter the restaurant."

"That will be fine."

"Is there anything else you require?"

"No. Thank you."

I dropped my phone, made sure the call was disconnected, and informed Mason, "One guard in the restaurant."

"That'll be me," he informed me back. "Fallon will post outside the door. Pete will stay with the car."

"Is it weird the restaurant Amir picked is one we can see from the apartment?"

"If you're asking if he knows where you're staying, possible but unlikely. But it wouldn't matter if he did. You're in a luxury penthouse. If we were staying at the Best Western in a shitty thirty-dollar-a-night room and he knew, that'd be a problem. But you up in the sky with your three guards, not unusual, nothing to question. And the restaurant he chose is a hot spot, a place to throw money around and be seen doing it. I'd have questions if he wanted to take you someplace quiet. He also knows taking you to a club like he does with the men isn't going to work. Women and booze won't impress you."

Mason was right. I was being paranoid because Jason was already in Dubai and close.

"Okay."

"Are we straight with everything else?"

I would not blush like a schoolgirl.

"We're straight."

Mason's smile came slowly, and when it fully formed, it was lazy. Pantie melting. Dangerously sexy. Thigh-clenching, mind-dizzyingly beautiful.

"You're gonna stop avoiding me?"

Um. No. I was going to avoid him the rest of the afternoon while I took a long, hot bath and gave in to the fantasy of Mason and what his mouth could do. Then I'd get down to mission prep. But before I could concentrate on my assignment, I needed to relieve the ache. I had to find a way to release the constant throbbing that wasn't only between my legs but around my heart.

Vagina first.

Mission second.

Heart later.

Chapter Sixteen

"Sweetness, you keep staring at me with those pretty eyes of yours, I'm gonna think you want that kiss now."

YES! Please.

"Fuck," he snarled, stepping closer and dropping his head so his mouth was at my ear. "Is that what you want, Calli? You want your kiss now, baby?"

My head bobbled in what I hoped was a nod, but with all things Mason filling my senses—including his hard body pressed against me—I wasn't positive I pulled off my approval.

"Then take it," he rumbled.

The gravel in his voice sent a bolt of electricity to my core. His taunt made me bold. But when his lips skimmed over my cheek on their journey to my mouth, desire turned into a craving. I *needed* him to kiss me. The urgency was fueled by primal want, a hunger so intense it felt animalistic. My heart was beating erratically, my clit pulsed, my breasts felt heavy. Every inch of my body readied itself for Mason.

"Please," I begged.

I fisted his shirt, pulling him closer. Or was I anchoring myself to him while the storm he created threatened to take me under?

A slow glide of his tongue over the seam of my lips gave me the answer—totally holding on for dear life.

"Open for me, Calli."

I parted my lips. Unlike mine from last night, there was nothing tentative about Mason's kiss. His tongue stroked mine, coaxing at first, then demanding. He deepened the kiss, taking it from hungry to downright intense.

This wasn't a kiss—it was possession.

"Christ," he groaned, breaking the connection.

I whimpered my protest. "More."

"Calli—"

"Please, Mase."

It didn't register he'd moved us until my back hit the wall.

"Keep your hands on my shoulders." He softened the bite of his command by brushing his knuckles along my jaw.

I followed his directive and let go of his shirt. When my hands were where he wanted them, he leaned in, kissed my throat, and issued another order. "Spread for me."

I shuffled my feet apart. His hand went to the space I'd created, and he used the edge of his finger to gently stroke. I groaned at the contact and shifted closer.

Mason didn't lift his lips from my neck when he spoke. The vibration tickled, but his question ignited a fire only he could extinguish. "You spread for me, Calli, but still I gotta ask, is this the more you wanted?"

"Yes."

"Like this?" He twisted his hand and circled my clit with his fingertip. "Or do you want me to fuck you with my fingers?"

My brain was short-circuiting from the gentle over-the-clothes maneuver. With each circle, he brought me closer to climax. I would've been embarrassed if I had any working brain cells, however, in my haze of euphoria, there was no shame.

My hips jolted and I moaned, "Mase."

That was as far as I got when he made the decision for me.

"I wanna feel you, sweetness. You okay with that?"

"Yes."

I momentarily lost his hand. When I got it back, this time under the spandex of my workout shorts, I couldn't stop my gasp. No one had ever touched me there, not bare. Teenage groping and over-the-clothes fondling was as far as I'd gotten.

And Mason was no adolescent fumbling around to find the spot—he zeroed in with expert precision.

My fingers curled around his shoulders while his teased my center, before pushing in.

My breath rushed out in a mix of "oh my God," which I verbalized, and "holy shit, this is so much better than a toy," which I amazingly kept to myself.

"Goddamn, you're fucking tight," he growled against my throat, and pushed his finger deeper. "Grind down on that, Calli."

With no other choice, my body obeyed, mindless in its pursuit of pleasure. His thumb engaged my clit, my eyes closed, and my orgasm inched closer.

"That's it, baby, come for me."

Was it possible to orgasm on command? Apparently the answer to that was a resounding yes.

Before the moan could escape, Mason pulled his face out of my neck and slammed his mouth on mine, swallowing my cry of ecstasy.

The tremors racking my body made it hard to keep my balance as my climax held me hostage. My inner muscles pulsed around Mason's unyielding finger. It was too much—the heat chased by chills racing over my skin, his tongue, his thumb working miracles on my clit. It was unending euphoria, a tidal wave of relief and the sweetest high.

Mason tore his mouth off mine. Slowly, my eyes opened to find the green of his irises swallowed up by his pupils, a look I could only describe as carnal saturating his features. A feminine thrill washed over me.

He twisted his finger, setting off a wave of aftershocks as my orgasm waned.

"Fuck me, you're gorgeous."

His forehead lowered to mine, and together we slowed our breathing. Well, at least that was what I was doing. I felt like I'd been tossed into the zombie apocalypse with no warning and had just spent the last ten minutes running for my life.

Really, Calista, you couldn't come up with a better analogy? Zombies?

Shut up, my brain isn't functioning after that big ole orgasm from Wonder Mason.

Great, now I was conversing with myself.

"You good, baby?"

I sagged against Mason and gave him the God's honest truth. "Oh yeah."

That simple movement set off a chain reaction of events I wasn't experienced enough to foresee. The first thing that happened was, I pressed against his rock-hard erection. The second was, his hand still down my pants twitched, causing my hips to chase the sensation. And third, Mason groaned. No, it wasn't a groan, it was a raw, untamed rumble that sounded wild and erotic. Like a man on the verge of throwing his woman over his shoulder, this after he dragged his knuckles on the ground and brought a saber-toothed tiger back to the shelter he'd made.

Unfortunately, the next thing he did was pull his hand out of my pants. Obviously that meant I'd lost his magical finger, which pulled a sorrowful whimper out of me.

I searched his features for a sign of what I should do next.

"No."

"No?" I repeated, but instead of a statement, mine was a question.

"Right now, I'm gonna walk out of here. Before I leave, so this doesn't get twisted, I'm telling you straight, I'm this close"—he lifted his hand and showed me his thumb and pointer finger almost touching—"to snapping and begging you to let me get more than a finger inside your tight, wet-as-fuck pussy. But before that, I'd beg you to let me spread you out on the sparring mat and eat your cunt until everyone in this whole damn building knows how good I can make you feel and how hard you get off for me. The consequence of that is I'd have to kill two men I respect because no one but me gets to hear you. That's mine and only mine."

Boy, he doesn't know how right he is.

"So, I'm going upstairs to jack off to the memory of your *tight, wet-as-fuck cunt* and pretend it's not my hand getting me there."

"I could help you with that?"

I wouldn't've thought it possible for Mason's eyes to get darker than they already were, but there, staring back at me, was proof they could.

"That already went further than it should've."

Shit.

Celibate for ten years, Mason had kissed me and finger-fucked me to orgasm.

Before I could apologize, he hooked me around the back of my neck and brought my face close to his. "Don't go there."

"You don't know where I was going," I protested.

"You're gearing up to say you're sorry. I already told you, I'm a big boy, no one makes me do anything I don't want to do. Not only was I with you every step of the way, I want more of you, Calli. I don't know what it is about you, or why I feel the way I do, why when I'm next to you, what makes me want to toss you over my shoulder and keep you captive. I also know I don't care why, I just know I do, and it feels right in a way it's never felt before."

There it was. I knew that look was pure caveman.

"I wasn't lying or exaggerating, sweetness. I'm edging toward losing my control. Before that happens, I need to leave. We straight?"

I nodded, not trusting I could hide my disappointment if I spoke.

With a soft brush of his lips over mine, he let me go and stepped back.

I immediately missed his hands on me.

Mason walked to the door while I stood rooted in place.

Then he was gone.

And I was left standing in a gym in a penthouse owned by a stranger, smiling after having my very first non-self-induced orgasm.

Vagina sated—check.

Heart under wraps—not even a little bit.

Time to mission prep.

◆ ◆ ◆

I was still in my robe, but my hair and makeup were done for dinner with Amir when the pull of the balcony got the best of me. Ignoring my dress laid out on the bed, I made my way to the slider.

Instead of sitting on a lounger, Mason was standing at the railing, hands curled around the metal banister, staring out at the cityscape, but when I approached, his head turned. After a top-to-toe eye sweep, he smiled.

"That tracks," he mumbles.

"What does?"

"You living dangerously."

I shrugged but kept my distance. "It's been a few hours. I thought I'd be safe."

"You thought wrong."

I took in his wet hair, black slacks, and crisp white oxford. He looked showered, ready to go play bodyguard, and edible.

My efforts to hide my smile were fruitless when I asked, "Were your . . . activities not successful?"

Mason's lips twitched. "Activities?"

"You know, your event, endeavor, deed." I tossed out a few synonyms.

"Come closer and I'll tell you."

Without permission, my feet took me to Mason. As soon as I was close, he let go of the railing and hooked me around the waist, drawing me flush with his side.

"Fuck, you smell good."

So did he, but now that I was back in his arms, all I could think about was what happened in the gym and how I really wanted it to happen again, preferably in a room with a bed.

"Are you worried about tonight?"

It took me a moment to recover from the conversational whiplash Mason had delivered.

I tipped my head back and to the side, taking in his strong profile. That five-o'clock shadow was now filled in to a proper beard, yet I could still see the tense set of his jaw.

"No."

I watched him nod.

Eager to get back to our original conversation, I prompted, "So, are you going to tell me?"

"Tonight when we get home."

"You're telling me I walked all this way only to be denied?" I teased.

Mason snatched my wrist, guided it to his crotch, and pressed my hand against his erection.

Holy hell, Batman. I'd felt it earlier in the gym, but not like this, not with my hand on it, feeling the impressive outline.

"Shower's worn off, sweetness. If I tell you the details of what I thought about while I stroked my cock, either you'll be missing dinner completely or I'll be escorting you with a stiff dick and no chance of hiding it. PDA is illegal in Dubai. I don't know for certain, but I'm thinking walking around in public with an erection is frowned upon."

Mason wasn't wrong about PDA. Even married couples holding hands in public was iffy. Kissing, absolutely not. Walking around with a tent pole would definitely garner unwanted attention.

"Well, we wouldn't want you to get a fine for your trouser tower, so I'll wait for the details until we get home." And since my hand was still resting on his package, I took the chance and gave it a squeeze.

That earned me a grunt and a "Jesus."

"You claim I like to live dangerously, yet it was *you* who put my hand on your cock."

"What can I say, I like living on the edge."

"Of insanity?" I shot back.

Mason tipped his chin, leaned close, and right before he kissed me, he shared, "We passed insanity a few hundred yards back, sweetness."

This kiss was nothing like the one earlier. He kept it light and gentle—a sweet tease. His hands didn't wander, but mine did—up and down his shaft until he broke the kiss with a groan.

"Go. Finish getting ready."

"Life sucks," I grumbled, not wanting to stop what we were doing.

"It'll suck less if you get your ass in gear and go change into what dress you're going to torture me with all night, so we can get to this bullshit dinner and get home and pick up where we left off."

"Promise?" I whispered.

"Yeah, sweetness, I promise."

I couldn't read Mason's expression, but I felt his words someplace deep inside of me where he shouldn't've been able to reach.

Maybe it was time to start reinforcing those walls around my heart.

Chapter Seventeen

"Keep your shit," Fallon's amused voice said through my earpiece.

Bad timing.

We'd arrived on the fifty-fourth floor before Amir could be seated. As soon as Amir's eyes landed on Calista, Fallon and I were immediately dismissed. Not that I could blame the asshole. Calista was a sight in her black dress.

Skintight black dress that covered more skin than it showed. But the high collar that covered her cleavage managed to highlight her large tits. The hem hit innocently just below her knees, showing off her curves. All of that before you got to her devil-red spiked heels that matched her lipstick. Shades of black and gray on her eyelids made her eyes impossibly blue. Whatever she'd put in her hair made the normally glossy strands gleam.

Hands down, she was the most beautiful woman I'd ever seen. Made up, she was striking. And I was going to rip Amir's arm from his body and beat him with it if he didn't remove his hand from Calista's lower back as he guided her through the dining room.

I could end this whole operation in the three seconds it would take me to kill him. There would be no invitation forthcoming because there would be no auction after I bled out the host in the middle of a swank, busy restaurant.

Fuck.

"Status." Pete came through in my ear.

"Amir's got his hand on Calista. I only got Mase from the back, but I think he's having his own personal earthquake. Might not want to stay in the garage in case his shaking becomes such that the building crumbles."

I said nothing in response as I followed Calli and Amir out onto the terrace.

The motherfucker didn't drop his hand when the hostess stopped at their cozy table. There was no quiet corner but only because the dining area was circular. A quick scan of the seating made it clear Amir had the tables on either side of theirs removed for privacy.

Slick motherfucker.

Before the hostess could move away, Amir stopped her. "Clase Azul Ultra Añejo."

Cheap motherfucker thought he could impress her with a three-thousand-dollar bottle of tequila.

"Moët & Chandon Impérial," Calista said, as the hostess backed away. "Vintage, please."

I bit back a laugh.

She saw his tequila and raised to a seven-thousand-dollar bottle of champagne.

Good girl.

I couldn't see Amir's face, but I did have Calli in profile. The catlike grin on her face was magnificent.

Amir pulled out a chair and dipped his chin. "Please."

Calista took her seat.

Amir turned to me and flicked his wrist. "That'll be all."

Oh, yeah, fuck yeah, I was going to beat him with his severed arm.

Before I could tell him he could fuck himself, Calli jumped in. "My guard is not to leave my sight, Mr. Bakir. I was clear about that with your secretary. He will step to the side while we dine but he will not be out of touching distance for the remainder of the evening. If this was a problem, it should've been conveyed immediately. I would hate for this evening to be a waste. My time is to be respected, as is yours."

Cool, calm, and firm.

Wordlessly, Amir took his seat. I stepped into the shadows, keeping the least amount of distance between us as I could manage.

"You're not what I expected, Ms. Hawthorne," Amir admitted.

"What did you expect?"

"Not you." There was appreciation in his tone, and a goodly amount.

Slimy motherfucker.

Amir made small talk about the city, pointing out all the buildings, giving her a history lesson I was sure she didn't care about. He only stopped his commentary when a waiter in a tux dropped off their drinks, making a show of setting down the gold bottle of champagne along with two flutes. The less expensive bottle of tequila, in its black decanter, was placed in front of Amir, and with it two long-stemmed glasses.

The waiter poured Calli half a flute of bubbly before Amir dismissed him with another wrist flick.

Jesus, the motherfucker had fewer manners than a drunken sailor at the Dirty Plank.

Out of the corner of my eye, I saw Fallon doing his walk-through.

"You look calmer." As soon as Fallon's voice came at me, Amir reached over and dragged his fingers down Calli's arm. "Spoke too soon."

I watched Calli stiffen, took a step toward the table, but halted when Calista's ice-cold response came.

"This is going to go one way, *Amir*." She dropped the respect bullshit and used his given name. Bold. "And one way only. I am not on offer. I'm here on business. That business being purchasing what I need through you. Respectfully, I hope we can do business. But make no mistake, this dinner is as much me vetting if I want to accept your invitation as it is you extending one."

Fucking hell, she was glorious.

"Your woman's got it going on," Fallon said, having heard her speech through the open mic.

"There's no reason we can't mix business with pleasure," Amir purred.

Having learned Calista didn't need me to intervene, I stayed where I was and waited for her to eviscerate the fucker.

"Your offer is noted. However, I did not get where I am by fucking my way to the top. My pussy's not for sale, nor is it on offer. Tell me, Amir, if I was one of your male clients, would you be offering him use of your cock? Or is your disrespect singular?"

Christ.

As superb as her comeback was, the disrespect was such that I was worried he'd lash out. I'd bet my left nut women did not speak to him that way. The kind of piece of shit he was would literally smack a woman down who dared insult him.

Never would I have guessed Amir's response would be to throw his head back and laugh.

When he regained control, he looked at Calista with something worse than lust. There was no missing his admiration.

"No. You are not at all what I was expecting."

"Never in my life will I forget your girl asking Amir Bakir if he offered up his cock to men," Fallon chuckled.

That was twice he'd called Calli mine.

Twice the area around my heart suspiciously tightened.

The knot just kept tangling.

Dinner was served without either of them ordering. My beautiful, brilliant girl made a show of picking at the lobster and pushing around the grilled broccolini. Nor did she touch the caviar. If Amir didn't get her show of dominance, he was an idiot on top of being a motherfucker. Calista had the upper hand, and at no point would she concede to him.

Fucking brilliant.

That brilliance continued when she declined dessert and ended the evening when it was clear Amir was enjoying sitting next to a gorgeous woman, with no intention of leaving anytime soon.

Hell, I wouldn't have been surprised if she didn't unman the asshole and pick up the check.

She opted for the power play.

"Thank you for dinner and the company," she started, as she placed her napkin on the plate, covering her half-eaten meal. "I'm looking forward to doing business with you, Amir. I've been told you put on an impressive show, and after meeting you, I have no doubt that hasn't been exaggerated. I have the funds available and ready to be transferred into your holding account. At your convenience, please have your secretary send me that information, and I'll see the transfer happens immediately."

Amir used his last moments with her to stare at her. Admiration had slid into adoration.

Fuck me.

"The pleasure was mine, Zara. Though, I must say, I now wish I'd met you under different circumstances that had nothing to do with business. I can think of a great many ways I'd like to possess the beauty that is you, dear."

Slimy, cocksucking motherfucker.

"I'll take that as a compliment, dear."

Amir smiled with a longing in his eyes that sent a shiver up my spine.

She'd pushed, and now the fucker was thinking about taking up the challenge of owning what was . . . mine.

Fuck that.

I stepped behind Calista's chair, managed to pull it away from the table without yanking the damn thing with her ass still in out across the terrace, and helped her stand.

"Ma'am." I grunted the syllable and gestured toward the doors.

"Thank you again, Amir. See you soon."

With my hand on Calli's lower back, I propelled her forward.

"On the move," Fallon told Pete.

"Copy."

We were halfway through the restaurant, passing the packed bar, when Calista's step faltered. My hand slipped around her waist to stop her from tripping. She made no acknowledgment of her stumble or of her being pressed to my side. Her gaze was fastened to something or someone at the bar.

I scanned, looking for the source of her discomfort. My eyes snagged on a man in an expensive suit, mid-forties, light hair, built but not bulky, too far away to see his eye color but not miss the way he was sizing up Calista.

"Who is that?"

She jolted out of her stupor, turned her body to give the man her back, kept her head high, and lied through her fucking teeth. "No one. Let's go."

That wasn't no one.

No one wouldn't have made her stop in her tracks.

No one wouldn't have made her look like she'd seen a ghost.

I waited until Fallon fell into step next to us, flanking Calli, and we were waiting for the elevator before I tried again. "Who was that?"

"I told you, no one."

"Damn, woman, you served that asshole some serious attitude," Fallon softly praised. "I'm impressed."

"Thanks," she returned on a distracted mumble.

The elevator ride was silent. As was the walk through the lobby. Fallon opened the back door to the blacked-out Wagoneer. When Calista was safely inside and the door was shut, I looked at Fallon and told him, "I want the security footage of the bar."

"Why?"

"Someone spooked Calli. I want a name."

"Did you see him?"

"Yeah. You get the footage, I'll point him out. Though when you see it, you won't miss it. The guy was staring at her, and not because she's gorgeous and he was looking to get laid. Like he knew her and was unhappy she was with me."

"An ex?"

Fuck.

"Maybe."

Fallon blew out a breath. "Or, she's into you, and he's an ex, and she doesn't want to talk about him to you."

I could buy that, maybe.

That was, if her reaction to him wasn't stumbling before she turned to stone in my arms.

"Will you do me the favor and call Shep?"

"Yeah, I'll call him when we get back to the apartment."

The drive back to the penthouse was filled with Fallon's blow by blow of the evening, with Pete interjecting here and there. The general consensus was, Calli was a badass and a verbal ninja. My commentary wasn't needed, thus I said nothing.

Which was problematic; it gave me time to stew. Not only that, but the unease I'd felt at the end of the night when Amir looked at Calli grew.

Men like him wouldn't see Calista as a beautiful woman to be cherished and spoiled. They'd look at her as a trophy to be paraded after they had her cowed. They wouldn't work themselves to the bone to make her happy and feel loved; they'd work to break her.

Thank fuck she wouldn't have to see Amir again. She'd get her invite and pass the location to Tom and be done.

As soon as Pete let us into the penthouse, Calli made a beeline to the stairs. "I'm going to wash this shit off my face."

I waited until she made it to the top of the stairs before I announced, "I'm going to take a shower."

"I bet you are," Pete mumbled. "I'll let you know when the team gets here."

Fuck. I forgot the team had landed and were on their way over.

I had my suit jacket off by the time I hit Calista's bedroom door. Without knocking, I pushed in, expecting she'd already be in the bathroom. What I didn't expect was for her to be standing in the middle of the room with her head bowed, deep breathing.

That man was no ex-boyfriend. Unless he'd hurt her, in which case I'd be heading back to the Sky View.

"Who was he?"

She righted her head, and her eyes came to mine.

Flames danced in the blue.

Gone was the sweet, pliant woman who I'd kissed a few hours ago, and back was the woman who'd greeted me in the hotel in Abu Dhabi.

Totally closed off and defiant.

Chapter Eighteen

"Drop it." Calli's demand was coupled with a deep frown. Her body language screamed 'back off or else.'

Fuck that.

"Drop it? You froze when you saw him. Now you're standing in your room breathing like you just jogged up the forty-two flights of stairs instead of taking the elevator."

"Fine, Mason, how about this? Who he is, is none of your business."

"Wrong answer." I slammed the door and tossed my jacket on her neatly made bed, which brought me within reaching distance of her.

"Mase—"

"Oh, no, don't Mase me, sweetness. Who the fuck was that?"

She took two steps backward. The retreat would've been smart except she'd backed herself against the wall. I followed and caged her in with a palm on the wall above her shoulder.

My advance was the opposite of smart. A fatal error bringing me too close to the sexy woman in her black dress, spiked heels, and that devil-red lipstick, all of which had been fucking with my head all night. Then there was that sultry perfume that wrapped around my senses and grabbed me by the balls.

"Step back." Her demand came out breathy.

"Not a fucking chance, baby."

Anger flared in her eyes. She inched closer. I braced for a verbal assault.

What came next was an assault of a different kind.

Calli's mouth hit mine, her hands went to the sides of my neck, and her tongue clumsily attempted to push past my lips.

I jerked my head back and looked down at her.

Pupils dilated. Erratic breathing. Flushed face.

Anger, definitely. Lust, absolutely.

"You want this?" I growled.

"Yes." Her answer was hissed.

"Warning, Calli. Later you tell me this was a mistake, I'm gonna be pissed. Call it now, baby. You want my mouth, it's yours, but you take it knowing I will *not* be your regret."

The last word had barely left my mouth when her lips were back on mine. This time, when her tongue touched my lips, I pushed it back into her mouth and guided the kiss, coaxing it deeper until her hands slid up into my hair and she was arching into me.

Heat flooded. Blood rushed south. My body alive and alert.

It had been a long time since I'd fucked a woman. But it could've been yesterday, and still the woman in my arms would've filled me with the same desperate desire. My need to have her was intrinsic, perverse, frantic.

Calli groaned. I slanted my head, taking more of her mouth. One of her hands slid out of my hair, down my neck, chest, stomach, until she was yanking my oxford up. With light fingertips, she traced above the waistband of my slacks. I didn't dare touch her until she asked. Didn't dare move until she was ready for more.

Her hand flattened on my stomach, traveled up. Her blunt nails grazed my nipple and my hips unconsciously bucked. Calli arched deeper. Her hand came out of my shirt and she went for my belt, but she abandoned that in favor of unbuttoning my shirt. She let out a frustrated growl against my tongue that nearly made me smile.

I slapped her hand away and undid the buttons without losing her mouth. Before I had the last one undone, both her hands were exploring. By the time the shirt hit the floor, she was groaning down my throat.

The eighth circle of hell I was in was exquisite torture.

She broke the kiss, panting. She didn't put any distance between us when she begged, "Touch me."

"Where?"

"Everywhere."

Fuck me. *Fuck me.* Fuck me.

I dropped my hands to the hem of her dress and slowly dragged it up her thighs.

"You want this off, Calli?"

Her reply was a moan.

I stopped right before the hem would expose her panties and prompted, "Sweetness?"

"Yes."

"Lift up your arms."

She complied without hesitation. I pulled the dress clear of her body, tossed it to the side, and found myself not breathing.

My gaze raked over her bare tits, flat stomach, down to the black silk covering her pussy.

I'd yet to finish my perusal when Calli's body collided with mine. Skin to skin. Her mouth latched back onto mine. My hands went to her ass and lifted her off her feet, her legs wound around my waist, and there it was—those fucking legs wrapped tight.

Christ.

I broke the kiss, planted my lips on her neck, hoisted her higher, and pulled a waiting nipple into my mouth.

"Oh my God," she groaned.

I drew it in deeper, gave it a swirl before I moved to the other side.

"Oh my God, Mason."

I could feel her hot, wet heat on my stomach. Her hips moving, trying to find the friction she needed.

With a light nip, I released her nipple and asked, "More?"

"Yes."

"You want my mouth on your pussy, sweetness?"

"Yes."

Fucking hell.

I turned, took the three steps I needed to the bed, toed off my shoes, put a knee to the mattress, and all but collapsed on top of her. It wasn't one of my finer moments, however, with all my blood now throbbing in my cock, it was the best I could do.

Calli's legs tightened. She arched deep, tilted her hips. I ground down, and the mewl that tore from her throat was sheer beauty.

Jesus, fuck me.

I broke the kiss and set about earning more of those throaty whimpers. I used my lips, tongue, and teeth to work my way down to her tits. Calli's legs fell open to make room as I lavished both nipples with attention until she was squirming and panting under me.

"More."

All thoughts other than her pleasure disintegrated.

I shifted my balance to my elbow, shoved my hand between us into her panties, and my thumb found her clit. Her body jolted and a sharp cry rent through the room.

"Oh my God!"

I gave her nipple a deep pull, rolled her clit. Her body strung tight, her hips bucked, and she went off.

Jesus fuck. I was going to come just listening to her orgasm.

My thumb slowed to a gentle circle, working her down from her climax until she was soft and panting under me.

"You want more, Calli?"

The question was unnecessary. Her hands already had fistfuls of my hair, and she was communicating her need by shoving my head in the direction she wanted.

The shy, timid side of Calli was sexy.

This bold, take-what-she-wanted side was hot as fuck.

"Words, sweetness. Tell me what you want."

"Your mouth," she slurred, sounding lust drunk.

"Here?" I asked, and lowered my mouth back down to her puckered nipple.

Instead of using my tongue, I scrapped my teeth over the sensitive bud and nipped until her back bowed and she yelped.

"Yes . . . I mean, no, lower."

I released her nipple, skimmed my mouth down to her belly button, and asked, "Here?"

"Lower."

Needing to relieve the ache, I pressed my harder-than-steel cock against the mattress and teased my tongue across her stomach just above her black silk panties.

"Here?"

"Lower."

I hitched her leg up over my shoulder, kissed her inner thigh, and groaned my question. "Here?"

The closer my lips got to her sex, the harder the point of her heel dug into my back. Marks I'd proudly wear, knowing it was me who made this stubborn woman mindless.

"Please, Mason. You're killing me."

Too far gone to continue my game, I yanked the gusset of her panties to the side and gave her a long, slow swipe of my tongue from slit to clit.

Her ass came off the bed and her breathy "Oh my . . . holy shit" filled the room—and I ate.

I couldn't control my desperation if I tried. I *needed* to taste her orgasm, *needed* to feel her come apart again, *needed* to hear her call out my name. That alone should've scared the fuck out of me, but I couldn't muster the fear. My attraction was all consuming, my desire borderline obsessive.

I wanted every part of this woman—not just her orgasm, but her trust.

"Mason, oh shit."

"Is this what you wanted, baby? My tongue fucking your sweet pussy?"

"I think . . . I'm going to . . ."

I shoved my hands under her ass and angled her higher. "Ride my face, Calli."

In spectacular fashion, she did as I asked. The harder she rocked her pussy on my tongue, the harder I ground my cock against the mattress, uncaring I was going to come in my pants.

"Mason," she mewled.

Her hips bucked wildly as I lapped her through her orgasm, moaning "Mine" against her pussy.

I couldn't remember the last time an orgasm had felt so fucking good.

"Mason!"

Shit, motherfucker, that was *not* Calli. It was Pete calling my name.

"Team's here!"

Calista's thighs clenched tight around my head.

I released her ass to tap her hip. She got the hint and released her hold so I could unfortunately roll out from between her legs, but not before I dropped a hard kiss on her clit.

That earned me a sweet, thankfully soft groan.

"I'll be right down," I shouted back.

Immediately, Calista tried to close her legs. I halted her movements, keeping her open for my perusal.

"Mason?"

My gaze tipped up from her pink, swollen, just-tongue-fucked pussy to her soft, sated, pretty face. "Yeah, baby?"

She looked sheepish and shy when she whispered, "What . . . um . . . about you?"

So, I was partly wrong. Bashful, just-had-two-orgasms Calli was hot as fuck.

"You offering to take care of me?" I asked even though not only was it not necessary, but we didn't have time for me to get off.

"I'd like to try."

Try?

There was something in her tone I couldn't put my finger on. It wasn't timidity or hesitation. It sounded more like insecurity.

Calista insecure about anything, but especially when it came to me and my desire for her, was not something I could stomach.

I righted her panties before I shifted up and over her, bringing us face to face.

"First," I started, and settled into the cradle of her legs. My new favorite place to be. "You okay with how that happened?"

Pink hit her cheeks, and for some perverse reason, I liked seeing the color bloom.

"Yes."

"You were pissed—"

"I know what I was," she cut me off. "Then I wasn't."

Right.

Moving on.

"Okay, then I feel the need to ask why you said you'd try to get me off, when you have to know how sexy you are, and on multiple occasions now you've felt my attraction to you."

She seemed to be mulling over how to answer. I'd bet if she had access to her thigh, she'd be tapping her fingers against it.

"There's no guarantee I could . . ."

Her trailing off should've given me concern, but I was too distracted by her pretty blue eyes.

I want to get lost in those eyes forever.

Just as quickly as that thought invaded, I shoved it away, not ready to contemplate why everything about Calista drew me in.

"Well, sweetness, the fact I need to change my pants before I go downstairs and meet my team says otherwise."

Her eyes widened before they darted to the side and her blush deepened.

"You . . . um . . ." she asked the wall.

"As much as it fucks me to admit, I came grinding against the bed like I'm not a grown man. At least I have a good excuse."

Good didn't quite cut it. More like a phenomenal excuse.

"Oh."

"Now, you wanna tell me again you'll *try* to get me off when all it takes is me tasting you and I can't hold back?"

"Nope."

"Right. I'm gonna go change. Are you going to come down and meet the guys? Catarina's with them."

She'd met Jack and Cat in Mexico but not Gavin and Aiden.

"I think I need to shower first."

I dropped my head to nuzzle her neck.

She smelled like sex and her perfume. As much as I hated her washing away what we'd shared, it was probably a good idea.

I pressed a kiss against her throat, before I went in for a real kiss.

Two seconds later, our tongues touched, and once again I was lost in her. It wasn't until my unruly cock jumped back to attention that I broke the kiss.

As soon as I pulled back, Calli's fingertips went to her lips.

"You taste like me," she whispered.

I couldn't stop my smile. "Yeah, baby, that's what happens when—"

Her fingers left her lips to cover my mouth.

"Don't start. If you turn me on, you won't have time—"

My brows winged up. "If?"

Calli rolled her eyes to the ceiling and left them there when she mumbled, "Smug bastard."

There was no heat to her insult. The last thing I wanted to do was go downstairs when Calli was being playful and sweet.

Unfortunately, duty called.

But not before I left her with something to think about.

"I wouldn't call it smug as much as I'd call it confident. And before you call me arrogant, there's no other way I can be when I barely touch you and you come for me." I felt her stiffen beneath me. "I don't know how you could twist that in your head, but I can feel that you did, so let me straighten you out." Calli's eyes narrowed along with her head jerking back on the pillow. I lowered my face so all she could see was me when I informed her, "It's hot, Calista. The way your body responds to me. Not only do I like it, I fucking love how quickly I get you off. It means I get to make you feel good—the more times I can do that, the better. We straight?"

"Yes."

The look in her eyes said we weren't, but I didn't have time to coax it out of her.

"We're not. But I need to get cleaned up, which means we'll continue this later."

"I said I was straight, Mason. No need to talk more about it."

With time being limited, I should've given her that play, but I couldn't.

"Do me a favor, Calista, and don't bullshit me. Not when I'm lying on you while you're naked. Not when I still got the taste of you on my tongue. Not about something as important as me making sure you're not only comfortable about what we've done but also needing to make sure you understand you're safe with me to react and talk to me when you're not clear about something I've said. But mostly, don't ever bullshit me about *anything*."

She completely relaxed under me, her face softened, and her eyes held mine when she softly said, "Okay, Mason."

I was positive it made me a dick, me wanting her to completely trust me when I knew I wouldn't offer her the same.

Yet I couldn't bring myself to feel guilty about it.

Chapter Nineteen

There was a saying about biting off more than you could chew. I wasn't sure if that was exactly the case, but I was definitely in over my head.

Still lying in the bed where Mason had just given me my first ever oral sex experience, I smiled at the ceiling.

I didn't care I was forty and too old to lie in bed, giddy that the boy I liked had gone down on me—the results of that were insanely spectacular. Somehow I didn't think that twentysomething men had mastered the skills Mason had, so for once I didn't feel like I'd missed out on anything. I doubted that many women had the same experience their first time. Or maybe they did, what the hell did I know.

Three orgasms in one day.

Three.

My smile deepened, and I didn't care about that either.

I was going to lie here and bask in my newfound good fortune.

I was going to lie here and pretend I was twenty and allow myself a few moments of immaturity while I remembered every detail of Mason's mouth on me.

I deserved it.

Hell, I'd earned the right to savor the moment.

Later would come soon enough, and reality would come crashing back in.

Later would also mean I'd have to face Pete, who I was pretty sure had heard the culmination of Mason's fantastic cunnilingus.

Good Lord, that was a cringy word.

On that thought, no longer glorying in all things orgasmic but instead embarrassing, I rolled out of bed.

I needed to wash off the five layers of makeup I'd worn out to dinner—which, after two orgasms, felt like a lifetime ago.

Silly but true. It felt like I'd lost track of time when I was with Mason. Like the outside world didn't exist, and it was just me and him in our own version of paradise. Not that I'd admit it to Mason, but even arguing with him made me feel . . . normal.

Up until a few days ago, I'd never exchanged a cross word with Atlanta. We didn't bicker or banter. Tom didn't count; I didn't argue with him. When we didn't see eye to eye, or in the rare cases he attempted to play overprotective overlord, I voiced my disagreement, he voiced his, and that was it. I didn't yell at him, my heart rate didn't elevate, and I certainly didn't get worked up to the point I wanted to jump him and hump his leg.

Oh God, more embarrassment. I'd blundered the whole unbuttoning his shirt, and I think I climbed him like a tree—I couldn't exactly remember that part, I was too turned on, but I was blaming that on Atlanta. She'd put the thought in my head.

I couldn't regret what I'd done, but damn if the timing didn't suck.

Now I had to face Pete and pray that he didn't tell Fallon.

Thankfully, my phone on the dresser rang, stopping my spiraling thoughts before they could get any worse.

Speak of the devil . . . my old pal Atlanta.

"Hey," I greeted.

"Hey?" she greeted back, but hers sounded more like a question.

I waited for her to go on. Normally I could withstand the silence, but not when I was in the middle of an embarrassment episode—was that a real thing?

"You called?" I broke and asked.

"I wanted to see how your dinner with Amir went, but now I want to know why you sound . . . squeaky."

Squeaky?

Great.

Perfect.

I traded my oral sex V-card for a squeaky voice.

"I don't know what you're talking about," I told her, as I made my way into the bathroom and closed the door. My gaze caught my reflection and my breath caught in my lungs. My one breast had . . . was that . . . beard burn?

"What's happening right now?" Atlanta asked. "You sound like you're having an asthma attack."

"Nothing's happening," I wheezed.

But something was. The evidence of Mason's claiming was right there on my breast.

His mark.

I clenched my thighs at the sight.

If Pete hadn't interrupted, would I have begged him for sex? Yes, absolutely. Yes, without question, I'd been ready for more.

"Calista," Atlanta snapped. "You didn't hear a word I said, did you?"

"What'd you say?"

"Okay, seriously, what the hell is going on? Did Amir do something?"

Shit, I knew that tone, it was Atlanta's *I'm going to ruin your life with a few keystrokes* voice.

"No. Dinner went fine. He's slimy, made a few passes, but I made it clear I was uninterested, and he let it go. Mason was there the whole time. Fallon too. But . . . Jason was there."

"What? At dinner?"

"At the bar. I saw him as I was walking out."

"Fuck, Calli."

Fuck was right. I'd lost my advantage.

"It'll be fine. I lost the element of surprise in the sense he knows I'm in Dubai, but he'd never imagine who I've turned into. The only thing he's going to find on me is that I'm a freelance journalist. Most of my articles are about crimes against women and children. With my background, that won't raise any red flags. I'm proceeding as planned. Which reminds me, did you get ahold of Tanner?"

Atlanta blew out a harassed breath. "Yes. I gave him the information on Sparkle." I didn't miss her chuckle slash sneer. "He said it would take him a few days to get a team together, but he'll take care of it."

"And my kit?"

"He's got a Steyr DMR and two Colt M-nineteen-elevens for you."

I would've preferred a Knight's Armament SR-25, but a beggar can't be choosy.

"What kind of glass on the Steyr?"

Her *pfft* made me smile. "Like I'd let Tanner give you shit optics. He sighted in a Leupold Mark 5HD for you at a thousand yards, just in case. But it's not like you're gonna use the Steyr."

She was correct. The long-distance rifle was a just-in-case backup. This particular mission would be up close and personal.

"Thanks."

"On a scale of a little mad to super-extra-double mad, where are you now?"

My exhale felt like I'd let out a breath I'd been holding for twenty years. Maybe it was because I was so close to finally getting peace for my sister, or maybe it was the three glorious orgasms Mason had given me, or maybe I was just tired of my life, but I felt like I could almost taste my freedom.

"A few notches up from a little mad but nowhere near *really* mad."

"Okay, now that we got the fun stuff out of the way, tell me why, when you answered, you sounded . . . strange."

"I thought you said I sound squeaky," I reminded her.

And why am I having this conversation in only my undies?

I snatched a towel off the bar and wrapped it around me.

"You did, which is strange. You normally have this husky phone-sex operator voice—"

"I do not."

"Girl, I've been on comms with you when you're working a mark. You add this almost Southern honey to your voice when you're trying to canoodle. I'm a chick who likes dick, but even I think it's hot. But I've never heard your voice get high pitched."

Canoodle.

I shook my head and stared at the floor. "It's . . . personal."

"You banged your fake bodyguard," she whooped.

"I didn't bang him."

"Why the hell not?"

Because I'm a virgin!

No, that wasn't the truth. I'd been ready to happily shed that designation.

"We were interrupted," I admitted. "Not visually. No one walked in on us. But Pete knocked on the door, and I think he heard." I rushed out the *heard* part.

"Oopsie."

"Oopsie? That's all you have for me? Mason's downstairs with his team now. Gavin, Aiden, Jack, and Catarina just got to the penthouse, and I'm hiding in the bathroom."

"Okay, now I get the squeak. You just did it again. But I don't get what the big deal is. You and Mason are two unattached . . . wait, he's single, right?"

"Of course he is."

"Right. Good. Two single, consenting adults fooling around. You said Pete didn't walk in on you, so what's the big deal, he heard a little moaning and grunting. Wait, you weren't getting all freaky-deaky asking to ride him like a camel, were you? Not that there's anything wrong with that, fly your freak flag, sis, but—"

"Camel?" I choked out. "Ride him like a *camel*? What the hell, Atlanta. That's not freaky, that's weird."

Why had I answered the phone?

"Sorry. I was reading a Brittney Sahin romance last night." *Wait, what? Atlanta reads romance books?* "Actually, the book takes place in

Dubai. The hero was after a terrorist, and the heroine was trying to free her best friend from jail before he was beheaded. There was a scene in the desert with a camel. The book's really good. You should try it. Oh, and shit, the hero was pretending to be her bodyguard too! And so you know, there was some well-written tent nookie. Maybe you and Mason should go rent a tent."

Unfortunately, my life wasn't a Brittney Sahin novel. Though I should look her up and stock up on some of her books before I slipped away to my no-people-allowed oasis.

"I think you've lost the plot of my story," I grumbled.

"No, I haven't. My point is, there's nothing to be embarrassed about. Sex is natural. Besides, it would seriously suck if Mason was giving you the business and he couldn't bring it home."

Mason had no problem bringing it home—quickly, as he pointed out. Something else to be embarrassed about. The man barely had to touch me and I was a sopping-wet mess primed to explode.

"Okay, well, thanks for the talk. I need to shower off the gallons of makeup before I get wrinkles."

Leaving makeup on doesn't cause wrinkles, dumbass.

"Right. Wrinkles," she called my bluff. "Tanner will be in touch. I gave him this number to arrange delivery."

Shit, he couldn't deliver my kit here. I'd need to set up a place to meet him.

"Great. Thanks."

"Before I let you go, Jason . . . did he recognize you? It's been twenty years. You're older now, and when you're all glammed up, you don't look like you."

I thought about the way Jason was staring at me. The bar was dimly lit and he was across the room. I was hoping (probably for naught) the way he was looking at me was nothing more than him noticing a woman in a tight black dress. I, on the other hand, could pick that asshole out of a crowded room without issue. But that's what happens when you look at a picture of the man you're obsessed with nearly every day for two decades.

I doubted Jason ever gave me or my sister a passing thought.

"I'd like to say no. But, maybe."

"We'll figure it out."

We wouldn't, but I would.

One way or another, this ended here. It had to.

"Talk soon."

Before she could give me any more horrible advice like mounting Mason like a donkey, I hung up.

Just because I was already in the frying pan, I figured I'd continue my stupidity and jump straight into the fire. Instead of going downstairs after my long hot shower, where I'd found more beard burn between my legs, I opted for our balcony.

This time, I was out there first on my lounger, with nothing but silence and my thoughts.

The skyline and lights did nothing for me. I'd much prefer a view of the mountains or ocean. I closed my eyes and let my mind wander. First back to Mexico, after Catarina caught me running from Ahmad's people after I'd escaped. I had to admit that was a close call . . .

Carlos Quintero, may his soul be rotting in hell, had taken the bait and me. Tom needed a connection between Ahmad and the cartel in Juárez. Unfortunately, after I'd put the word out that a blonde-haired, blue-eyed virgin was roaming the streets alone in Juárez, Carlos had gone rogue and taken me on a joyride across Mexico to sell me directly to Ahmad, cutting out the cartel.

That had been a bust, but in true Tom fashion, he'd spun it to higher-ups and still got approval to take out Ahmad. I'd been hoping Carlos would reach out to Jason Anderson and I'd be taken to Berlin. But not every op goes according to plan.

PACE.

Primary, alternate, contingency, and emergency.

I'd moved to the contingency part. Tom jumped the gun and went to emergency and sent in Pete and his team to rescue me.

At the time, I'd been furious. Now, I wasn't sure I had it in me to be angry Tom had unintentionally brought Mason into my life. Same with Atlanta. Maybe that's why I was slowly forgiving her for going behind my back. At this point, I was nursing my grudge on principle. If she hadn't texted him, I wouldn't've had *this*—our balcony and stolen moments with a man who made me feel alive, human, like a woman . . . and not the one I'd turned into under Tom's tutelage.

"With that frown, I'm not sure if I'm waking you up from a nightmare or interrupting you plotting murder."

Both.

My eyes popped open to find Mason sitting on his lounger, elbows resting on his black sweatpants-covered knees.

Too bad they weren't gray, then the Instagram-inspired fantasy would be complete. Was he commando under those sweatpants? Did I want to find out? Hell yes, I did. Jeez, I'd gone from not thinking about sex to being a horny virgin.

Gah. I hated that word. Actually, I was beginning to hate both of them.

"Calli?" he prompted.

"Sorry I didn't go downstairs," I mumbled, not offering an explanation that would likely lead to questions I didn't want to answer.

"It's late, and it was a long day for them. Nothing more than hellos were exchanged before they took off to find a bed."

With me having my own room, the guys would have to double up. Unless they were going to sleep on the mini couches in the living room. I didn't know what Gavin and Aiden looked like, but there was no way Fallon, Jack, Mason, or Pete would fit on any of the sofas.

"I don't know if I ever apologized for threatening to shoot you back in Mexico," I blurted out.

Mason chuckled good-naturedly. "If memory serves, your magazine was empty."

It had been, and at the time, he'd pointed it out.

"I was just pissed Tom sent a team to rescue me."

"So you've said."

"I have an irrational aversion to feeling beholden to someone. My father and Tom had this relationship where each of them felt obligated to the other. Neither of them actually respected or cared about the other. It was a circle of debt. My father provided intel to Tom. Tom kept my family safe. My father saved Tom's life. Tom offered more protection. The circle was never ending—or it should've ended when my father died, but instead I stupidly jumped on the merry-go-round."

I should've found a way to take out Jason without Tom's involvement. But hindsight was twenty-twenty, and at the time, I'd been blinded by grief and anger.

Hard green eyes held me captive when he asked, "Is that what you feel, Calista? Indebted to me and my team?"

Instead of telling him what I knew he wanted to hear, I searched my feelings. Did I feel indebted to Mason? Was that why I was so drawn to him? Because he'd shown up for me, twice now, to have my back when no one else did?

That couldn't be it. I didn't feel the same connection to Pete, and he was there.

"No," I finally answered. "I feel grateful but not beholden. I feel linked to you but not obligated."

I saw the tension bleed from his features, but more than that, I saw relief sweep over him.

"It's late, Calli. You should get some sleep."

It was well after midnight, and I was exhausted, but I wasn't ready to go back to my room and climb into an empty bed, ending *Calli and Mase* time.

"Where are you sleeping tonight?"

"Out here. Gavin took my bed."

It was a warm evening. Sleeping on the lounger wouldn't be uncomfortable, but still, I didn't want him spending the night out on the balcony.

"We can share my bed," I offered.

Mason's smile was quick, but it morphed into a smirk just as fast.

"Not sure either of us would get much sleep if we shared your bed."

One could hope that was the case.

I shrugged, uncaring my robe gapped open at the movement. At this point he'd seen my breasts, sucked and licked and left his mark of ownership. My thighs clenched at the memory. I dared not look, but I wondered if the beard burn was visible. I hoped so. I wanted to see it again in the morning when I got dressed.

Mason's groan cut through my thoughts.

"You sure?"

"Absolutely."

Mason stood and offered his hand.

I stared at his calloused palm that had touched nearly every inch of me. Maybe not every inch, but all the important ones. But it wasn't the memories of what he could do with those long, thick, magical fingers that had me captivated. Something about this moment felt different, life altering, and not in a give-up-my-V-card kind of way. As if by taking Mason's hand, he'd change the course of my entire future.

"Calli?" he called. "If you've changed—"

Before the moment slipped away, I reached up and grabbed Mason's hand.

When his fingers curled tightly around my hand, I knew I'd made the right decision.

Chapter Twenty

"Is this okay?" Calli whispered.

Was it okay she'd rolled into me as soon as we got into bed and rested her cheek on my chest? Ten years ago and with any other woman, I would've stopped the progress before she'd made it to my side of the bed. But Calista wasn't any other woman. The reason still escaped me, but it couldn't be denied there was something there.

I curled my arm tighter and answered in the same soft tone she'd used. "Yeah, baby."

Calli relaxed into me before I could get a lock on exactly why the feel of her pressed close calmed my mind, while at the same made my heart rate kick up.

I couldn't shake the feeling something was about to happen, something big, something I wasn't ready for. Something that would make it difficult to allow Calli to walk away from me.

"Are you happy?"

The way she asked, like she genuinely cared and my answer would either break her heart or fill her with joy, made my gut clench.

"In general, yeah, I'm happy. I've got good friends, work that I can't say I like because the nature of what we do isn't likable, but it saves lives. I have a bar that gives me headaches, but that has to do with trivial shit, nothing life or death, so it's easy, most days enjoyable. I live in paradise and drink my coffee on my deck with a view of the ocean."

Now that the words had left my mouth, was that happy or was that content? Was I missing out on the kind of happiness Jack had found because I'd closed myself off to the possibility of love, or was I playing it smart, choosing a bachelor life over potential heartbreak and a messy end?

I didn't bother asking Calli if she was happy. I knew the answer to that.

But I was curious . . .

"Right now, are you happy, baby?"

"Yes."

Straight out, no hesitation. Fuck me, I liked that.

"Good."

The silence stretched, neither of us filling it. I tried to shove my wandering thoughts back into the box where they belonged, musings of what life would be like with Calli by my side. The fights we'd undoubtedly have because that was us. The woman would drive me crazy. She'd go head-to-head with me and not back down. And why did I find that so appealing? Why did I suddenly want to know what it would be like to wake up and find Calli out on my deck, soaking in the peace of the early-morning rays?

What if she didn't walk away? What if I could give her the peace she needed?

What if we ended in a disaster, where would that leave me? Emily had destroyed me. Calista betraying me would annihilate me.

"Can I tell you a secret?" Calista's voice wobbled, causing me to brace for the worst.

I tried to inject calmness I was no longer feeling into my tone, but my answer sounded rough to my own ears. "Sure."

She didn't immediately tell me her secret. She cuddled closer, like she was attempting to transfer whatever she wanted to tell me telepathically.

"Calli," I prompted.

"I'm a virgin."

Her words were a barely there whisper. So faint they were almost inaudible. There was no way I'd heard her correctly.

"I didn't hear you, sweetness. What'd you say?"

"I'm a virgin," she repeated. Then added, "At forty."

The impossibility of that hit me in the gut, but before I could muster the anger over her lying to me, I remembered her shy, tentative touching. Her barely there tongue touch.

What you tasted like.

I've never had a man.

Never had a man, not in a relationship way like we'd been talking about, but physically.

What. The. Fuck.

How was that possible?

"Say something," she pleaded.

Calli was a virgin, and I'd finger-fucked her twice and eaten her out.

I had so many questions, but I settled on "Why?"

"Why am I telling you, or why am I still a virgin?"

"Both."

I felt her draw in a breath, then felt her exhale.

"I was a virgin when Lili was taken. After, with everything going on, sex was the last thing on my mind. Then we found out she'd been trafficked, and sex became evil. It was the reason she'd been taken from me. The thought of someone touching me made me sick. My sister was kidnapped, sold, and her body used. She had no control over hers, but I had control over mine.

"I wasn't going to tell you." Her admission was coupled with another deep breath, this one shaky. "But not telling you first felt wrong. It would make me worse than all those women who screwed you over in the past combined."

I could understand how Calista would equate sex with being evil. Extreme grief had a way of twisting shit up. But Calli was right, her sister had been taken so that disgusting, vile men could use her for sex. Though the act wasn't evil, the men who used her were.

Wait.

What?

"First?" I questioned.

Without warning, Calli moved. A long leg slid over my thigh, and she hoisted herself over me to straddle my hips, and thank fuck it was dark in the room and the eyeful of her breasts was shadowed when her robe parted.

Fuck me, not the best position for a newly discovered virgin like Calista to be in. Not when my cock had a mind of its own around her.

"Another reason I never let anyone touch me is because there's trust involved in allowing someone close, at least for me there is. A vulnerability I was never comfortable giving anyone. Until you."

Until me.

Jesus, fuck me.

"Calli, baby, I can't—"

"You can't or you won't fuck me, now that you know I'm a pathetic virgin?"

Pathetic?

Hell no.

"There's nothing pathetic about you. There's strength in your decision. The gift you have to give should be given to someone special."

"And you're not special?"

My throat got tight. Emotion clogged my airway. I didn't know what to say to that, but if I had, I still wouldn't've been able to speak.

Special?

Me?

"And you're right," she went on. "It's mine to give. My choice. And I want to give it to you. I want you to be my first. I trust your honesty. I can be me with you. I know I'm being selfish, asking you to break a promise you made to yourself. But I'm still asking because, if I don't, I'll regret it for the rest of my life."

The promise I'd made to myself didn't apply to Calista. She could never be an empty orgasm. But the gravity of what she was asking gave me pause. It wasn't the gift of her giving me her virginity, it was what receiving it would do to me.

I was already having a hard time reconciling her leaving. Watching her walk away from me, knowing I'd forever carry a piece of her with me, made my stomach roil. We'd be tied together in an unforgettable way.

A few hours ago, if Pete hadn't interrupted, I was ready to slide inside of her, vows and promises and consequences be damned. But this felt different.

She misread my indecision and mumbled dejectedly, "I get it. It's too weird."

I halted her swinging off of me by grabbing two handfuls of her sweet, round ass.

"You don't get it, Calli. This is cliché as fuck, but it's not you, it's me. Nothing about you is weird. It's about what I'm feeling. How *much* I'm feeling. And truthfully, it scares the fuck out of me."

"I get that."

I wasn't sure she understood the enormity of my feelings, and I didn't miss she felt something for *me*. I just didn't think it was on the same level.

Yet, I couldn't fucking deny her, even knowing in the end she'd break me.

"You need to tell me exactly what it is you want."

Her hands hit my chest, she leaned forward, the robe split wider, and her breasts were now dangerously close to snapping my sanity. Not that I already hadn't lost my mind.

"You. I just want you."

An unhealthy need exploded in my chest. My stiff cock hardened painfully, ready to take what she so beautifully offered.

But, fuck.

"I don't have a condom."

I wasn't sure if that was my saving grace to stop my recklessness or if this was the true meaning of hell on earth. Having something I wanted more than my next breath so close but not being able to take it.

Torture.

"Well, since I've never . . . and you haven't for a long time . . . and I have the birth control implant, we're covered."

I didn't ask why she had birth control covered. I knew. And the thought of why she'd cover herself against pregnancy—just in case she was violated—made me murderous. Burn-cities-to-the-ground homicidal.

"I've never had sex without a condom," I admitted.

"Neither have I," she teased.

Her body shook in silent laughter above me, doing a number on my self-control. There was only so much I could take with her pussy shuddering over my rock-hard, ready-to-go erection.

But she had to guide this. All of it.

"Kiss me, Calli."

Without delay, her palms glided from my stomach up to my pecs as she brought her mouth closer. By the time her lips touched mine, every muscle in my body was strung tight in anticipation. When our tongues met, my hands on her ass gave an encouraging squeeze.

She was in control.

Her pace.

Even if every soft slide of her tongue killed me, I wouldn't rush her. When she started rocking her hips, I knew death was a real possibility.

Calli broke the kiss long enough to issue a demand. "Touch me."

I lifted her ass up enough I could slide a hand between us, shoving the robe out of my way as I went. *Fuck me.* No panties. My knuckles grazed my eager cock as my fingers went in search of heaven.

"Christ," I groaned, finding her sex drenched.

"Yes," she purred, and nudged herself against my finger toying with her opening.

Using every ounce of restraint I could muster, I slowly pushed a finger inside. Calli had other ideas when she immediately started rocking.

"More."

I ignored her request and gently built her excitement until she was panting. I pulled my finger free and pushed back in with two.

"Mason."

Jesus, fuck me, her breathy whimper hit me square in the chest—the left side to be exact. With each choppy exhale against my lips, the barbed wire around my heart started to loosen. Every shudder, every agitated jerk of her hips, felt like a defibrillator shocking my heart back into a rhythm that was as painful as it was impeccable.

"More, Mase."

With my pulse pounding, my dick aching, I needed clarification. "You want my cock, baby?"

"Yes."

I pulled my fingers free, slid them through her wet, toying with her opening. I tried again. "You sure you want this, Calli?"

"Yes. Now."

The need to claim, to get inside of her, to feel her wet heat take my cock was overpowering.

"Robe off."

Calista easily complied. My hands went to her hips, gliding up her silhouette, moving in to cup her breasts. She immediately arched.

I swept my thumb over her nipple and invited, "Lean forward."

As soon as she was in reach, I pulled a nipple into my mouth. Calli arched deeper, groaning her approval.

I released the taut bud and, on my way to the other side, I ordered, "Pull me out, baby."

As consuming as my desire was, I needed her to take this next step.

Her movements were clumsy and frenzied when she reached between us to free my weeping dick in the limited space she had.

Her hand wrapping around my shaft had my hips thrusting into her fist, nudging her clit and pulling a groan from both of us. I went back to her abandoned nipple, and with each drag of my tongue, Calli circled her hips, bringing the crown of my cock precariously close to her center until she had the tip lined up.

Her thighs tensed as she started to lower herself down.

"Slow," I gritted out, as I felt the head of my cock glide through her excitement.

"I need—"

"Slow, Calli," I interrupted her. Needing her to go easy for both of our sakes.

"I need . . ." She trailed off, wheezing out a breath.

I knew what she needed. That same need was coursing through my veins.

"Calli." I growled her name as a warning.

One she didn't heed when she dropped down on my cock, taking half of my length.

"Jesus," I grunted, clamping down on my back teeth tight.

"God!" Her oath was nothing more than a gasp as she pulled up to the tip.

On her second attempt, she slammed down, taking all of me.

Calista's reaction was borderline violent. She half screamed, half moaned. Her tight-as-hell pussy clamped around my cock and her body shuddered.

Home.

Time stood still.

And in that moment, I finally experienced what it meant to physically feel beauty.

I used my free hand to cup her face, forcing her to look at me.

"Are you okay?"

"Yes," she rasped.

Her thighs clenched my hips, and her nails dug into my shoulder.

"Relax, Calli, and breathe."

"I need to move."

I needed her to move, but not before I knew she wasn't in pain.

She's a virgin, asshole, of course she's in pain.

Or was one until she'd impaled herself on my cock.

Christ.

"Please don't make me stop," she pleaded.

She squeezed her thighs tighter, her cunt clamped around my cock painfully as she inched up and slid back down.

"Take what you need, baby," I groaned.

"I want you on top."

"I want you in control. I don't want to hurt you."

"You won't hurt me, Mason. I want you, all of you. I trust you."

Jesus. Fuck me. *Fuck me.* Fuck me.

"You promise to tell me—"

"Yes."

The word had barely left her mouth when I flipped us over.

I closed my eyes and dropped my head to her forehead.

Good Christ, this woman owned me.

I'd dig to the deepest depths of my control to give her what she needed, to make this good for her even if I died in the process.

And while she was at it, she could have my heart and soul if it meant she wouldn't walk away.

Chapter Twenty-One

Mason lifted his head to look down at me.

I was mesmerized by the sight. Big, beautiful Mason Hughes on top of me, connected bodily, skin to skin. As amazing as the sight was, I needed more. My breasts felt full and heavy, my nipples were ultrasensitive from Mason's mouth, and my core clenched and ached at the same time.

"Calista," Mason groaned, sounding pained.

"I need . . ." I trailed off, unable to communicate what I needed.

Mason eased out of me. "I know what you need."

All right, okay, yes, he knew what I needed. That felt good. He slowly pushed back in, and that felt better.

"Okay?" he asked.

"Oh yeah," I breathed.

Mason gave me a few more slow, sluggish, languid strokes. The ache intensified. I was hot and shivering at the same time. I felt restless. My skin tingled.

"I need to move, baby. You ready for more?" His rough, hoarse voice sent a tremor through me.

"Yes."

Mason's lips went to my neck. I tilted my head back, giving him better access. His tongue blazed a trail down to my throat, and there, he told me in that same coarse, raw voice that made my blood heat, "Wrap your legs around me."

I did as I was told. Then something amazing happened—Mason slid deeper.

Now *that* felt great. Overwhelmingly, astoundingly great.

"Fuck, Calli, you feel beautiful."

So did he, but my breath left my lungs in a whoosh, taking my voice with it when his hand skimmed over my breast. All thoughts vanished when his thrusts became more powerful—deeper, not faster. His thumb strummed my nipple. I arched, wanting more of something I didn't understand.

Instinctively, my hips surged up. "Oh my God."

Tremors shot through me. My legs tightened. My hands decided to get in the game, moving around to his back where hard, smooth, hot skin awaited. I could feel his tension under my palms, muscles coiled, straining to keep control.

I didn't want Mason's control. I wanted him to feel what he was giving me.

"More," I whimpered.

His fingers captured my nipple, his thrusts turned into drives, the tension in his back tightened. The throbbing between my legs became unbearable. I squirmed with each plunge of his cock, grinding, reaching, craving.

Mason groaned against my throat. I felt the vibration. I memorized it. I locked it away to revisit it later—every feeling, every thrust, every breath, every groan, touch, kiss. They were mine for eternity. I could lose everything, I could never have it again, but I'd never lose this. I'd never forget.

"Christ," he rasped. "So fucking beautiful. Nothing better than your sleek, tight pussy taking my cock."

I felt a rush of wet. My breath hitched. My orgasm floated just out of reach. I felt like I was going to come out of my skin, fevered, frantic, desperate.

"Look at me, baby."

I opened my eyes, not remembering when I closed them, but happy he'd ordered them open. No, seeing the stark desire swirling in his eyes, the normal jade green now emerald, I was ecstatic.

"You're gonna let go and come with me," he told me with a swivel of his hips, grinding down hard.

That desperate feeling strengthened with each drive of his cock. My pulse went wild. The air around me felt like I was in a sauna, hot and humid and hard to breathe.

"Mason," I pleaded, trembling all over.

He forged deeper, harder, faster, angled his thrusts just right.

Then everything disappeared, his hot skin under my palms, the air in my lungs, my legs, his eyes. All that was left was the sweetest euphoria I'd ever experienced. An explosion that swept me away into a place where all I could feel was intense pleasure.

"That's it, Calli. Fuck, baby, fuck!"

I sucked in breath, only to have it stolen again when Mason's thrusts turned ruthless, uncontrolled, brutal.

"Oh my God!"

Every nerve was alive with sensation. My inner muscles clenched and clutched, greedy for more.

For the first time in my life, I felt alive. I gloried in it, succumbed to the bliss, flew apart, and danced in the flames.

Mason buried his face in my neck and groaned. Two more thrusts, he planted himself to the root, and he followed me into ecstasy with his body jolting, his cock jerking, his heart pounding against my chest.

Together.

Connected.

For one beautiful moment in time, I had everything.

I had Mason.

The exquisiteness of it was branded on my skin for only me to know.

My brain slowly came back on station. If this was the only time I was going to have this, I was taking everything I could. With that in mind, my hands went back to exploring. The tension had eased from his frame, but he was still hot—hard muscle under silky, damp skin. God, I loved how he felt, his weight, his lips on my neck, his cock, his hands.

I wanted to keep him, stay with him, have this for always.

But he wasn't mine to keep.

Later, I would miss this.

Mason slowly lifted his head. His gaze immediately found mine. Searching in his Mason way, looking for something that was not there. I would not tell him this was a mistake, because it wasn't. I wouldn't apologize because I wasn't sorry he'd given me something I'd never forget. I wouldn't regret a single second.

I knew he found what he needed when he brushed his lips over mine, finishing with a soft kiss to the corner of my mouth. It was sweet, made sweeter when lips moved to my temple and kissed me there, then to my forehead, my other cheek, and my jaw.

Who knew Mason Hughes could be tender, peppering my face with kisses? I wouldn't have guessed, but now that I'd been on the receiving end of all that tenderness, I gloried in that too.

He shifted, taking away some of his weight, and his hand came up to brush some errant strands of hair off my face.

"Unwrap, baby, so I can get you cleaned up."

I didn't unwrap. I tightened my legs, and my muscles clenched in a new, frightening way.

"Calli," he moaned. "Christ, baby, you already milked every last drop out of me."

I didn't understand what he was saying. Obviously, he read my confusion because he went on to explain, and that, too, was frightening.

"When you tighten like that, I feel it. Just not those long, sexy legs holding me close, but inside."

"Oh."

He was quiet for a second. His eyes roaming my face, taking me in, not in study but in something else.

"I took you rough," he whispered.

He had. It was glor-ee-ous. I couldn't help the clench.

"Jesus," he grunted. "Your pussy is a miracle."

Not exactly a flowery compliment but a damn sexy one.

"I need to pull out, baby."

That was disappointing.

"What if I don't want you to?" I asked sheepishly.

Now that the desire was at a simmer instead of a rolling boil ready to scald me, it was easy to remember up until a little bit ago, I'd been a virgin. And just because I no longer carried that particular card, I still had no experience in what happened next.

Mason swept his thumb over my cheek. "Trust me, sweetness, the last thing I want is to lose your tight, wet heat. But I've got a few more seconds before I'm hard again."

That didn't sound like a bad thing. "And?"

A slow, lazy smile formed. No, a slow, lazy, satisfied smirk formed.

He didn't answer. Instead, he told me, "You're crazy beautiful, Calista."

"You're crazy hot, Mason," I returned.

"I took—"

All right. Enough was enough.

"You didn't take anything," I interrupted. "It was mine to give, and I gave it to you. You didn't hurt me."

"Baby, your scream said otherwise. And if that didn't do it, the tears brimming in your eyes would've."

I had to give him that.

"It was a shock. A pinch of pain. But you didn't hurt me." He looked unconvinced, so I added, "I promise, Mason."

"Okay, Calli. You trusted me with that, now I need you to trust me again and unwrap so I can see to you."

That sounded scary. But I unlocked my ankles. He slowly slid out. I groaned. He moaned. As soon as I lost him, he scooted down and pressed his mouth between my breasts, then another to my belly, and one more lower still, right above where my panties would've been if I'd been wearing them.

I felt that in my womb.

"Be back," he told me, as he exited the bed and hitched up his sweats. But he didn't walk away until he yanked the corner of the comforter up and covered my naked body.

I watched him disappear into the bathroom, thinking there was something erotic about me being fully nude, while he'd only had me pull his sweats down far enough to free his cock.

I'd had sex with Mason with his pants pulled down to his thighs.

Frantic. Desperate. Desire fueled.

Now that was the way to lose your virginity.

Mason came back into the room, his lean hips and six-pack on display. All of that was hot, but it was his chest and shoulders that had me enthralled. And his biceps. He was muscled and cut all over, but I had a special affinity for his chest and arms; the former was the first part of him I'd touched. And those arms had carried me to bed—twice now.

Two times I'd been carried by Mason—two times I'd been safe there.

He stopped by the side of the bed, stared down at me but didn't speak. I gave him a few seconds of silence before fear inched in.

The slap of reality hit me.

I haven't fucked a woman in ten years.

Just because I didn't regret what we'd done didn't mean *he* didn't.

"Everything okay?" I whispered.

"Better than a dream," he mumbled, like he wasn't talking to me. "You ready to trust me some more?"

"Yes."

Without preamble, the covers were thrown off me. Mason scooped me up off the mattress. My arms went around his neck, and he made his way into the bathroom.

Three times.

In a perfect world, there'd be hundreds more.

But the world sucked, so I'd remember this time too.

He set me on my feet next to the partially filled bathtub.

I tried not to allow my disappointment to show. He was taking care of me by running me a bath, but I wasn't ready for him to leave.

Do not get clingy, I warned myself.

"Oh, yeah, better than a dream," he declared with a top-to-toe perusal.

I tried not to squirm under his scrutiny, but I failed. Especially when his fingers grazed up the inside of my thigh, gathering the wetness that was leaking.

"Fuck," he growled, and tipped his eyes up. "I know it says something about me, how much I like my come dripping down your thigh, but I can't begin to give a fuck what it says."

My breath was stuck in my throat. So it was a good thing he didn't seem to want a response when his lips gently pressed against mine and he gave me a gentle shove.

"In, baby."

Damn. Overtime was over.

I would not show disappointment.

I stepped into the tub, inhaled, and turned to say something that was likely going to be stupid because there were no words to express how much he meant to me. He'd broken his vow to himself and given me something I'd cherish.

Some girls dreamed of roses on the bed and declarations of love upon losing their virginity.

Not me.

If I'd ever given it any thought, what Mason had given me was exactly what I would've wanted.

Respect.

Control over my choice.

And care and gentleness.

On top of that, he made it good for me—phenomenal, actually. He'd given me everything and didn't make me feel silly for holding on to something most people lost by the time they were in their twenties.

But when I'd turned, his sweats were off and his very large penis was on display.

"Holy shit."

"Calli." I heard the humor in his voice but ignored it.

"Holy shit."

His humor turned into a chuckle. "Sweetness."

I knew it was rude to stare, but for the love of all things holy in the universe, I'd never seen a dick in real life. He was thick, and even flaccid there was a good deal of length, then there was the bell head . . . all of that making a very pretty picture.

"That's um . . ." I cleared my throat. "That's . . ." I ran out of words, even though I'd technically only said one and made a nonsensical sound.

"You gonna let me in or stand there and stare at my cock?"

"I think I want to stare at it a bit longer. I'm trying to figure out how it fit."

"It fit," he reminded me.

I don't know if it fit as much as I'd muscled it inside of me, and my vagina had no choice but to accept the intrusion.

"I think I need another demonstration."

"Goof," he muttered, and moved to turn off the water.

Since I lost sight of his dick, I took in the rest of him. My first look of him completely naked only cemented my earlier assessment—he was hard everywhere, like he was carved out of stone.

Mason stepped into the tub behind me, and for the first time since I'd stepped foot into the penthouse, I appreciated the extravagance. Or maybe I just appreciated the gigantic bathtub that could hold five adults comfortably.

His hands went to my hips. With a gentle squeeze, he ordered, "Sit, sweetness."

Mase helped me down. His back against the tub, my back against his chest, his legs bracketing mine, I was in a perfect cocoon of Mason Hughes safety. This was better than our cone of silence on the balcony.

"Okay, Calli, we need to talk about what happened."

I felt every muscle from my toes to my scalp tense.

"Relax."

Such a man, telling a woman to relax, like him ordering it will make it so.

Spoiler alert: I didn't relax.

"Mason—"

As if I didn't speak, he went on. "First, I want you to know I'll never forget all that you gave me, how precious it was, how gorgeous. Straight up, Calista, no lie—I will cherish that gift forever." I started to melt against him. Unfortunately, that was short lived. "But, sweetness, you held on to that for a long time."

There was an unasked question in his statement, even though I'd told him why. Probably more than one. And truth was, I owed him more of an explanation.

I had nothing to be embarrassed about, and I wasn't, but it was awkward and uncomfortable, which was stupid because I'd had this man inside my body.

"I blamed sex for killing my sister. Then I started working with Tom, and I learned what was *really* happening. Porn. Prostitution. Slavery. All of it evil. All of it solely based on sex.

"Logically, I knew it wasn't the act of sex. I just had no interest in sharing that part of myself with someone. At some point, me being a virgin was just weird, and the thought of telling someone why or talking about my sister wasn't something I wanted to do."

"Just to point out, Calli, *I'm* someone, and you just explained it to me. And there's nothing weird about you not giving someone something you don't want to share. Especially your body."

"But you're not someone . . . you're Mason," I lamely retorted.

His body went rigid behind me, and his thighs pushed tighter against mine.

"I am that," he said, his voice thick with an emotion I didn't understand.

"You get it," I softly told him. "All of it. I'm safe with you."

His hands came out of the water, his arms went around me, and he held me tightly to his chest.

"Yeah, Calli, you're always safe with me."

Always.

I wished that were true.

I wished I could live for always in the cocoon of Mason Hughes.

Chapter Twenty-Two

I knew she was awake, but I wasn't ready for her to roll away—wasn't ready to lose her to any regret she may have.

That would kill my soul.

It had been a long time since I'd woken up in bed next to a woman. So long, it felt like another life—and not a good one worth remembering. And I'd certainly never curled around a woman with the sole purpose of holding her close, not wanting to let go.

"What are you thinking about?" Calli asked softly.

Of course, my smart girl knew I was awake too.

"How much I like lying here with you."

Calli shifted her ass deeper into my crotch but abruptly stopped when her bare ass met my hard-on.

"Ignore it."

"It's kinda hard to ignore."

I didn't want to be that asshole who couldn't control his base urges. I'd done what I could so she wouldn't feel what her warm, soft body was doing to mine. Now she knew and, like me, she'd have to ignore it for now.

"What about you?" I asked. "What are you thinking about?"

"That I wished we weren't ignoring your penis."

Penis.

Christ, she was cute.

"Just to say, Calli, boys have penises. Men have cocks. Dick is also acceptable. Never peen, penis, or willy."

"Is that in the Man Rulebook?"

"Yep. Page one, paragraph two, right under the one that explains how to be a gentleman."

"Did you read paragraph one or skip straight to two?"

"I skimmed it."

Her hand resting on my forearm started *skimming*. "I don't believe that. I think you read every word."

I was far from gentlemanly, though for her, to her, I always would be. If gentlemanly included introducing a plethora of new-to-her things I could do to her body that would culminate in her having more orgasms.

"Love you think that, baby, but stop being a smart-ass and tell me what you were lying there thinking about before my cock took your attention."

I felt her body start to shake before I heard it. My mind rewound and I tried to remember if I'd ever heard her laugh. I couldn't remember a single moment since I'd met her back in Mexico where she laughed. I lay statue still and took in the sound.

"Before your cock caught my attention, I was wishing I could stay here all day and not have the world intrude. That for the first time maybe in my whole life, I feel . . ."

I gave her a moment to finish her thought. When it was clear she wouldn't, I prompted, "You feel what, Calli?"

It took a couple more seconds before she answered, "I feel like the world doesn't suck. That maybe, I don't know . . . I could be happy, be normal, be safe."

"You can be all those things. But normal, that shit is overrated," I teased, and kissed the top of her head.

Her hair was still damp from last night's bath. A first for me. The thought of crawling into a tub and washing a woman's hair had never occurred to me. The comparison wasn't close, but I liked that after

Calli gave me what she gave me, I could give her something clean and untainted. That was hers and hers alone.

"I've made my decision," she announced. "After I get Tom what he needs, I have one more thing to do, then I'm out. I don't know what I'll do. I have money. I can take my time, find a place, figure out what I'm going to do . . . but whatever it is, it won't be this."

I didn't have a good feeling about this. Mostly because I didn't want to think about what happened next. That invite could come in anytime, then she'd be gone.

My gut cramped at the thought. I didn't want her to leave me. I didn't want her to find a place that would take her far away.

"Will Tom let you go?"

Not that it mattered. If he had a problem with it, Shep and our team would help her get out from under him.

"I don't officially work for the CIA."

"Officially?"

"I don't know where he gets his budget. But I'm not the only one who works for him. Atlanta used to do what I do, but she had enough and moved to admin. She's a brilliant hacker, she takes care of travel and gets me things I need wherever I am. Tom's also got three other shooters I know of."

Fuck.

"He ever ask you to take out someone who wanted to walk away?"

She snuggled back deeper into my chest and pulled my arms around her tighter.

"No. But Atlanta told me she stopped doing fieldwork because Tom asked her to take someone out who went against her moral code. But I don't think it was someone who worked for him. It sounded more like Tom wanted a pawn removed from the board. Atlanta had no problem putting a bad guy in her crosshairs, but she'd never take someone out unless it was righteous. But, I'll figure it out."

I wanted to tell her *we'd* figure it out.

"Can we talk about last night?"

I rolled closer, pinning her back to my chest. "We can talk about anything as long as you don't use the words *mistake*, *shouldn't've*, or *regret*."

"Do you regret it?"

"Fuck no, and if you have to ask that, then you weren't listening last night when I told you I'd never forget the gift you gave me."

"Okay."

I gave her a squeeze, and asked, "Is that what you wanted to talk about?"

"I was worried you'd wake up this morning and be mad at me. I took something you weren't offering, and in doing so, made you break a promise to yourself that was obviously important to you because you kept it for ten years."

I didn't fuck empty pussy.

Calista was so far from empty, she was in a different universe.

"You didn't take anything, I gave it." I used her words from last night. "The promise I made to myself wasn't about sex, it was about meaningless orgasms. And there was nothing meaningless about the ones I've given you, or mine."

"I just . . . Okay."

"You just what?"

"I couldn't bear it if what we did meant nothing to you. Even if all it meant was two friends sharing a really good time that both will look back on and smile."

I rolled away, pulling Calista with me so she was on her back, then rolled again, coming up on top of her. Immediately, her legs opened to make room for me. I took the invitation and settled in. Our new position was dangerous. All she had on was her robe. No panties. Nothing stopping my bare cock from tunneling back into his new home.

As if on cue, the fucker twitched.

"Fuck, you're gorgeous."

I hadn't meant to tell her that. I had something important I needed her to understand. But her beauty hit me straight in the chest. Her sexy man-eater getup to go out to dinner was hot. But fresh faced, sweaty from working out, hair wet from a bath, lounging on our balcony, lying under me, that Calli stole my breath. Even pissed and angry Calista did it for me.

"You're pretty handsome yourself, hotshot."

Fuck, yeah, she totally did it for me.

Time to get back on track.

"We're friends?"

Her head pressed back on the pillow, putting another inch between us. "We're not?"

"This doesn't feel like friends," I told her.

"Um. What does it feel like?"

"Like you're mine."

Her lips parted, her eyes went soft, and her features gentled.

Her phone rang from somewhere across the room.

Fuck.

"Shit."

She couldn't ignore it. It could be Amir's secretary.

I rolled off. She scrambled off the bed with a muttered "Sorry." Giving me a great view of her perfect ass. My cock gave an appreciative jerk.

The world had intruded.

"Hi, I'm Calista." Calli introduced herself as soon as we hit the kitchen.

I stood back and watched my team greet her.

With an appreciative eye sweep, Gavin offered his hand. "Gavin."

"Nice to meet you."

As soon as Calli released Gavin's hand, Aiden stepped up with a crooked smile I knew got him laid, and regularly. "Good to meet you, Calista. I'm Aiden."

"Aiden," she returned with a smile.

Pete was sitting at the table, staring at me with concern.

Fallon's gaze was ping-ponging between me and Calista.

Both men were trying to puzzle out what was happening, while Aiden and Gavin just looked confused at the tension.

"Where's Jack?" I asked.

"He went upstairs to wake up Kitty," Fallon told me.

"One of these days Jack's gonna kick your ass if you don't stop calling his woman Kitty," Gavin noted.

"He can't be mad. I gave her that nickname before she was his woman," Fallon shot back, like that was a rule carved in stone.

Pete hadn't stopped studying me, using his superior reasoning to suss out what was going on between me and Calli. He knew me best, and if he watched me close enough, I'd give something away.

Fallon's approach would be different. He'd work hard to annoy me in hopes I'd get irritated and break. Normally his tactic worked, but not with this. What had happened, or what was going to happen with me and Calli, was no one's business. Unless she made it theirs.

"Sheesh, Fallon, you're going to give yourself a seizure if you don't stop with the eye thing," Calli complained.

"You look different," he taunted.

I sighed.

Calli smiled. "Sweet of you to notice."

Fallon looked confused. "Notice what?"

"How refreshed I look after a bath and a good night's sleep."

The saccharine smile she flashed at Fallon was what did it for me. I couldn't stop my laugh. Through it, Calli's smile changed from phony to knowing—a secret smile just for me.

"That's a euphemism for something, right?"

"Give it up, Fallon." Pete entered the conversation.

Fallon winked at Calli and went back to eating his sandwich. "There's more crab salad in the fridge."

"Did you make it?" I asked.

"Yep."

"Hard pass."

Calli looked at me in question.

"Trust me, baby. It's swimming in mayo."

Pete's eyes immediately narrowed, as did Aiden's.

There it was. I gave it away and Pete picked it up, and Aiden didn't miss the endearment either. Gavin coughed into a closed fist, likely to hide his smile.

"I need to call Tom," Calli declared, completely oblivious to my team watching us.

Dread hit my chest. For reasons I didn't understand, it felt like I was on the verge of disappointment. One wrong move would change the course of my life. I'd learned to ruthlessly control every aspect of my life. Withhold my trust. Never allow vulnerabilities.

Emotion was the great disruptor.

Yet for the last few days, I'd been playing fast and loose with every set-in-stone rule I had. The consequence of that was this—emotional turmoil.

"When did Amir's secretary say the party was?" Pete inquired.

"Friday."

Today was Wednesday.

Two days.

Or would she leave today since she had the address?

Panic flared and stole my breath.

"Tight timeline. Is it even possible for Tom to have a team on standby?" Aiden asked.

"I would assume the team is close, but unless I'm directly involved, he doesn't share his plans with me."

No, he just used her, and in the between times or when it suits him, he lets her ass swing out there. I hated that fucker.

She was staring at her phone like she was stalling.

"Calli," I called, and her eyes came to me. Her gaze was full of trepidation. "What's wrong?"

"The world feels—" She stopped when she remembered we had company. "Nothing's wrong. I'm just procrastinating because every time I talk to Tom, one way or another, he pisses me off. I'm in a good mood. I don't feel like getting into an argument with him."

"Almost done," I reminded her.

"Right." She picked up her phone. "Almost done."

Almost fucking done.

Then what?

The phantom ache in my heart intensified. I was short on time, without a plan. I didn't have a move ready. No movement meant Calli walked out of my life. Asking her to come back to California with me was risky, maybe *too* risky. What if she said yes, then in a few months the lies started, tiny mistruths, secrets—deception came in many forms.

What if she *didn't* want to come home with me? I didn't know if I could absorb that blow. She wanted out to find her peace, find normal. My life was anything but.

Maybe when she got to where she was going, I could visit her. Visiting someone wasn't committing. It wasn't sharing a life. It wasn't expectation and betrayal. We could share a few days here and there, then go our separate ways. No harm, no foul.

Jesus, did someone turn on the heater?

I couldn't take my eyes off Calista. But worse, I couldn't get the band of fear around my chest to loosen.

I didn't know this woman. I didn't trust her. But for some godforsaken reason, my heart thought otherwise.

But the heart lied.

I had to let her walk away.

I wouldn't survive a betrayal from Calli.

Chapter Twenty-Three

I couldn't place the exact feeling hammering in my chest. The prospect of speaking to Tom was never particularly pleasant. He had a way about him—that way being invoking anger and annoyance. Speaking to him was like walking through a minefield of lies and manipulation. He could teach a master class on gaslighting.

Oh, wait, he did.

But that wasn't what had my pulse thumping. It was Mason, the way he'd reminded me that I was almost done. He'd meant to calm my nerves. However, his reminder had done the opposite. This was it. One phone call to Tom, and it'd be over. I'd have no reason to stay here.

I wasn't naive. I knew that just because we'd slept together didn't mean anything had changed.

We were two ships passing in the night or whatever that dumb idiom was. We'd crossed paths. We'd shared a few nights. I'd given him my virginity. He'd broken a personal promise to himself. I'd waxed poetic about Stevie Nicks. Nothing more.

Then why did my heart feel like it was breaking?

The call connecting pulled my derailed thoughts back to my current problem—Tom.

"Yes," Tom answered, sounding wide awake, which made me wonder where in the world he was.

Not that it mattered, but I found it interesting he never answered the phone sounding groggy. Did they teach that skill at the Farm, or was Tom a vampire and never slept? He'd sucked all the life out of others over the years, so I was going with the latter.

"I have your location." I cut straight to it.

There was no sense in drawing this out. Not only because I didn't make it a habit of speaking to Tom longer than necessary, but if my heart was going to be torn from my chest, it was better to make it quick so I could break down later in private.

"Good."

My situation was far from good. I quickly rattled off the information he'd hired me to find.

Now it was done.

All over.

I wondered how long it would take Mason to pack. Did Pete already have a flight scheduled to take them back to California? Was Fallon itching to get back to whatever it was that Fallon did when he wasn't helping the CIA shut down sex-slave auctions? Would the others be mad they'd wasted a trip if Tom actually came through and dispatched a Ground Branch team?

"I need you to attend the party."

Tom's order banged around in my head, making it pound to the same beat as the drumming of my heart.

"That wasn't the mission," I reminded him.

"The mission is always fluid." His neutral, relaxed tone pissed me off.

My gaze snagged on Mason's angry face as I replied, "I'm not attending—"

"You are, Calista, and you know why. This will be two birds—you take out *my* target and you'll have access to yours."

I locked down the slew of obscene names ready to spill out of my mouth. Unfortunately, I couldn't block out the three sets of male eyes staring at me in censure. I'd never mentioned I *had* a target. And the other two men in the room were now also laser focused on me, which made me twitchy.

"Listen to me carefully, Tom. I am not attending. Your team can take out your target, and if they can't, call in one of your other mercs. I don't care what you do, but it won't be me."

"The team's too far out. I need you to go in."

Bullshit. Bull-fucking-shit. He'd once again lied. There *was* no team. He'd always intended for me to attend the party.

I glanced at Pete. The hard set of his jaw said it all—he was furious. And relieved he'd brought his team to Dubai.

There was no way I could attend the party after last night. My cover wouldn't hold.

Not that I'd explain my reasons to Tom, nor would I tell him Pete would now be going in to rescue the women and give him the chance to manipulate the situation.

"I'm not going to the auction," I declared. "If you don't have a team close, I suggest you start calling around."

Before I could disconnect the call, Tom blew my world apart.

"I'm delivering Jason Anderson to you on a silver platter."

"Who's Jason Anderson?" Mason interjected.

"Mason Hughes," Tom drawled. "Calista didn't explain?"

Motherfucking dick canoe.

Piercing green eyes fixed me in place. The unbridled accusation almost made me flinch.

"Explain what?"

"There's nothing to explain," I warned. "And, Tom, I was going to wait until after your mission to talk to you, but with this bullshit, I'm thinking now's the perfect time to tell you I quit."

"Tell me, Calista, how does one quit doing what you do?"

Was that a threat?

"I don't know, you tell me. Do I need to email you my resignation, or will verbal notice suffice?"

"You're smarter than this."

No, I wasn't. This morning was proof of that, when I lay awake in Mason's arms, wishing I could wake up next to him every morning, wishing that was my life—Mason and peace. But neither of those would ever be mine. Even after I walked out of my old life, I would never be walking into his. My world would never be perfect. I'd never get even a little bit of what I wanted.

"Don't ever call me again. I'm out. If you come after me, I'll come out of retirement. And warning, before you think to fuck with me, remember you're a good teacher, Tom, and I never forgot a lesson. I'm all for mutual destruction—and you taught me that too."

I stabbed the screen of my phone and refused to look up. I knew what I'd find, and I wasn't ready to deal with it yet.

Jack and Catarina walked into the kitchen hand in hand. Jack took in the room and asked, "What's going on?"

Mason ignored Jack and launched right in. "Who's Jason Anderson?"

"No one."

"No one?" he echoed. "The same no one from last night or a different no one?"

Why did the damn man have to be so smart? I was backed into a corner with no move. My best play was to stay silent. He didn't need my help puzzling out conclusions.

Unfortunately, Fallon had something to say. "Jason Anderson was at the Sky View bar last night."

"How do you know that?" My question was yanked painfully from my chest.

"I had the security footage pulled," Mason told me.

Indignation had me in its firm grasp. Fury was familiar, it felt good, like a warm blanket wrapped around me on a cold night. Rage, I could work with. I knew what to do with these feelings. I knew how to control them and use them to keep myself safe.

What I didn't know how to deal with was the feeling of my heart shriveling with the knowledge that Mason had gone behind my back.

"Why would you do that?"

"Because I knew you were lying to me." His cold tone should've been a warning. Yet it fueled my outrage.

"I didn't lie to you, Mason. Not everything is your fucking business." I shoved back, the legs of my chair sliding over the marble floor. When I was on my feet, I slammed my palms on the table, giving myself that small outburst. Not that it made me feel any better. "You know what your problem is? You mistake transparency with lying. You're not entitled to everyone's thoughts. You don't have the right to demand truths someone doesn't want to give. But I bet it makes it easier for you to sit there in your judgment of me, like I did you wrong when it was *you* who crossed the line and invaded my privacy.

"And let's hark back—it was *you* who inserted yourself into this situation. Even if you came here thinking I contacted you, I told you the truth, and it was your choice to stay here. Then you forced that decision on me. I didn't invite you into my life and offer you my secrets."

Okay, so that last part was a big fat lie. I'd done more than invite him into my life, I'd invited him into my heart. And just like Atlanta, he'd betrayed me and gone behind my back.

My phone vibrated on the table. Atlanta's name appeared on the screen, like I'd conjured her up by merely thinking about her.

Fuck my life.

I snatched up the phone, debated walking it to the sink, dropping it in, and turning on the garbage disposal. Until I could secure a new phone, I didn't have that option available to me. I also couldn't decline the call, in case Tom had already put a kill packet out on me and that was why Atlanta was calling.

Reluctantly, I answered and put the phone to my ear. "Hey."

"What the hell is going on?"

Shit. Tom was wasting no time. I had to get out of the UAE, especially since Tom would have a team close for cleanup after his target was taken out at the auction.

A chill washed over me. He wouldn't send Atlanta to take me out, would he?

Uncaring I had an audience, I asked, "Is he sending you in?"

"Is who sending me where?"

Her tone hinted at confusion, but Atlanta was a skilled mercenary.

"Calista," Mason growled.

I didn't have time to deal with Mason and his anger or with pussyfooting around with the truth. The more I could get Atlanta to talk, the better chance I had at detecting a lie.

"Tom. It would make sense, him sending you to take me out. You'd know my plays before I made them."

There was five seconds of silence. Five seconds was a long time for someone with Atlanta's cleverness. She'd have a ready lie for every question. She'd taught me the art of anticipating your target's moves. She'd also know I wouldn't lead with feigning stupidity. I'd go with a direct approach.

"Why would Tom send anyone to take you out? You're his prized possession."

Yes, that's all I was, a possession. Tom Washington's personal assassin. His favorite toy, yet somehow still expendable.

"If you don't know, then why are you calling me?"

"We'll come back to that, but only because what I have is time sensitive. Are you with your team now?"

My team.

That felt like a blade sinking into my heart. Mason, Pete, and Fallon were never my team. But last night, it felt like they were. It had felt good knowing they had my back. And the night before felt like it, too, when we worked together to save two young women. I hoped Mira and Kiara were safe and would be able to find that ever-elusive peace after trauma.

In a moment of weakness, I allowed my gaze to travel around the room. As pissed as I was at Mason, I was glad he had these men and Catarina.

I refrained from telling her they weren't my team and never would be.

"Yeah, they're here, why?"

"Put me on speaker. I need to talk to them."

I'd learned that lesson once today.

"Not until you tell me why."

"Someone's digging around, and I need to ask them a few questions."

Son of a bitch.

I focused on Mason but told the room at large, "Atlanta has a few questions." I put the phone on speaker. "Go, Atlanta. But before you ask your questions, you should know Mason had the security footage pulled from the restaurant where I had my dinner with Amir. Whoever did the hack must've triggered the alarm."

"Why the hell would he do that?" Atlanta spat, not hiding her anger.

Because he was an entitled asshole.

"I don't know," I told Atlanta. Then asked Mason, "Why'd you go behind my back?"

Mason's jaw clenched, a clear sign he was seriously unhappy with my attitude. Not that I gave a shit what he was or wasn't happy with at the moment. Depending on who was digging and what they were after could mean a delay in taking Jason down once and for all. It could mean years before he left the safety of Berlin again, where he'd built an empire of filth.

No, he hadn't built it—his father had. Jason just erected the protective walls around the fortress. He bought protection from local and government authorities, had connections his father never managed. Which made him untouchable. He rarely left the city. My only chance of taking him out was when he only had a few guards with him and not the full force of the establishment.

"You know what, that doesn't matter," Atlanta said diplomatically. "For the last eight hours, someone's been digging into you. You, *Calista*, not you, Zara. Which led them to digging into Mason and Fallon."

"We know," Pete said. "Or I should say, Fallon and I and the rest of my team know. We hadn't briefed Mason and Calista yet. But it was to be expected, and whoever's looking has hit roadblocks, and the deeper they dig, the easier it will be for us to track them."

I narrowed my eyes on Pete. I didn't have to ask how he knew—Shepherd Drexel was how. It was on the tip of my tongue to confirm for

Atlanta they had Shep in their pocket, but for some asinine reason, my loyalty to the three wouldn't allow me to.

"I already know who it is," Atlanta announced. "Archie Evans."

Jason's guard.

Yeah, I was royally fucked. Up shit's creek with no paddles in sight.

"Who's Archie Evans?" Pete inquired.

"Former SBS turned scumbag protection," I told him.

He could find out the specifics from Shep if he felt so inclined. I had bigger issues to worry about.

"There goes any hope he didn't recognize me," I grumbled.

It had been twenty-one years. I was hoping I'd at least have age on my side and it would take him a few minutes to figure out who I was. Time I would use to end him. Now I'd lost the element of surprise. Jason knew I was in Dubai. He knew that *I* knew who he was.

"Is there any way I can spin this?"

"Spin what?" Mason rejoined.

I ignored his question and asked another one of my own. "Is that all you had for them?"

"Yeah. I felt compelled to warn them, but that's all I had, and they seem to have it under control. So I won't interfere." That was nice of her to give them the consideration she hadn't given me when she'd interfered to get them there. "But you could use them. Keep your cover and go to the party. Get close to him that way. There will be cocktails before the auction. You could get him alone before the inspections begin or he has time to burn you."

Inspections.

Another reason I was glad I was done. I couldn't stomach having these conversations anymore. I never really could, they'd always left my stomach in knots, but now I felt the bile crawling up my throat, threatening to choke me. I'd lost whatever it was that had driven me for years to continue down this dark and murky path. I was one step away from a new road, one that wouldn't make me want to vomit and cry at the same time. My new route would have me burying my head in the sand and pretending the world where women were inspected before they were sold didn't exist.

"That won't work," I told her. "I need to think. But before I let you go, you should know I quit today and told Tom never to call me again."

"About fucking time," she breathed.

I had to believe she meant that.

"The only thing I ask is, if he sends you in to take me out, that you show me respect and do it while looking me in the face."

Mason made a feral sound that wasn't quite a growl and more of a beastly snarl.

"If I wasn't in Berlin, I'd smack you, Calista, for even thinking I'd do such a thing."

I had to believe she meant that too. I was out of options. I needed to be able to trust that Atlanta would have my back on one more thing.

"Berlin?"

"Yes, bitch." Her insult held no heat. "Berlin. You know, where Jason runs his den of debauchery. I'm looking for his traitor, though I hate to say it, I'm coming up with nothing. But that doesn't mean I'm going to give up until you put him in the ground. After that, it won't be necessary, because he'll take the power, and we'll know who was looking to overthrow the king."

"I'm sorry I said that to you."

"You're forgiven, but only because I know why you think the worst of everyone. Call me back when you're done thinking or if you need help coming up with something. You've got three days to make your move, then he's scheduled to fly home."

"Got it. Thanks."

"Who's Jason Anderson?" Mason seethed.

He could seethe and foam at the mouth for all the answers he wanted. None would be forthcoming.

He'd fucked me—in more ways than one.

"Ask Shep," I tossed out, and started for the archway that would lead to the foyer. "I'm going out to get a coffee from the corner. I'll be back in thirty minutes to get my stuff and get out of your hair."

"Calista, I don't think you should go anywhere until we understand what's going on," Pete said. His tone was neutral and placating; however, the pinch of his brows and stiffness in his shoulders told the real tale. He was anything but relaxed. He was firmly on Team Mason and pissed I hadn't divulged my plans.

"I appreciate all your help, please believe I mean that. But this isn't your business either. Mason has the information for the auction. Obviously I cannot attend. I can hook you up with my man here in Dubai. He can get you whatever weapons you'll need. But I'm out."

Mason stood so quickly the chair he'd been sitting in wobbled before it fell back on its legs. Too bad I couldn't have my foundation shaken and land back on my feet so quickly. A decade's worth of planning and maneuvering and obsessing—all leading me to this very moment—could go up in flames.

I no longer had the upper hand.

Jason knew I was coming.

"You're not going out to coffee," Mason denied. "We need to talk."

"I have nothing to say to you, Mason. You took something from me I wasn't offering, and in doing so, you might've taken away my only opportunity to find the peace I desperately need."

I didn't wait for his rebuttal. I turned and stomped into the foyer. It wasn't my most graceful exit from a room. I was no less infuriated when I stabbed at the button to call the elevator, but the guilt of my low blow had started to form.

"Calista, wait!" Catarina called from behind me.

Goddamnit.

"I'm sorry I didn't get a chance to talk to you, but I need to leave." My new plan was slowly starting to come together as I waited for her to try to talk me out of going.

"Let me come with you. We can get your coffee and catch up."

As appealing as it was, I wasn't going to entertain her idea. I didn't need to get close to another person only to have them torn from my life. And I needed to focus on Jason before it was too late and he bolted.

Thankfully, the doors in front of me slid open.

"We'll talk when I get back," I lied. "I just need some fresh air and a little bit of alone time."

Not that I'd get either of those if I could flush Jason out.

"Calista, I really wish you'd let me come."

I stepped into the elevator and smiled at Catarina. "I know I was bitchy back in Mexico and didn't properly thank you for the assist, so I'll do that now. You had my back, I'm grateful. Maybe one day I can repay the favor."

I hit the close button on the panel.

"You can do that now—"

"I can't, Cat. I have somewhere I need to be."

With that, the doors closed.

By the time I was walking across the stupidly lavish lobby, a tiny bit of logic had seeped in. It wasn't Mason's fault Jason knew I was in Dubai. That was the universe's doing—wrong place, wrong time.

Mason's only crime was being an asshole thinking he had a right to something I didn't want to share. But even that didn't sit right, because if I thought about it—which I didn't want to—I'd know he'd only stepped over the line because he'd felt my reaction to seeing Jason. He had a front-row seat to my shock at seeing the man who'd stolen my sister from me.

Over twenty years had passed and still the wound was fresh. I'd accepted her death, but until Jason was dead, I couldn't mourn the last years of her life—how she'd died, what Jason and his father had caused, the ripple effect it had on my family.

Only vengeance could right that wrong.

Jason had to die by my hand.

He owed me his life.

As soon as I stepped out onto the sidewalk, the heat of the day smacked me in the face. Clearly, settling in the desert was out of the question. A nice mountaintop somewhere sounded perfect.

Or the beach with Mason, my treacherous heart filled in.

If there was one thing to be said about downtown Dubai, it was clean. Spotless. Gleaming. Polished. Healthy green trees lined the boulevard.

I waited until I rounded the corner before I stepped off the curb and waved down a taxi.

The red-roofed car glided to a stop in front of me. There was no reason for me to waste my time roaming the streets, hoping Jason would find me.

Not when I could walk right up to his hotel room and knock on the door.

I heard footsteps pounding on the sidewalk behind me. When I turned to look, Mason was running at me with a face like thunder.

"Calli! Wait!"

I slipped inside the cab and slammed the door. "Go. Please."

The taxi shot forward. My gut roiled and my heart painfully shriveled back to its pre-Mason size.

Chapter Twenty-Four

I was still out of breath from my jog around the corner. Of course, my timing was shit, and I'd lost sight of the taxi Calli was in before another had shown up. I had no choice but to get back to the penthouse and my team.

I have nothing to say to you, Mason. You took something from me I wasn't offering, and in doing so, you might've taken away my only opportunity to find the peace I desperately need.

Calista's words echoed in my head, ricocheted around, and sliced me to shreds. I'd taken a lot from the woman in the last twenty-four hours. Raw pain took a tour around my bleeding insides, leaving its own damage.

I held my phone up to my ear, getting Calista's voicemail for the third time.

"Mase?" Not even Pete calling my name could fully pull me out of the last vision I had of her getting into the taxi, looking devastated. Her last words to me had been angry, but her face was a mask of suffering.

After I get Tom what he needs, I have one more thing to do, then I'm out.

I hadn't asked her what that one last thing was. I'd been too caught up in the feel of her. Too busy fighting an internal battle to comprehend what she'd said.

"Mason!" Pete snapped.

"I need a minute."

I dialed Calli again.

Jason Anderson had to be that one thing.

"We don't have a minute," Pete said.

Goddamn voicemail. I stabbed at the screen of my phone and asked, "Who's Jason Anderson?"

"Shep's working on it. Now, what's going on?"

Nothing. Everything. If Jason was her endgame, I hadn't taken that from her. Not only because there was no way in hell Shep would've left a digital footprint when he got the security footage, but even if he had, seeing Calista in person would've tipped Jason off.

You're not entitled to everyone's thoughts. You don't have the right to demand truths someone doesn't want to give.

Fuck, but the woman was right. I'd become the one thing I hated only a little less than a liar—an entitled prick. I needed to explain why I'd overstepped. I didn't think she understood the way she'd trembled, the fear that had rolled off of her, the way she'd flinched at the sight of him.

I might not have been entitled to her every thought or secrets, but when it came to her safety, while she was a part of the team, I would do what I had to do to keep her safe. I'd blow through every boundary, step over lines, and be the dick she loved to call me. I'd take whatever hate she wanted to throw my way as long as she was safe.

"Are you okay, brother?" Gavin inquired.

"Not even a little bit."

"You care to explain that?" Pete pushed.

Fuck. I scrubbed my hands over my face and blew out a frustrated breath that did nothing to extinguish the burn of her verbal blows. The woman served up one hell of a tongue-lashing. She knew exactly the right buttons to push.

"I think I . . ." No, that wasn't how I wanted to start. "I was going to . . ." That wasn't right either.

I needed to recalibrate my brain and get my shit straight. We needed a plan and answers from Shep about this Jason character. But before we did that, I had to convince my best friend and teammate I hadn't gone completely around the bend, which wouldn't be easy to do, because I was fairly certain I had.

"I changed my mind. I'm actually fine."

"You have the emotional intelligence of a toddler." Pete thrust his hand through his hair. A clear sign I'd pushed him well past his patience.

Gavin, Aiden, and Catarina all looked like they agreed. Fallon was straight up looking at me like I was an idiot, and Jack looked like he felt sorry for me.

My best friend didn't lose control, not even of his own hand, giving away his frustration. Before our plane had touched down in Dubai, I'd had that same detached cool. Seeing Calista in her black dress had frayed whatever control I'd thought I had. But it wasn't the dress or the sexy shoes, or the long legs that I now knew felt better than I'd imagined wrapped around my hips.

It was that split second of wide-eyed shock when she opened the door and saw me. It was that zap of electricity. It was the energy surrounding us that I wanted to deny but couldn't.

"I fucked up," I finally admitted.

To my shock, Pete leaned aggressively close and narrowed his eyes. "Wake. Up."

I reared back to put distance between me and my best bud. It wouldn't be the first time we'd worked shit out with our fists, but we didn't have time for that shit.

"Come again?"

"I heard."

"Heard what?"

"I. Heard," he repeated. "This place is big, but it's not a palace."

Gavin shifted uncomfortably, and I wondered if he'd heard too.

Irrationally, anger hit me square in the chest. Her sounds were mine—all mine. They were just for me and not for anyone else to hear.

"You listened to us," I growled, intentionally allowing him to hear my displeasure.

"Fuck no. The two of you weren't exactly quiet. Fallon and I went into the far TV room and put on a movie as soon as we realized what was happening. We were the only two still awake."

Jesus. Fuck me.

"So why are you getting in my face, telling me to wake up?"

"You know I love you like a brother, but you are a dumb son of a bitch."

Now he was just being rude, calling my mother names. Not that he was wrong. My mother *was* a bitch. A lying, grasping bitch, and if I was being thorough in the description of her, I should also add cheating, money hungry, and useless.

"I don't know why you gotta bring my mother into it."

Redirection was my new best friend. I no longer wanted to participate in this conversation. I knew what came after Pete's name-calling—truth bombs. And I was in no mood to be hit with another verbal assault. It would appear Calista and Pete had something in common with their choice of armaments. Neither of them started with a nice small Mk 81—tear through some flesh, cause some injury. No, they went straight to the JDAM and dropped two thousand pounds of mass destruction.

You took something from me I wasn't offering.

Calista's blow slammed into me again.

"I've waited a long damn time for this moment," Pete went on.

"What moment?"

My gaze sliced to Fallon, standing next to Pete with his arms crossed over his chest, looking like he'd happily deck me. What was *his* problem? The only person who should be pissed off at me was Calista, and the only reason her anger was valid was because I'd gone behind her back. I should've told her I'd asked Fallon to pull the footage.

Thankfully, the rest of my team hadn't been around the last few days to witness my downfall, or they'd be in on the riot act too. Although Catarina looked like she wanted to take a swing at me. Was that a sisterhood thing? Did she think I'd hurt Calli, so now she was pissed on her behalf?

"This moment." He jabbed his finger toward the floor. "When you finally care about a woman enough to put yourself through the emotional wringer. So I'm going to give you some friendly advice—wake the fuck up and deal with your shit before you lose her. She is not your mother."

"My mother?"

What the hell was he going on about my mother for? I hadn't seen or spoken to the woman in ages.

"You're going to let Calista walk out of your life before she can turn into your mother. You think control equals strength. You're dead-ass wrong, brother. Strength is facing your shit. Strength is besting the ghosts of your past instead of allowing them to haunt you for the rest of your life. You talk a big game about your control, and I'll give it to you, Mase. No way in hell I could've turned down all the ass that's been thrown your way. There's not a chance I would've gone ten years without a woman. No doubt you have control."

"Pete," I warned.

"But you're weak as fuck, because you're going to let that woman—the only woman in ten years who, for some magical reason, you let in—walk away. She didn't break down your walls and storm the gate. You opened those fuckers up wide open and invited her in.

"Now you're getting cold feet. You're scared, so you're trying to push her out and close the gate. But you can't even do that. She fucking gutted you, and she wasn't wrong, Mase. Your measure of truth is in place as an excuse to keep everyone locked out. No one can live up to your standards unless they bare their soul."

I blocked out every word Pete hurled at me, not ready to deal with the truth. Everything he'd said was on the money. I *had* opened the gate for Calista. But first, I'd unlocked the sixty-five padlocks I used to keep it closed. Then, after it was open, I'd rolled out the red carpet.

Fallon shifting snagged my attention. Happy to have a target rather than having to admit to myself I was what Pete said I was—weak as fuck—I focused on him.

"What?" I asked.

"I've known you a long time," he started. "Knew you didn't see your parents, but I had no idea you had problems with your mom."

Fuck me to hell and back.

I twisted my neck, trying to relieve some of the tension. Though the stiffness could've been from the guilt that kept piling on.

"I hate my mother." There, I said it.

Fallon's brow winged up, silently calling me out on my bullshit.

"My mom and dad had this on-and-off relationship before she got pregnant with me. When she found out she was pregnant, she went back to my dad because the new guy she was screwing wanted no part of a kid—his or not. My dad took her back and married her. I guess everything was okay for a few years. Then when I was around five, she took off.

"She comes back a few months later, my dad takes her back. The next time she did that, I was around twelve. Now, that time I remember clearly, and it wasn't a few months—she was gone six. She comes back, cries, begs, tells me and my dad she's sorry for leaving us. She had a hundred bullshit excuses why she needed to find herself or be alone or whatever lame shit she said. My dad lets her move back in. It takes me a while, but I forgive her. She's my mom, I love her. I want to believe she loves me.

"The next time she bails, it was a few weeks before my seventeenth birthday. She doesn't show her face again until my eighteenth birthday. But now, I'm an adult. I gave my dad the choice—her or me. He picked her, so when her lying bitch ass walked in the door, I walked out."

"That's fucked, Mase," Fallon muttered his understatement. "Straight up, brother, she's a bitch. *She.* Is. Calista's not—"

"Calli was never going to stay." Fuck, that bitter pill of rejection hurt like a mother when it got stuck in my throat. "She was always going to leave. I knew she was going to quit before we came downstairs. I knew after she gave Tom the intel he needed she was going to take off and go find her peace. Find a better life. And damn, she deserves it. But that doesn't make her walking away hurt less."

"You asked her to come back to SD with us?" Fallon asked.

"No. I . . ." I paused.

That hesitation meant Pete could jump back in. "You chickened out, you dumbass. I don't get it, but whatever the hell you two have going on has both of you tangled together. Did you ever maybe think she *wanted* to come back to California with you, but didn't want to . . . I don't know how chicks think . . . seem clingy?"

"You're right, okay?" I exploded, lifting my right hand to squeeze the back of my neck. "But why the fuck are we talking about this now when she's out there somewhere doing God knows what?"

"Because while we're waiting on Shep to call," Fallon started, "we're sorting your shit out so that when we have actionable intel, you're ready to roll out, and when we get to her, you won't have an excuse to puss out."

My hand dropped from my neck to my chest. Christ, was I having a cardiac episode? Was the ache from the thought of losing her completely or her coming back to California? From the moment she'd walked out the door, I felt the pressure building, and it was only partly because she was pissed at me. If the thought of losing Calista forever made my chest feel like I was having a heart attack, the reality of that would surely kill me.

"Mason." Catarina called my name. "I *do* know how women think. And I know what I saw when she got into the elevator. She's scared. Of you, of being rejected, of accepting help, of failing. I get the feeling the two of you are exactly the same—too afraid to trust because both of you know how bad it hurts when the person you trusted burns you. It's going to have to be you, asking her to stay. She won't let herself hope for a life with you. If you let her, she'll run."

Isn't that what she'd already done while I stupidly hesitated, too caught up in my anger to stop her? Instead of nursing my pride, I should've tossed her over my shoulder and locked her in our room until I'd talked some sense into her.

Our room.

Christ.

Before I could come up with a response to what Cat had said, Pete reached into his pocket, pulled out his phone, and frowned.

"Unknown caller," he announced. Then answered, "Who's this?"

Pete frowned again, but it wasn't until his shoulders tensed and his eyes fell to the floor that I knew something was wrong.

"What's—"

"Let me put you on speaker," Pete spoke over me. "You still there, Atlanta?"

"Yeah. Like I was saying, I've been calling her for the last ten minutes."

"She bolted," I told her. "Before I could get to her, she got into a taxi."

"Any idea where she'd go?" Aiden asked.

"To Tanner."

Who the fuck was Tanner?

"Who's Tanner?" Pete voiced my thought.

"The man who has everything Calli needs to take out Jason Anderson."

Now we were getting somewhere.

Chapter Twenty-Five

"I'm sorry, Calista, Amir—" The rest of what Tanner was going to say was cut off by Arlo's vicious blow to his jaw.

His head jerked to the side, but the chair he was tied to stayed upright.

I felt his pain, seeing as just moments before I'd been on the receiving end of Arlo's right hook. The Aussie had one hell of a power punch, although he obviously pulled his punch to my temple since he hadn't knocked me out like he had Tanner. That didn't mean I wasn't seeing stars floating in my peripheral.

"It's been a long time, Calista."

Just hearing Jason's voice made my stomach roil. Memories from the last time I saw him raced to the forefront of my mind, bringing with them excruciating pain that rivaled the blow to my head.

"Amir sends his regards," Jason continued.

Fucking hell.

"He wasn't pleased to learn that the woman he'd dined with wasn't who she said she was. He drove a hard bargain. You cost me a pretty penny. Luckily for you, I've already had a Ventura woman . . . and liked the taste of her. I'm sure you'll find your time with *me* more pleasurable than what Amir had planned."

I glanced around Tanner's living room. He'd put up one hell of a struggle before he was tied to the chair, if the broken coffee table and overturned chairs were anything to go by. Not to mention his face looked like he'd gone through all twelve rounds with a heavyweight champ and lost.

"If you're feeling sorry for your friend Tanner, don't. He sold you out. All it took was a phone call from Amir and the guy sang. Told Amir everything, down to today's pickup. All I had to do was wait. And voilà, here you are."

And there I was, unarmed, with no phone, and a headache after Arlo got the drop on me. I would've felt like a schmuck about this, but Arlo was six-three, two-fifty pounds (by my guesstimation) of pure muscle, and he'd had the added benefit of knowing I'd be walking up to Tanner's door at some point.

Atlanta must've called Tanner after I'd spoken to her, knowing I'd want to pick up my kit sooner rather than later. Ironically, the woman's efficiency might get me killed today. If only I hadn't tossed my phone out the window of the cab, she could track my location, but that was exactly what I was trying to avoid—Mason calling Shep to get my location.

"A Steyr DMR. I'm impressed," Jason went on, taking his gun off of me to wave it at the table. "Tell me, Calista, was that for me or for Amir?"

I bit my tongue.

Time.

I needed time to figure a way out of this clusterfuck. I couldn't make a move with Archie guarding the door, Arlo standing sentry next to Tanner, and Jason pointing a gun at me. I had yet to see Bodhi, but he'd be here too.

"Not that it matters, now that you're coming home with me." Jason paused and smiled. "I'll have your sister's room prepared. I'm sure you'd like to see where she lived all those years she stayed with me."

I willed the pain not to lacerate my insides as the memories of my sister reared up.

"Wait until you meet him, Calli." Lili beamed and patted her pink cheeks.

"Is he hot?"

"Like you wouldn't believe. But he has this voice. It gives me goose bumps."

Goose bumps.

The man who would be the death of her gave her goose bumps.

I was going to enjoy every second of killing Jason Anderson.

Back in high school, I had this history teacher who was into watching *Dateline*, and once a week, she'd tell the class about the episode she'd seen.

The bad guys always look so normal.

At the time, I hadn't known how right Mrs. Hill had been. Most of the time she relayed the stories, I didn't pay attention—something like murder or kidnapping didn't happen to people like us. Naively, I didn't think horrible things could touch my family. My father owned a dry-cleaning business, my mom was a stay-at-home mom until my sister and I went to high school, then she worked part time helping my dad at the cleaners. We had a good family. We loved each other.

Bad things didn't happen to good people.

God, I was stupid. Bad things happened to everyone.

"Nothing to say? My Lili used to give me the silent treatment too. When she'd get mad at me and not speak, I'd tell her, her Russian was showing."

My Lili.

I was going to throw up, and not from the blood all over Tanner's small bungalow.

My dedulya had once told me a story about growing up in Moscow. He called it a gangster's paradise. Crazy stories. But the one that stuck out was him telling me that he saw a man through a shop window, hanging from a hook and being electrocuted. My parents hadn't been happy he'd told me the story. For the next week, I had nightmares of a man hanging on a hook.

That was how I was going to start. Jason would see my Russian.

Apparently, he liked the sound of his voice as much as my sister had, since he kept going without any input from me.

"I was surprised to see you last night."

I bet you were.

I kept that comment to myself and my eyes on the table across the room.

So many weapons just out of my reach.

"You were a beautiful teenager," he grossly went on. "I almost picked you. But you were too young."

That confession settled in my stomach. If he'd picked me, Lili would still be alive. I couldn't help but wonder if it had been me instead of my sister, if my mother would've found a way to go on.

"You're totally Dad's favorite." Lili shook her head, smiling, holding up my birthday present from our dad—a new MP3 player. "This thing costs almost two hundred dollars."

"So? You're Mom's favorite. She bought you a pair of Guess jeans for no reason. Do you know the last time Mom bought me a present for no reason?"

"You're right." She smiled wider. "But do you know who my favorite is?"

"Mom. She buys you expensive jeans."

"You, you dork. You're my all-time-forever favorite."

I stared at my sister, thinking she was my favorite too. Unfortunately, the thought never left my mouth.

"We need to go," Bodhi announced.

Jason ignored his guard. "I had Arlo look into you."

Arlo . . . not Archie. My gaze swung to the door. Archie had his arms crossed over his wide chest, eyes narrowed on his boss.

"You've done well for yourself. Commercial real estate, impressive."

That cover was so old, and I'd used it so often, I wasn't impressed Arlo had found it. We left it out there dangling for people like Jason to find.

I waited for him to say more. It wasn't like he had a problem with carrying on a one-sided conversation while Bodhi stood watch over a passed-out-cold Tanner. I wondered if they ever got tired of him talking.

If that was why one of them had turned traitor—just to get him to shut up.

"I would think a woman with your wealth would know better than to travel with second-rate bodyguards." He sounded like he was actually scolding me for not having more protection. "But then, a woman in commercial real estate wouldn't be dealing with an arms dealer, now, would she? Tell me, Calista, why are you really here?"

Since there was no reason to hide the truth, I didn't.

"To kill you."

Jason's mouth tipped up into a smile, the one that I knew my sister had fallen in love with. But it was his obnoxious laugh that triggered a memory so painful, I had to grit my teeth.

"I think I love him," Lili said, and plopped down next to me on my bed.

I looked up from my notebook and couldn't stop my smile. She looked so happy.

"Where'd you guys go today?"

"The miniature golf place."

"The one with the arcade or the one next to the bowling alley?"

"Arcade." She glanced down at the textbooks cluttering my bed. "You need to find a boyfriend, Calli. There's more to life than studying."

"One day." I brushed her off, not telling her last weekend I'd gone on the lamest date ever, worried I'd never find my Jason. "Tell me everything."

"He's . . . I don't know . . . perfect! And when he laughs it's like . . . I don't know, I just want to sigh. He said he wants me to meet his family. I want to meet them, but I don't know if I'm ready. What if they don't like me? I don't want to lose him. Jason Anderson is the best thing that ever happened to me."

Jason Anderson was the devil.

"Lili told me you were an idealist, always coming up with wild stories in your head. I see you haven't changed."

I'd changed more than he knew. I wasn't the same naive girl who'd cried in his arms at the police station after he'd given his statement. He'd played the part of worried boyfriend like an Oscar winner. His story never changed, not a single detail. That should've been a red flag. It had been rehearsed and memorized.

And I should've known it was a lie. I knew my sister, and there was no way she'd ask Jason to end a date and take her back to her apartment because she got a headache. She loved him, wanted to spend every waking moment with him. She would've suffered through a headache to spend time with him.

The timing of his story had been impeccable. His alibi solid. Sometimes I wondered if he'd driven the route from my sister's apartment to his friend's house at the exact time of day, so he'd get the traffic right. Twenty years ago, there weren't cameras on everyone's front doors and on street corners. It was easier back then to kidnap someone and get away with it.

"It's time, Jason," Bodhi pressed again.

"Do you believe in fate?"

That question caused actual physical pain.

"Why do you look so happy?" I asked Lili as she tossed her purse on the kitchen island.

"Are Mom and Dad home?"

"No. Dad's still at work, and I don't know where Mom is."

"I think Jason's going to ask me to marry him."

Marry him.

"Isn't three months too soon to get married?"

"I said ask me to, not run off and elope tomorrow." Lili had this dreamy look on her face, which seemed to be her permanent state of being these days.

"Did he take you to a jewelry store or something?"

"No, last night we were lying in my bed, and he asked me if I believed in fate. I told him I wasn't sure. He told me he did. That he knew we were fated to be together."

"Absolutely," I replied.

From the second the thought had crossed his depraved mind to take my sister from me, his fate had been sealed.

Quicker than I thought Jason could move, he swung his Colt—or was it mine that I'd ordered from Tanner—in Arlo's direction and fired.

Two-hundred and thirty grains of stopping power slammed into the man's head.

Before Arlo could drop, Jason had Archie in his sights and double tapped.

What the fuck just happened?

The pounding in my head got a friend called tinnitus.

Jason turned back to me. "Let that be a lesson to you, Calista. I don't tolerate traitors or incompetence."

Well, fuck. So much for me using the traitor for help.

Chapter Twenty-Six

The tall dark-haired woman standing in front of me did not match the voice I'd heard earlier this morning on the phone.

"You lied to her," I fumed. "Again. That's twice since I've known her, and you want me to trust you?"

The corner of Atlanta's mouth hitched up, but she schooled her features before the smile could fully form. "I love this for her."

My patience was nonexistent. The anger I was barely keeping in check was in danger of spilling out and eviscerating Calli's friend.

"My woman's missing." My woman? Fuck. "I'm not sure what you love, but I'm not loving *any* of this, including the part where you told her you were in Berlin when obviously you're standing in front of me."

"I know it looks bad," Atlanta began, taking in my team huddled behind me. "Fine, it is bad. I lied, but I did it for a reason. I had no idea she was going to quit today. And when she asked if Tom had contacted me to take her out, I knew she'd freak if she found out I was here. She's a lone wolf and has serious trust issues."

"Can you blame her when the people who are supposed to be closest to her lie to her?" I snapped.

"You're one of those black-and-white guys, aren't you?"

The growl that slipped out of my mouth sounded feral. I was beyond social graces—not that I had many to begin with, but I could oftentimes stop myself from snarling like an animal.

How the fuck did I get here, debating with some woman I didn't know about my moral compass? Oh wait, I knew. The woman showed up in the lobby and told us to ring her up.

"I'm as gray as they come, lady. Except when it comes to loyalty and lying."

Atlanta shrugged like it was all the same to her, and she didn't care where I fell on the moral spectrum—lily white to pitch black to every shade between.

"Technically, I *was* in Berlin today. My flight landed here at eight this morning. If she wouldn't have quit, I wouldn't have lied. But I needed to make sure she trusted I had her back, so I told her I was in Berlin."

I wanted off this merry-go-round.

"Who's Jason Anderson?"

I'd asked Atlanta, but it was Pete who answered. "Liliya's boyfriend at the time of her disappearance, and the man responsible for her kidnapping."

All of the pieces locked into place, revealing the whole picture.

Fuck me. *Fuck me.* Fuck me.

"Jason Anderson is her endgame. Her one more thing."

"Yes," Atlanta confirmed.

"Before we go down that rabbit hole, what else did he say?" I asked, intentionally not mentioning Shep in front of Atlanta.

"Amir's changing the location of the auction," Aiden told me, holding my gaze. There was more, I knew it. "No word on where to. Calista's cover is blown."

It was Gavin who delivered the kill shot, and when he did, pain sliced through my gut, leaving carnage in its wake that almost took me to my knees. "Amir put out a bounty for Calista. It has since been rescinded."

Rescinded?

"What the fuck does that mean? Did Amir pull the bounty or was it paid?"

"The working theory is paid," Catarina gently told me.

"Rescinded," Atlanta contradicted. "Jason wouldn't let this opportunity slip through his fingers. He'd pay Amir to find her for him."

The calm tone in which Atlanta had rapped out that Calli was being hunted by a sex trafficker—the same one who'd taken her sister two decades ago—pissed me right the fuck off. The lack of urgency was infuriating.

"I need to make a call," Atlanta announced.

Jack waited until Atlanta was in the living room, out of earshot, before he told me, "Jason is staying at the Bvlgari Resort. Shep hacked the security camaras. Two hours ago, Jason and three guards left the property in a black SUV. Shep tracked it but lost it when it headed out of the city. He's still trying to pick it back up. He's also got feelers out for the new location of the auction."

"What about the taxi Calli was in?"

"Shep lost it twelve miles past the Dubai Safari Park."

Fuck.

I took my phone out of my back pocket to pull up a map. "There's nothing but desert out there," I noted. "Why the hell would she go out there?"

"Tanner," Atlanta said as she came back into the foyer.

"Who, exactly, is Tanner?" Catarina asked.

"He's my contact in Dubai, former merc turned arms dealer, among other things. I called him earlier to tell him to expect Calli early to pick up her kit—rifle, pistol, and body armor. At Calli's request, I also asked him to call in some guys to handle the brothel at the bazaar. He lives in a tiny village, twenty minutes past the Safari Park."

I wanted to feel relief Calli had gone to pick up weapons and was now armed. However, the gnawing in my gut made it impossible.

"Jason left his hotel with three guards," Pete told Atlanta. "What can you tell us about them?"

"Bodhi Lee, Arlo Brown—both former SAS—and Archie Evans, former SBS. It's not Jason who you need to be worried about. The guy is a total tool. He inherited the brothel and the high-class service from his father. Rumor is there's a traitor in Jason's crew. My bet is on one of them."

"Prostitution's legal in Berlin. Why kidnap women and force them when there are willing women?" Gavin pointed out.

Personally, I didn't give a shit about the history lesson. I wanted a locale and to move.

"Old man Anderson got greedy and wanted something to offer his clients who had rougher tastes, but he couldn't find any girls to offer those services, so he picked a few from his stable, got them hooked on heroin, and suddenly they don't mind being punched in the face by a john. This proved to be popular, but he didn't want to keep pulling beautiful women from his brothel, and those men didn't care what the women looked like, so he started snatching runaways and putting them into service."

"Inherited? So, the father's dead?" Aiden asked.

Atlanta's dark hair shifted when she turned to look at Aiden. "Yes, he's dead. A stroke."

Quick and painless. The bastard deserved worse. But there was nothing I could do about that.

"How'd Lili wind up over there?" Catarina's inquiry had me grinding my molars.

Who the fuck cared? Calista was out in the desert alone with a rescinded bounty on her head and two men who'd either like to see her dead or sold.

Neither option was acceptable.

Jesus fuck, my heart felt like it was crawling up my throat.

"This is a guess," Atlanta started, before I could put a stop to it. "But Jason wanted Daddy's attention. He saw his father four times a year. Twice in the US, when his dad flew there, and twice when Jason flew to Germany. Jason was twenty-five when he gave Lili to his father, and wanted to make a statement he wanted in on his dad's gig. Or, another guess, old man Anderson told Jason it was time for him to prove himself, because he wanted to groom his son to take over the business. So he handed over Lili."

And now Jason was after Lili's sister. Chills ran down my back, chased by fire licking up my spine. Oddly, if it was just Calista against Jason, with her pent-up rage, I wouldn't be worried. She'd tear him apart. But with three former Special Forces guys in the mix and Amir and his army, I had a bad feeling. Even if one of them was a traitor. He wouldn't turn on Jason until he felt confident he could do it and take over Jason's operation, and he wouldn't give two shits about Calli.

"It's time to go," I told Pete.

"I'm coming with you," Atlanta demanded. "If Calli's already come and gone, maybe she told Tanner her plan, and he won't talk to you. Besides, he'll sell to anyone who has cash in hand, but he saves the good shit for people he knows."

I must really be going insane if I was contemplating going into an unknown hostile situation with a woman I didn't know and who I didn't trust.

No, not contemplating, that was exactly what I was going to do.

"Call him. Tell him we're on our way."

"I already did. He's not answering."

"Is that unusual?" Gavin asked. "Does he always answer when you call?"

"No, he's hard to get ahold of. I left him a message to call me."

"Mason—"

"You told me to wake up," I interrupted Pete. "You told me not to fuck this up. This is me with my eyes wide fucking open, not fucking this up. I'm going in to get Calli. Either you're coming with me or you're not."

Pete's jaw clenched at my outburst. "Fallon and I are coming with you to Tanner's. Jack and Cat are going to hit Jason's hotel. Gavin and Aiden are going to pick up Samuel Allard. Calli said he didn't have the same buying power as Maxwell Lancaster. We're hoping he's the weak link that'll get us the new location."

"And me," Atlanta spoke up again. "I'm coming with you." Her gaze traveled to Pete. "Calli's right, Samuel Allard is the bottom of the barrel at this auction. He has a penchant for Russian girls—the younger the better. He won't use a massage girl. He'll want high-class hookers. Find who's got them to offer and you'll find Samuel."

Jesus Christ, sick fucking bastard. I hoped Gavin and Aiden took their time torturing the prick before ridding the world of a pedo sex trafficker.

"Let's roll."

Atlanta stepped in front of me. The stubborn set of her jaw and narrowed eyes said I wasn't going to like what came next.

"Do *not* take out Jason. She'll never forgive you if you do. She's lived and breathed her vengeance for a long time. If you take that from her, you'll lose her forever."

Lose her forever.

"I'll do whatever I have to do to get her safe. If that means taking out Jason and her never forgiving me, I'll do so happily, knowing she's out there somewhere breathing."

"Mason, I'm serious."

"I get that. But get *me*, Atlanta. Calli walking away alive is my only goal. Anyone who gets in my way is dead."

She held my gaze for a moment, then nodded.

"Okay."

"Holy fuck."

That was Atlanta, and *holy fuck* was an understatement.

Fallon lifted his fingers from the neck of the man tied to a chair. "Dead."

The blood pooling at the man's feet from the holes in his chest left no question how he died, but the why remained, and the who.

"Is that Tanner?" Pete asked.

"Yes," she gritted out. "The one on the floor next to him is Arlo. The other one over there"—she tipped her head toward the body lying near the kitchen table—"is Archie."

Three dead bodies. No Calista.

Jason Anderson was a dead man. I didn't give the first fuck about Atlanta's warning. I was going to strangle the life out of him.

I couldn't find my voice.

Fallon didn't seem to have the same problem. "The traitors?"

"That'd be my guess. I thought there was one, but seeing as two are dead, I think it's safe to say Arlo and Archie were conspiring together."

Since we'd cleared the house and there were no other bodies, that left one guard.

"Bodhi—"

"Hold that thought, call coming in," Pete interrupted me.

Please, God, let that be Shep with intel.

"Update," Pete barked.

There was a lengthy pause. I used the break to look around the room, hoping to find something to give me a clue about what happened here. The only blood spatter was directed around the dead guys, with the exception of the red smear Archie's body left as he was dragged across the room. He was done near the door, which was likely his post, to keep Calista from running.

She hadn't gone for the weapons piled on the table—thank fuck. She'd been outnumbered, and in the small space, there was nowhere for her to take cover if she instigated a shoot-out. So either Jason or Bodhi took out Arlo and Archie, or maybe both men had opened fire at the same time. Assuming Jason had accompanied his guards to intercept Calli.

But there was no other blood on the floor. I prayed that meant Calli was uninjured.

Not that it mattered if Jason had personally come to snatch Calli. He'd still pay for his part. His blood would spill in the most painful of ways if there was a single mark on my woman.

"Copy that," Pete said, drawing my attention back to his conversation. "Gavin and Aiden will check in with you after they pick up Samuel Allard. Call Jack or Catarina and reroute them. We're leaving Tanner's now, and just to confirm, he's dead. So is Archie and Arlo." There was another short wait before Pete ended the call. "Appreciate it. Later."

Seeing as I was on the verge of snapping, Pete didn't delay. "Grab some weapons and as much ammo as you can carry, we need to roll."

Thank fuck.

I walked over to the collection of weapons to choose from scattered on the table. I didn't take time to peruse. I picked a P226, Fallon and Pete grabbed Glock 17s and, to my surprise, Atlanta went straight to a Sig Cross chambered in .308. I had questions on her choice of long gun, but I didn't ask, nor did I question Pete when he picked up a stack of papers as I was shoving all the boxes of nine-mil ammo I could into the pockets of my cargos.

Fallon grabbed what I couldn't fit. Atlanta nabbed the only two boxes of .308.

Then we finally rolled out.

As soon as we were back in the Wagoneer, with Fallon behind the wheel, I pressed Pete for information.

"Tell me."

"Atlanta was correct. Jason Anderson approached Amir and offered to buy his problem. Amir saw the wisdom in this, rescinded the bounty, and helped Jason find Calista. Tanner was well known for getting people what they wanted, not just weapons but information. Apparently, he was also an idiot."

Pete handed me back one of the pieces of paper he'd taken from Tanner's. It was a handwritten note with a man's name, Ali Khan, boldly scrolled on the top. Written below his name was his order: fifteen fully auto MP5s.

"Amir sent one of his men out here to talk to Tanner, saw Calista's name, and reported back."

I closed my eyes and shook my head.

So fucking stupid. Unbelievably stupid. The man handwrote his orders and left them out in the open.

"If he got that intel, does that mean he finally got access to someone on the inside?" Fallon asked, referring to Shep.

"Yes, low-level errand boy, which was who Amir sent. Gavin and Aiden still need to break Samuel to get the new location."

"What else did he tell you?" I asked, knowing Pete was holding something back.

"Mason—"

"Tell. Me."

"Jack and Catarina are en route now."

"That's not what I asked," I growled, unable to keep the dread from seeping in.

"Amir's got a private fleet of jets. One is being fueled."

Fucking hell.

"Flight plan?"

"Germany. Three passengers, bogus names."

Dread turned into terror. Jason was taking her back to Berlin.

"Who do we know—"

"If we miss them, a team will be waiting in Berlin for them."

If we missed intercepting Calista at the airport, she'd be on a six-hour flight alone with Jason. Six hours was a long fucking time to be at the mercy—

"Calli won't get on that plane," Atlanta cut through my thoughts. "She'll fight and buy us the time we need to get there."

What Atlanta didn't say, but what she meant was: Calista would fight to the death—hers or Jason's.

Her endgame.

She'd take him out or die trying.

That razor wire that had been wrapped around my heart was gone. Calli had unraveled the barbs until there was nothing left of the old pain, leaving me vulnerable to this new emotion—abject panic.

A fear I'd never known threatened to choke me. Calista would choose dying for her cause over waiting for me to find her. A terrifying reality sank in, a truth there was an overwhelming likelihood I'd lose her—and faced with that possibility, I could no longer deny I'd fallen in love with Calista Ventura.

Chapter Twenty-Seven

It was now or never.

Bodhi was occupied, speaking on his phone with his back to me, eyes out the open hangar, not paying attention.

Jason was standing next to the airstairs, talking to the pilot.

If I got on that plane, that would be it. Atlanta could plead with Tom to send a team to Berlin to get me, but unless he was feeling altruistic, I'd be fucked. I had no doubt Mason would come for me, and when he did, he'd rally his team—eight against Jason's army was a battle I didn't want to consider.

I couldn't let Mason get hurt because of me. He'd try to save me without regard for his safety.

They'd left me to sit in a chair while the jet was being prepared for takeoff.

My only chance at keeping Mason safe was to escape.

Abandon my mission and sneak away while both men were occupied.

I had Jason in profile. He was a classically handsome man. Back in the day, I understood my sister's fascination with him; he'd been good looking then too. He'd been attentive and affectionate. He'd made her laugh, called her *pretty girl*, and he'd even pretended to be a gentleman, opening doors for her and my mother.

Until someone experienced trauma, they couldn't fully comprehend all the ways it takes over your life. How your brain latches onto a particular thought until it's all you can think about—obsess over. The inconsequential consumes your every waking hour even when, logically, you know it's trivial.

My sister had died in the ugliest of ways. She'd lived through years of abuse and torture, yet my mind kept circling back to the moment Jason had turned on her. The moment when she realized the man she loved was not the gentleman she'd thought, but Satan. The confusion and fear she must've felt. The pain of his treachery.

Every kiss, every touch, every sweet word a lie rolling off his forked tongue.

Did she fight? Did she try to run? Did he tie her up, drug her, did he hurt her before he'd handed her over to his father?

The answers wouldn't bring Lili back. Knowing would only give my brain more information to torment me with, yet that's where my mind went.

My trauma response was the need to revive the trauma—keep it alive. Endure more pain so I never forgot Lili.

I couldn't stop the cycle.

I now associated my big sister with suffering—hers, my family's, my mother's drinking. Any memories of happiness had been lost to me. My sole focus had been on her final years.

My need for revenge.

I'd convinced myself the only way I'd find peace was if I killed Jason.

Then I met Mason . . . and within a few days, he'd proved me wrong.

Could I give up a twenty-year vendetta for a man who I'd known for a handful of days?

This doesn't feel like friends.

Um. What does it feel like?

Like you're mine.

Was I Mason's? He sure made me feel like I was.

I looked away from Jason, out the hangar, and took in nothing but brown sand as far as the eye could see, with a makeshift air traffic tower next to the runway.

Was it too late? If I managed to slip out, there were only a handful of buildings I could hide in or behind. My white T-shirt and jeans would do me no favors blending into the wasteland. I had no weapon. Both Jason and Bodhi were armed.

Shit odds.

However slim the possibility, I had to try to run.

"You always win!" Lili yelled from behind me.

"Not always," I huffed, and bent double to rest my hands on my thighs.

I glanced over at the Atlantic and tried to catch my breath while Lili caught up to me, standing on the finish line we'd drawn in the sand.

"I wish we could move here," Lili said when she made it to me.

"You just want to tell people you live in Kill Devil Hills."

My sister's laughter drowned out the sound of the ocean.

"Not true. I want to build sandcastles and skim board and twirl in the ocean."

I watched Lili spin on the wet sand, and the white foamy seawater danced around her ankles.

"I want that too," I told her.

Lili stopped spinning and smiled at me. "You don't always have to want what I want, CeCe."

Her declaration felt like a punch to my stomach. Did she not want me to like the same things as her? "But you're my sister."

Lili skipped back to me and grabbed my hand, pulling me into the water until it lapped at our knees.

"You'll always be my sister, even if when we grow up, I move to Paris and you move to New Zealand."

I didn't want to move to New Zealand.

"But—"

Lili squeezed my hand and gave my arm a slight jerk. "What I'm saying is, no matter what, we're sisters. You don't have to like the beach or softball or painting. I'll love you even if you don't like what I like. I just want my little sister to be happy."

"I want you to be happy too, Lil."

She tugged my hand, stepping farther out into the surf.

"Lil and CeCe, best friends forever!" she shouted, lifting our hands above my head.

"Lil and CeCe, best friends forever!" I echoed.

With a rebel yell, my fearless sister dove under the water, taking me with her.

I shook free of the memory—our last vacation to North Carolina. The next year, my parents had taken us to Daytona, and Lili discovered the orange-sand beach at Flagler. From that year on, every summer until Lili went missing, we'd spent a week together in Florida.

Good times I'd forced myself to forget.

The best of times.

Lil and CeCe, more than sisters—best friends, happily sitting on the beach doing nothing but spending time together. Just being us.

I glanced back at Jason, the truth slamming into my chest with such force it knocked the air from my lungs. A truth I'd buried because it didn't fit my narrative. A truth I'd ruthlessly denied so I could plan and plot and do so free of guilt.

Liliya would hate this.

She'd hate all the years I'd wasted, keeping the worst years of *her* life alive and forgetting the love we'd shared.

My sister would be pissed, and when Lili was angry, she was hell on wheels. She'd chew me out and not hide her disappointment.

It was time.

To give up the past.

To stop resuscitating the pain.

To start healing from the loss of her.

But first, it was time I got my ass up and out the door.

Fuck Jason Anderson.

God would be the judge of his soul.

Bodhi abruptly dropped his phone. The clatter of it hitting the concrete echoed through the hangar. I watched as he yanked his rifle up, the combat sling smoothly adjusting as he fitted the rear of the stock to his shoulder. His gaze swiftly cut to me, but he spoke to Jason. "We have company."

Company?

"Get ready to leave," Jason said to the pilot as he drew his sidearm.

I bolted out of the chair, uncaring it fell back in my haste, and took off running.

I was nearly at the door when Jason's hand caught my hair. With a vicious yank that made my scalp scream in pain, he spun me around. I only had seconds to lift my arms and cover my face before he hammered down the butt of his gun.

My temple exploded in pain. The flow of blood fast on its heels.

Before I could get my bearings, Jason used my hair to drag me back into the middle of the hangar, toward the plane that would be my death sentence.

I spun, ignoring the pain of my hair being wrenched in the process, and punched his forearm. As soon as the pistol flew out of his hand, I elbowed the bicep of the arm that still had my hair in his grasp.

"Fucking—" he shouted.

If he meant to say more, it was cut off by gunfire.

Before I got hit by one of the bullets that were slamming into the back wall of the hangar, I needed to end this.

I kicked the inside of Jason's knee, the resulting howl of pain making my heart swell with joy. Unfortunately, my elation was short lived. On his way down to the concrete, Jason grabbed ahold of my shirt and took me down with him.

I landed on my hip. More pain exploded up my spine as Jason tumbled on top of me.

I twisted to my side, freed my elbow from under Jason, and swung it back as hard as I could. I heard his grunt. I reached behind me, feeling for any soft tissue I could pinch, pull, or gouge.

I swung another wild elbow, connected with something hard right before Jason punched me in the back of the head. I blinked away the blood, now flowing freely over my brow and impairing the vision in my right eye.

I felt the tip of a knife press on the right side, just below my ribs, and froze. I didn't know how long I'd make it if he stabbed me in my liver.

Jason maneuvered to his knees, digging the tip of his blade into my side.

"I should've just killed you," he ground out.

For the first time in twenty years, I cared if I died.

Wasn't that inconvenient. Here was my chance to kill my sworn enemy, but I could die in the process.

Out of the corner of my eye, I saw a black-clad body sneak into the hangar, followed by a second one with broad shoulders. The men were masked, but I'd know Mason anywhere, and those shoulders were Fallon's.

"Should've taken both of you. Bet that sniveling bitch would've been easier to break if I had you as incentive. Instead, all she did was beg and cry. Took fucking *months* to shut her up."

Red.

Blood red.

Murderous red.

My vision blurred with it. The room went hazy with it. My veins throbbed with fury.

The snap of a bullet rang out.

Jason's body slumped over me. But no sooner had it landed on my chest than it was being pulled off.

"Calli."

I looked at Jason Anderson, face down on the floor.

Dead.

Not by my hand.

"Calista."

Gone.

No more one more thing.

"Calli, baby." Mason's gloved hand wrapped around my upper arm and pulled me up. "Sweetness, I need you to talk to me. There's too much blood. I don't know where you're hurt."

"Head," I said by rote.

"Fuck me. *Fuck me.* Fuck me," he groaned, and pulled me to his chest. "We need to get you out of here."

I shook my head.

"Calli, before Amir's men get here, we need to exfil now."

I shuffled around Mason. I needed to see him one more time.

Dead. Just dead.

"Come on, baby."

When I didn't move, Mason swept me up into his arms.

Four times.

I wasn't sure if I wanted to commit this one to memory, but just in case, I closed my eyes and let Mason carry me away from the man who had stolen everything from me.

Chapter Twenty-Eight

"On a scale of super-double pissed and over-the-top, ready-to-commit-murder pissed, how angry are you at me?" Atlanta asked.

I glanced around Mason's bedroom, then back at the phone.

"This feels like déjà vu," I told her, my attention going back to the whitewashed dresser.

Who knew Mason Hughes would decorate his badass condo in a classy beach theme. There were some Navy memorabilia and nautical-themed pieces scattered around, but it was mostly pastel blues, creams, sage, and whimsical.

I loved it, and not because my sister loved the beach. Because it was Mason's.

"Well?" she pushed.

I blew out a breath and gave her what she was looking for—absolution.

"You did hack some pretty scary places to make the evidence against me disappear," I reminded her.

"That's what friends do," she huffed.

I didn't think that's what normal law-abiding-citizen friends did for each other, but I didn't point that out. There was nothing law abiding about Atlanta, and I doubt there ever would be.

"And you did have my back with Tom and told him you'd cut him from throat to ball sack if he ever tried to contact me again. And you got him to send in a GB team to back up Pete, Jack, Cat, Gavin, Aiden, and Fallon when they crashed Amir's auction and took him out."

Something I wished I'd been a part of but instead was nursing a head wound back at the penthouse, with Mason standing guard at my side.

"Calli," she snapped. "Just tell me how mad you are and if you're ever going to forgive me."

I snatched my phone off the bed, and on my way to the living room, I told her, "There's nothing to forgive."

"I killed Jason," she reminded me.

A few months ago, I never would've forgiven her for taking his life, thus taking away my opportunity for revenge.

I spied Mason sitting out on his deck, beer bottle in hand, enjoying his view of the ocean.

"While I was sitting in that hangar, I remembered how much my sister loved me. After all the years of not wanting to reminisce about the real her, who she was, how much she enjoyed life, my brain finally allowed the good stuff to pour back in."

Mason's head turned, and when he noticed me standing in front of the sliding glass door, he smiled.

It was that smile, the way he looked at me, the invisible tether that rooted me to him, that had given me back my sister.

Killing Jason wouldn't have given me peace.

Revenge wouldn't have soothed the ache.

Mason did.

"She called me CeCe," I told Atlanta. "We were sisters but best friends forever. She'd hate that I lost two decades of my life. She died. It was brutal and ugly, but I'm still alive, and she'd want me to be happy and live . . . maybe even for the both of us. Jason's dead, and you know what?"

"What?" she asked softly.

"Nothing's changed. I don't feel the joy and happiness I thought I'd feel. The cloak of darkness didn't lift because he's no longer breathing.

I'm not sorry he's dead. The world's a better place, but honestly, as weird as it sounds, I just don't care. What I care about is, you made it possible for me to come to California. But before that, you gave me Mason. I can't be mad at you for going behind my back when what you did gave me the one thing I was desperate to find."

"I'm glad you found it, Calli."

"No, Atlanta, I didn't find it. You went behind my back to give it to me. Then Mason gave me the rest while I stubbornly fought him. Now, not only do I have the peace I'd been missing, I also have six men who act like annoying brothers and Catarina, who has unreservedly welcomed me. I'm going to enjoy my peace and write books and love on my man."

"I don't want to look a gift horse in the mouth, and I'm over-the-moon happy for you. But damn, woman, this new you is not the Calista I knew."

Thank God for that. The old Calista was miserable.

"That's the nicest thing you've ever said to me."

Her laugh made *me* laugh. What could I say? I was deliriously happy.

"So when's the wedding?"

"Tomorrow," I teased.

"What!" she screeched, nearly taking out my eardrum.

"Kidding. I don't know if we'll get married. Maybe we'll just live happily ever after and not worry about a piece of paper and tax breaks. Or maybe we will. Who knows, and if I have Mason, I don't care."

Mason jerked his chin, reminding me we had somewhere to be.

"Listen, I have to go. We're meeting the team at the Dirty Plank for drinks."

"One more thing. I'll be over-the-top, ready-to-commit-murder mad if you don't invite me to the wedding. Okay, two things." She paused, then added quietly, "I'm happy you have your Lili back. Don't ever forget her again."

With that, she rang off.

I waited for the sharp pain to hit at the mention of Lili. But like all the times in the last three weeks since I'd let my sister back in, it never came.

Mason came through the sliding glass door, his intelligent eyes scanning my face for any signs of distress. This look was different than his Mason stare back in Dubai—he wasn't examining me to uncover deceit. This perusal was a man who loved his woman and wanted to make sure she wasn't upset after having what he thought would be a hard conversation.

"All good?" he asked.

"Yep. Atlanta says she'll be over-the-top, ready-to-commit-murder mad if she's not invited to our wedding," I blurted out.

Mason's hot-guy smile lit his face. "Are you asking me to marry you, sweetness?"

"And if I was?" I teased him back.

"I'd drive us to the courthouse tomorrow. Unless you wanted a big wedding, then I'd tell you to start planning."

I blinked away my shock, but I didn't have time to think of a proper comeback before Mason's arm shot out and tagged me around the waist, bringing me flush to his chest.

"Do you want to get married, Calli?"

Did I?

I told Atlanta I didn't care, but maybe that wasn't the truth.

"I want to be Calista Hughes," I told him. "I want to have your name. I want us to be a team, a family."

The green of Mason's eyes darkened, and I knew what that meant. Since we'd been home, the floodgates had opened. I'd seen that hungry look on his handsome face for less of a reason than me telling him I wanted to be his wife. Heck, I'd told him his stoneware was rad, and that had earned me an orgasm on the kitchen island.

"We're gonna be late meeting our friends," he threatened.

"Fine by me."

Mason swept me up into his arms and stalked to the bedroom—his go-to place when he was feeling creative. I'd learned the couch worked in a pinch or when Mason felt like bending me over the back of it. Shower sex was hot. Wall sex, phenomenal. But Mason in his big king-size bed with room to get adventurous—otherworldly.

"Love you, hotshot," I whispered, still shy saying the words, which was silly since he told me ten times a day.

His hand came up to gently trace the scar along my right temple, as if his touch could erase the reminder that Jason had hurt me.

"Love you back, Calista. Don't ever forget, yeah?"

"I won't."

Not that he'd ever let me.

As soon as he stepped over the threshold into the bedroom, he lowered his lips to mine, but before he could kiss me, I mumbled, "Eleven."

"One day, that count will be so high, you'll lose track."

He was right. One day, the count would be ridiculously high. But he was also wrong. I'd never lose track of the times he swept me off my feet.

"Kiss me, hotshot."

Mason didn't kiss me, he chuckled, so I kissed him. With his happiness on my tongue, a kiss had never been so sweet.

Chapter Twenty-Nine

Chloe Baughman
San Diego, California

"Sorry, sorry. I know I'm late. Summer traffic is the worst," I grumbled as I rushed past one of my bosses, Ryan Strong, who unfortunately was a dead ringer for the actor Ryan Gosling, which made him distracting in an 'I can't stop thinking about banging you' kind of way.

"You're five minutes early," he contradicted.

"Five minutes early is ten minutes late," I countered.

My dad had taught me that back before the dementia had started eating away at the man who'd been the wisest person I knew. Now there were days when he barely recognized me.

Stop.

Recalibrate.

"I'll be out on the floor in a minute," I told Ryan, as I pushed into the locker room our awesome management had given us, taking half of a storage room to give the female staff members a fully kitted-out place to change and store their stuff. Pete had even put a couch in the room that was super comfy.

"Hey, Chloe," Poppy greeted from in front of her locker.

"Hey."

I busied myself opening my locker in an attempt to ignore my friend. I could feel her giving me the side-eye, and I was not in the mood for another lecture. She'd given me one last night before our shift ended, and again this afternoon when she called me. Luckily, I was at my other job and had a valid excuse to cut the talk short.

"You can't keep this up, Chloe."

Here we go.

I tossed my purse into my locker and pulled out my pen holder and notebook, diligently focusing on my tasks.

"You were up at five this morning," she told me, something I knew. "You worked until three. Now you're here and won't get cut until after one. After you cash out, do your side work, and drive home, that leaves three hours' worth of sleep if you're lucky."

She wasn't wrong, and I was feeling every hour of sleep I'd missed out on this week. But I needed the money. I had no choice but to work two jobs or move in with my mother, and as much as I loved her, I would rather work seventeen jobs and never sleep another wink.

Just because I loved her didn't mean she didn't drive me batshit crazy. I'd last approximately three days, give or take a few hours, living with her before I'd give up the comforts of a bed in favor of a cardboard box.

"I can get you a job at the Vault."

Not this again.

"No."

"I work a three-hour shift and walk out with a minimum of five hundred dollars. You make twenty an hour at—"

"I know how much money I make."

Sadly, I couldn't forget my twenty-dollar-an-hour job didn't even cover my rent on my one-bedroom apartment. Maybe I should see if there were any studios coming available in my building. That would save me a few hundred dollars a month. That would go a long way, and maybe I'd be able to afford a to-go coffee again one day in the next millennium.

"You'd be perfect—"

"Poppy, I love you with all my heart, but I'm not cut out to take off my clothes in public."

"You say that like the Vault's a strip club. It's not. Think *Coyote Ugly* but themed."

Every time Poppy tried to sell me on the idea of going to work in the bar nestled up in the hills with a steep cover charge and a drink minimum I couldn't afford, she always referenced the movie where the bartenders and servers danced on the bar top in cutoffs and crop tops. The movie was the bomb, but I didn't think I could even manage to climb on a table *or* the top of a bar.

And showing copious amounts of skin wasn't my thing, unless I was in my bikini on the beach. But that felt different, especially seeing as I was a SoCal girl and grew up running on the sand and in the surf.

"How about this," she continued. "Tomorrow night, come with me. Just watch the show we put on, and if you really hate it, then I promise to never mention it again."

I'd do anything to get Poppy to stop mentioning the Vault. "Fine."

She slammed her locker, bopped over to me, and kissed my cheek. "You're gonna love it."

I wasn't, but I *did* love seeing my friend smile.

"Yeah, yeah." I waved her off. "See you out there."

I heard the door close and dropped my chin to my chest. I was exhausted. So tired I was becoming delirious. I didn't know how much longer I could keep up this pace.

"We're going to have to move him, Chloe. We have no choice," my mother had shared with tears in her eyes.

We did have a choice—me working two jobs so I could help pay for my father's home that the insurance didn't cover.

I'd looked at the home the insurance company had suggested. Over my dead, broken, tired body would my father move an hour away from the women who loved him and live in a small white box of nothing. And that was what the rooms were—boxes. White, boring nothingness.

Hell to the no.

The truth of my situation penetrated my fatigued brain—I was going to have to work at the Vault.

For my father, I'd dance around half dressed.

For my mother to keep the love of her life close, I'd swallow my pride.

I swiped away the only tears I'd give in to and headed out to the floor.

◆ ◆ ◆

Ryan Strong

"Yo!" Pete called and waved me over to a table in the corner he'd commandeered before the early evening rush started.

I took the chair opposite his. "What's up?"

"Shep called. He needs us to look into something for him."

The team had been home from Dubai for a month. It wasn't unheard of for us to go out for back-to-back missions; neither was it abnormal for us to be home for a few months. So I didn't understand the look on my friend's face.

"Where we going? I'm up on rotation. Mase sitting this one out?"

We rotated who stayed stateside to manage the bar. Since Mason now had Calli and they were newish, it made sense he'd be the one to stay behind.

"The Vault," he said, weirdly.

"The Vault? The gentlemen's club?"

"Not so much a gentlemen's club as it is a private club. The servers don't strip, and they don't show any more skin than on an average Friday night here. Membership is astronomical, but twice a month, they allow nonmembers to pay a cover charge. Shep has intel there might be a member there scouting."

Scouting for women to sell, right in our backyard.

Hell no.

"When's the next nonmember night?"

"Next Wednesday."

Out of the corner of my eye, I saw Chloe walk out into the bar.

Beautiful, smart, hilarious Chloe Baughman—the woman who set my blood on fire and haunted my dreams.

My employee.

If I was a different man, I'd fire her just so I could have the woman.

Unfortunately, I had scruples . . . and a case of blue balls to go with my morals.

Needless to say, my condition was painful.

About the Author

Riley Edwards is a *USA Today* and *Wall Street Journal* bestselling author, wife, and military mom. She writes heart-stopping romance titles featuring sexy alpha heroes and even stronger heroines. Her favorite genres to write are romantic suspense and military romance. Born and raised in Los Angeles, Edwards now resides on the East Coast with her husband and children.

Connect with Riley Online

Riley's Facebook Page

www.facebook.com/Novelist.Riley.Edwards

Follow Riley on Instagram

www.instagram.com/rileyedwardsromance

Follow Riley on TikTok

www.tiktok.com/@rileyedwardsromance

Find Riley's Books on Goodreads

www.goodreads.com/author/show/15080716.Riley_Edwards

Find Riley on BookBub

www.bookbub.com/authors/riley-edwards

Website

www.rileyedwardsromance.com